THIS VIOLENT LAND

A SMOKE JENSEN NOVEL OF THE WEST

WILLIAM W. JOHNSTONE

with J. A. Johnstone

PINNACLE BOOKS
Kensington Publishing Corp.
www.kensingtonbooks.com

PINNACLE BOOKS are published by

Kensington Publishing Corp.
119 West 40th Street
New York, NY 10018

All Kensington titles, imprints, and distributed lines are available at special quantity discounts for bulk purchases for sales
promotions, premiums, fund-raising, educational, or institu-
tional use.

Special book excerpts or customized printings can also be cre-
ated to fit specific needs. For details, write or phone the office
of the Kensington sales manager: Kensington Publishing
Corp., 119 West 40th Street, New York, NY 10018, attn: Sales
Department; phone 1-800-221-2647.

PINNACLE BOOKS and the Pinnacle logo are Reg. U.S. Pat.
& TM Off.

ISBN-13: 978-0-7860-3644-8
ISBN-10: 0-7860-3644-3

First Kensington hardcover printing: August 2015
First Pinnacle mass market paperback printing: October 2016

10 9 8 7 6 5 4 3 2 1

Printed in the United States of America

First Pinnacle electronic edition: October 2016

ISBN-13: 978-0-7860-3645-5
ISBN-10: 0-7860-3645-1

CHAPTER 1

Northwest Colorado Territory, August 1870

The snowcapped crag known as Zenobia Peak towered above the two men on the small, grassy plain at its base. At some point in the past, a slab of rock in the shape of a crude rectangle had tumbled down into the field from those rugged slopes above. The rock was small enough that one man could move it—if he was a very strong man.

The rock sat up on its end, the passage of time having sunk its base slightly into the earth. That, along with the sheer weight of it, discouraged anyone from tampering with it—which was good because the stone marked a place special to the two men who stood beside it.

A simple legend was chiseled into the rock.

EMMETT JENSEN
BORN 1815 DIED 1869

The few words couldn't sum up the man's life. It took memories to do that.

Smoke Jensen stood at the grave of his father, his hat in his hands, and remembered.

The images that went through his mind seemed to have a red haze over them. *His father and his older brother Luke going off to war. The evil in human form riding up to the hardscrabble Jensen farm in the Missouri Ozarks. His sister being raped, his mother brutally gunned down. And the vengeance he had ultimately taken on the animals responsible for those atrocities, Billy Bartell and Angus Shardeen.*

Red was the color of that vengeance. Red for blood . . .

The memories cascaded faster and faster through his thoughts, out of all order. They were each part of what had made him the man he was. *Hearing about the death of his brother in the great conflict that had split the nation. His father's return after the war, to find nothing left to hold him and his son—the only remaining Jensens—on the farm. His sister Janey leaving. No telling where she was or if she was even still alive. And the day Emmett Jensen and his son, whose given name was Kirby, set off for the frontier, bound for the unknown.*

Battles with the Indians, meeting the old mountain man called Preacher who gave him his current name. "Smoke'll suit you just fine. So Smoke it'll be." His father's killing. The long and so far fruitless search for the men responsible.

Smoke scrubbed a boot in the dirt. *And the reputation building around him as one of the fastest guns the West had ever seen . . .*

Years of memories—long, bloody years—had come back to him in a matter of heartbeats.

He drew a deep breath and looked down at the rock-turned-tombstone, glad that time and the elements had not erased the words he had chiseled there. Preacher stood some distance away, having told Smoke that he needed some private time with his pa.

It was hard to know if Emmett could really hear him, but Smoke spoke to his father anyway, telling him what he had done, how he had settled part of the score for the wrongs done to the Jensen family.

And that he wasn't done yet. Not by a long shot.

He stood there in silence for another moment, then he put his hat on and turned toward Preacher.

"He was real proud of you, boy," the old mountain man said. "I know that for a fact. Same as I am."

The lump in Smoke's throat wouldn't let him reply.

"Where are you goin' now?" Preacher asked as they walked back to their horses.

"I'm heading back to Denver to turn in my badge. I don't reckon I'll be needing it anymore."

Preacher scratched his beard-stubbled jaw. "Oh, I wouldn't be so quick to do that, Smoke. A tin star can come in mighty handy from time to time." He paused, then added, "Most 'specially iffen you're still wantin' to go after them fellers what kilt your pa."

Denver, Colorado Territory

The low-lying building was made of white limestone. A United States flag flew from the flagpole out front, flapping gently in the breeze. Chiseled above the doorway were the words *United States Federal Office Building*.

Smoke Jensen, taller than most men, with shoulders someone once described as "wide as an axe handle" walked inside. On his shirt, he wore the star of a deputy United States marshal.

"Hello, Deputy Jensen," Annie Wilson greeted him as he hung his hat on the hat rack just inside the door. Middle-aged but still quite attractive, she flashed him a welcoming smile.

"Hello, Miss Wilson. Is the marshal in?"

Uriah B. Holloway was the chief U.S. marshal for the Colorado District. A while back, he had appointed Smoke as a deputy U.S. marshal for the purposes of locating Angus Shardeen, who had once ridden with John Brown and had personally taken part in the Pottawatomie Massacre in which several pro-Southern sympathizers were murdered.

After John Brown's death, Shardeen had started his own group and made his presence known by burning homes and killing innocents in Southwest Missouri. Shardeen had killed Smoke's mother, then stood by and watched as his men had used Smoke's sister Janey.

Smoke would have gone after Shardeen anyway, but the appointment, though temporary and without pay, had made his vendetta legal.

"He's in his office, Deputy. If you wait just a moment, I'll let him know you're here."

Smoke walked over to look through the window as Annie went into the office to announce him. He saw a couple boys sitting on the ground with their legs spread, playing mumblety-peg with a pocket knife.

"Ha! You lose, you lose! You have to root the peg out with your teeth!" one of the boys said triumphantly.

Smoke smiled as he recalled playing that game with his brother, back before the war. They'd played a different variation of the game. The object had been to see who could throw the knife into the ground and stick it the closest to their own foot. When Luke left for the war he was still carrying a scar on his right foot from where he had thrown the knife too close.

That was a much more innocent time. In fact, as Smoke thought back on it, it was the only innocent time he had ever known in his entire life.

"Deputy Jensen?" Annie said, coming out of Holloway's office. "The marshal will see you now."

"Thank you, Miss Wilson."

Holloway was standing behind his desk when Smoke stepped into his office. "Hello, Smoke," he greeted as he extended his hand.

Smoke took it and shook.

"How's that old horse thief, Preacher?"

"Preacher's doing well," Smoke said, speaking of the man who had become not only his mentor but also the closest thing he had to a father since his own pa had been killed.

He took the badge from his shirt and placed it on the desk in front of Marshal Holloway.

"What's that for?" Holloway asked with a puzzled frown.

"I want to thank you, Marshal, for putting your trust in me and making me your temporary deputy. That helped me take care of my business."

"It wasn't just your business, Smoke. If it had been, I would have never let you put on that star in the first place. There were federal warrants out for Shardeen and his men." Holloway pointed to the star. "There's too much prestige attached to wearing that badge, and too many men have died defending its honor, to give it out to just anyone. I would have never let you wear it if I hadn't thought you deserved it."

"I appreciate the trust, Marshal."

"Do you appreciate it enough to wear that star permanently? With proper compensation, I hasten to add."

"Are you offering me a full-time job, Marshal?" Smoke asked.

"Yes. You do need a job, don't you? I mean, you don't plan to eat off Preacher's table forever, do you?"

Smoke laughed, admitting, "I am getting a little tired of game and wild vegetables." He reached for the star, picked it up, and held it for a long moment, examining it.

He looked up at the man across from him. "Marshal, you do know that I'm after Richards, Potter, and Stratton, don't you?"

"Those are the men who killed your brother?"

"Yes, sir. And as far as I've been able to determine, they aren't wanted anywhere."

"You suspect that they killed your father, too, don't you?"

"I more than suspect. I know they did."

Marshal Holloway held up his finger. "Listen to me carefully, Smoke. You *suspect* they killed your father, don't you?"

Smoke wasn't sure where the marshal was going with that statement, but he picked up on the inference. "Yes, sir, I suspect they did."

"Then as a deputy U.S. marshal, you can always hold them on suspicion of murder."

"You do know, don't you, Marshal, that they aren't going to let me do that?"

Marshal Holloway smiled. "You mean they might resist arrest?"

"Yeah, they might." Smoke smiled, too. "They might even resort to gunplay in resisting."

"Well, as a deputy U.S. marshal, you would be fully and legally authorized to counter force with force."

"All right, Marshal." Smoke pinned the star back onto his shirt. "You've just hired yourself a new deputy."

Holloway shook his hand. "And now you'll be drawing forty dollars a month and expenses."

"Sounds good to me."

"But I'll be expecting you to do more than just look for those three men. Are you ready to start earning your pay?"

That surprised Smoke. "You have a job for me already?"

"Yeah," Holloway said. "I want you to go to Red Cliff over in Summit County. Go see Sheriff Emerson Donovan. He's a friend of mine . . . who was once my deputy, by the way. An outbreak of cattle rustling is so severe it's causing some of the ranchers to go out of business."

"Cattle rustling? Wouldn't that be a state crime?"

Holloway smiled. "It would be, if we were a state. But Colorado is still a territory, therefore any crime that's committed here is a federal crime." He handed

Smoke a piece of paper. "Here is an arrest warrant signed by a federal judge. You can put whatever name or names on it that you need."

"What if the names are Stratton, Potter, and Richards?"

"Who knows? Someday, those may be just the names you put on there."

CHAPTER 2

Bury, Idaho Territory

The town began as a "Hell on Wheels" settlement. As an End of Track location during the building of the Union Pacific, there had been high hopes for the town in the beginning. It had a bank, probably the best school building—a large two-story—in that part of the country, and a weekly newspaper, the *Bury Bulletin*. Businesses included a large mercantile store, several saloons and cafés, a large hotel, a leather shop, and a brothel. It boasted a sheriff, a deputy, and a jail. A handful of ranches and a lot of producing mines lay around the town, as well.

Nearly all of it was owned by three men—Muley Stratton, Wiley Potter, and Josh Richards.

Some citizens resented the presence of the three men, believing that they were bad for the town. Others thought differently.

"You have to admit that the town has grown considerably since they arrived," someone had said.

"Yes, but grown how?" asked another, pointing out

that there were more saloons than any other type of business. "Most of the newcomers who work for Potter, Stratton, and Richards are riffraff of the lowest element. Why, I believe most of them are gunfighters and outlaws. How can a town grow, and survive, with such people?"

What was not owned by Stratton, Potter, and Richards was the Pink House.

Billing her place as a "Sporting House for Gentlemen," Flora Yancey even advertised her services in the town, hiring boys to tack up handbills.

The Pink House
Is a SPORTING HOUSE *for* GENTLEMEN
Where Beautiful and Cultured LADIES
Will provide you with every
Pleasure

She made no apologies about running a brothel. "Why should I be ashamed of it?" she would reply to anyone who questioned her. "I give my girls a clean place to stay and I insist that the gentlemen callers be on their best behavior. If they are not well-behaved, I don't let them return."

Flora had been in town for more than four years, having arrived as a member of a theater group. The owner of the repertoire company for which she'd worked had lost all the box-office receipts in an after-show poker game. Rather than face his troupe with the disgrace of his betrayal, he'd made an attempt to recover the money at the point of a gun. That attempt had failed, and he was shot dead. He now lay buried in the Bury Cemetery under a marker sporting an epitaph.

Here lies McKinley Hall
A thespian of renown
He took his final curtain call
When one slug from a .44 put him down

Disgruntled and betrayed, the rest of the theater company had left town, but Flora, seeing potential business opportunities, had stayed. She was a beautiful woman and her role in the theater had inflamed the fantasies of many men. She knew that she had only to play upon those fantasies to become very successful. It was rumored that she had once been the mistress of Crown Prince Ferdinand of Austria. Another rumor had it as Prince Leopold of Belgium.

Whenever questioned as to whether or not the rumors were true, and if so, just which crowned head had she been with, Flora always replied, "A lady never informs upon the indiscretions of gentlemen of station." She knew that such rumors fed the fantasies of men who wanted to "do it with a woman who had done it with a prince," so she did nothing to dispel the rumors.

When Flora had made enough money she'd built the Pink House and hired only the most attractive women she could find. She then went into semiretirement, preferring to manage the affairs of "her girls" over providing her personal services to the customers.

Janey Jensen, who had been calling herself Janey Garner, sat in the parlor of the Pink House with

Flora, one of her "girls" named Emma—no last name available—and Sally Reynolds, the local schoolteacher.

Sally had met Janey the day she first arrived in Bury and found herself in the middle of a shoot-out. Shortly thereafter, Sally had learned that the Pink House was a brothel, that Flora was the owner or madam of that house, and that Janey Garner was not only the business manager of the PSR Ranch, she was also the mistress of Josh Richards, who was the majority owner of the ranch.

Despite what she'd learned, Sally passed no judgment on anyone. On the contrary, Flora and Janey had become her closest friends. She'd also become friends with all the girls who worked at the Pink House.

At the moment, Emma was Sally's partner in a game of whist. It became obvious that they were losing the hand.

Emma sighed. "Oh dear. I'm afraid I overbid the deal. I'm such a nincompoop."

"Nonsense, you are just a woman who bids with a degree of unbridled courage," Sally said, and the others laughed.

As the game continued, conversation picked up.

"You being from the Northeast, you more'n likely didn't see much of the war, did you," Emma asked Sally, making the sentence more a declarative statement than a question.

"I didn't see any of the war, except for what I read in the newspapers," Sally replied.

"You were lucky," Emma said. "I lived in Corinth, Mississippi.We had a very big battle real close by."

"Yes, I read about Pittsburg Landing," Sally acknowledged.

Emma shook her head. "No, it was Shiloh."

"In the South, you called it Shiloh. In the North, we called it Pittsburg Landing."

"How odd. Well, I remember all those wounded boys being brought into town. I was very young then, but I remember it very well. Wounded boys were lying out on the lawns of people's houses, on their front porches, even." Emma shook her head again and sighed at the memory. "It was just awful."

Sally reached across and put her hand on Emma's. "Oh, you poor dear. I'm sure it must have been bad for you."

"Let's change the subject. I see no reason we should talk about such horrid things." Janey had her own terrible memories of the war, memories that she didn't want to share. "Tell us about New York," she said to Sally. "I know you once said you had been there."

"Yes, I've been there. I have an aunt who lives there."

"Oh, please do tell us about it," Emma said.

"It is almost indescribable. Trains whiz along on elevated tracks throughout the city. The streets are crowded with carriages and wagons that never seem to stop. And at night the entire city uses gaslights, so that when you look out your window it is as if you are gazing at a huge, sparkling jewel.

"But it is most impressive at Christmas. All the stores, even the lampposts, are decorated for the holiday. Swags of green are stretched between lampposts from one side of the street to the other so that when you travel, you are traveling under a green canopy."

"Did you ever attend the Woods Museum and Metropolitan Theater?" Flora asked.

"Yes. I saw a delightful production there, called *Ixion*."

Flora laughed. "I was in that production."

"Oh, my!" Sally said. "How wonderful to meet someone famous!"

"I wasn't famous, dear. I was just one of the women wearing tights and a bodice that revealed my bosom."

"Oh, I would love to go to New York one of these days," Emma said. "But I know I never will."

"Why not?" Sally asked.

"Because I think such a large place would just scare me to death," Emma replied breathlessly.

"Besides, I could never let her go," Flora said. "If I did, I'm afraid all the cowboys who have fallen in love with her would riot in protest."

"Yes ma'am, we more'n likely would." Unnoticed, a cowboy had come into the parlor at that precise moment. He stood there holding his hat in his hand.

"Do you see what I mean?" Flora asked with a little chuckle.

Janey recognized him as one of the cowboys who worked at the PSR Ranch, and she knew that he was probably there for her. "Hello, Cecil, are you looking for me?"

"Yes, ma'am, I am. Mr. Richards, he sent me to fetch you."

"To *fetch* me? Is that what he said?" The inflection of Janey's voice displayed her irritation at the word.

"Well, uh, no ma'am. He didn't quite put it like that. What he said was, would I go to town and find you and bring you back."

"What if I don't want to go back?"

"If you don't want to go, I don't reckon there's anything I could do about it," Cecil said. "But Mr. Richards would more 'n likely be atakin' it out on me if I was to go back to the ranch without you."

"All right," Janey said, smiling. "I wouldn't want to see you get in trouble. Go on back. You may tell him that I'll be there, shortly."

"Ma'am, if it's all the same to you, I'd just as soon ride alongside your surrey."

Flora set her cards on the table. "You don't have to go back, Janey. You don't have to go back ever. Just tell Richards that you've decided to come work for me."

Janey laughed. "Ha, wouldn't he like that?"

"Why do you work for him, anyway? You could make as much money here as you do working for him. You could make even more money. I know you don't have any qualms about our business because someone could say you are doing the same thing for Richards."

"That's true," Janey said, making no attempt to deny the charge that she was Richards's mistress.

"And, my dear, your position with him is tenuous at best. Someone is going to shoot him dead one of these days. Richards's enterprises, by your own admission, are suspect."

"That's true as well."

Janey had no idea that the men she was working for were the same men who had killed her father. She didn't know, and had no way of knowing, that her father was dead. She had no idea that someone named Smoke was looking for her employers. Even if someone had told her that he was, it wouldn't have meant anything to her. She didn't know anyone named Smoke. As far as she knew, her brother, if he was still alive, was named Kirby.

Denver

Because there was train service from Denver to Red Cliff, Smoke decided to board his horse at a local livery stable while he was gone.

"Seven?" the hostler asked. "Your horse's name is Seven?"

"Yes."

"Why did you name him that?"

"I didn't. He named himself. Look." Smoke pointed to the white markings on the horse's face. The markings formed the perfect numeral seven.

The stable man nodded. "Yeah, I see what you mean. Well, don't you worry none about Seven while you're gone. He's in good hands."

Seven looked over at Smoke, who smiled and patted him on the face. "You be a good horse for this nice gentleman. Just rest for a while. I'll be back soon."

Leaving the stable, Smoke walked down to the depot where he bought a round-trip train ticket with a voucher that Marshal Holloway had given him. "Is the train on time?"

"We got a telegram from its last stop," the ticket agent said. "It's runnin' no more than fifteen minutes or so late. It won't be too much longer. Just have a seat and make yourself comfortable, Deputy."

"Thanks, I will." He bought a newspaper, then

took a seat on one of the padded benches in the waiting room.

A young mother was sitting just across from him, and he touched the brim of his hat in greeting. She nodded her head in reply. Her son was sitting on the floor in front of her, playing with a carved horse and wagon.

Smoke began carefully reading the newspaper, looking, as he always did, for any mention of the names Richards, Stratton, or Potter. It didn't seem likely that he would find them as easily as seeing their names in the paper, but he didn't want to leave any stone unturned. People like those three might wind up with their names in the paper. If there were no wanted posters out on them, they would have no reason to worry, so he was pretty sure they would be vain enough to have their names in the paper for just about any occasion.

After a long perusal of the paper, he put it aside, writing it off as a fruitless attempt.

"Folks, the train for Golden, Central City, Eagle, Glenwood Springs, and points west has arrived on track number three," the ticket agent said, holding a speaking tube to his mouth. "If you are holding tickets for that train, you need to proceed to track number three now."

The town of Red Cliff wasn't announced, but Smoke knew it was between Central City and Eagle.

"Mama, that's our train!" the little boy shouted, and started running toward the door.

"Johnny, come back here!" his mother called out in panic.

Getting up quickly, Smoke ran after the boy, swept him up in his arms, and brought him back to his mother.

"Oh, thank you, sir," the grateful mother said. "He is so excited about this train trip. I fear he might get too close to the track and get careless."

Smoke tapped the star on his shirt. "You see this badge?" he said to the boy.

The boy nodded.

"I'm a United States marshal, and if you don't want to get into trouble with me, you'll stay close to your mother. Do you understand?"

"Yes, sir," the boy replied in an awed voice.

The mother smiled. "Thank you again. He'll stay close to me now. He doesn't want to go to jail. Do you, Johnny?"

Johnny reached up to take his mother's hand. "No, ma'am. I don't want to go to jail."

"Then you hold my hand, and we'll go outside together to board the train."

"Yes, Mama."

Outside the depot was the smell of smoke under the car shed, though the roof was high enough that the smoke wasn't oppressive. Six tracks could be seen under the shed, with concrete walks extending out between them. Four of the tracks were currently occupied, including track number three.

Smoke glanced toward the faces in the windows of the cars in the train on track number two, which was slowly pulling out of the station. He wondered, in passing, if one of them might be Stratton or Potter or Richards.

He had never seen Richards, but Smoke somehow knew he would recognize the man if he saw him. He couldn't explain exactly how—just something in his gut.

He climbed aboard his train and settled into his seat, then stared out the window as the train departed the station, rolled through the city, and finally into the unsettled countryside.

His assignment had nothing to do with finding the three men he had sworn to bring to justice, but the badge would give him more flexibility in his search.

When he asked questions from behind that star, the response was a little quicker and more detailed. The biggest advantage to the badge was that it gave him the freedom an ordinary citizen wouldn't have when taking the law into his own hands.

He didn't have to worry about that. He *was* the law.

CHAPTER 3

Bury

As Janey drove the surrey down the road toward the PSR Ranch in response to Josh Richards's summons, the clop of the hoofbeats, not only of the horse pulling the surrey, but also the one Cecil was riding, built a cocoon of sound around her, allowing her to think without distraction. She considered Flora's offer to come work for her, and she knew that the idea wasn't all that far-fetched. She had worked in such a place before, for a madam in Dallas known as Chicago Sue. Sue had given her the name she had used for a while, Fancy Lil.

It was during that time of her life she had met the man known as Big Ben Conyers, one of her customers who had wanted more than an hour of lust, paid for and promptly forgotten. He had fallen in love with "Fancy Lil," who was touched enough by his devotion to reveal her real name.

With more between them, Janey had gotten pregnant. When he heard the news, Big Ben had been

eager to marry her. He had even taken her to his vast
Live Oaks Ranch, north of Fort Worth, and seen to it
that she had the best of care until she gave birth to
their daughter, beautiful redheaded Rebecca. Janey
had promised Ben that they would be married as
soon as she recovered from giving birth.

Instead, she had cut and run, unwilling to saddle
him with the disgrace of marrying a fallen woman.
And she never, ever wanted Rebecca to hear the vi-
cious taunts of other children about her mother
being a kept woman. She wouldn't doom a child to
that sort of life.

It had been easier to leave, knowing that Ben would
raise Rebecca with all the love in his gigantic heart.
Easier . . . and at the same time, the most difficult
thing Janey Jensen had ever done in her misadven-
ture of a life.

"There's Mr. Richardson out on the front porch,"
Cecil said as they approached the house. His comment broke her reverie. "I'll put your horse and surrey away, ma'am."

"Thank you, Cecil." Janey brought the surrey to a
halt, then stepped down and handed the reins to the
young cowboy, who led both horses toward the barn.
As she approached the porch she could see that
Richards was impatient and irritated.

"Well, I see that ignorant cowhand found you."

Janey climbed the steps to the porch, which extended all the way around the big house. "What do
you want, Josh? I told you I was going into town for a
while."

"No doubt to visit with Flora."

"Flora is my friend."

"She is also a madam who runs a brothel," Richards said derisively. "If people see you going there enough times, they'll believe you're one of the same."

"What makes you think they don't believe that now?" Janey asked. "They all know what I am. It's just that I'm *yours*."

"You don't have to be. You could be my wife, you know."

Janey started to reply that she would rather be what she was than be his wife, but she held that response in check and forced a smile. "I know that, Josh. And I appreciate the offer. But let's leave things as they are for now. I enjoy being the business manager for this ranch. It gives me a sense of purpose."

"But wouldn't being my wife give you a sense of purpose?"

"Not as much. If we were married, I would lose my identity as business manager and just be the wife of one of the owners."

"The majority owner," Richards said quickly.

Again, Janey managed a smile. "Yes, you would be the majority owner, but I would still be just your wife. Josh, don't you see that it's better this way? Besides, why do you need to marry me? Don't I share your bed from time to time? And don't you know that wives get headaches a lot more often than mistresses?"

Richards laughed. "By damn, you're right. Anyway, that's not why I had Cecil come get you. I need a paper signed by someone in Denver, and I want you to take it there in person, get it signed, and bring it back to me."

"I'll need five hundred dollars," Janey said without hesitating an instant.

"Five hundred dollars?" His eyebrows rose in surprise. "Janey, are you telling me that you are going to charge me five hundred dollars to take a paper to Denver and bring it back?"

"I'm not going to charge you anything to take a paper to Denver. My goodness, if I couldn't do a simple thing like that for free, why, I would be the biggest ingrate you ever heard of."

"So you aren't going to charge me for delivering the paper?"

"Of course not," Janey said. "Why would I do something like that? It's like I told you, I'm doing that for free."

"I don't understand. What is the five hundred dollars for?"

"Darling, you don't expect me to go to Denver and not buy several new outfits, do you? That five hundred dollars is just a gift. After all, I know you want me to look good. And don't tell me you can't afford it, darling, because I do your books, remember? I know full well that you can afford it."

Richards looked at her with narrowed eyes for a moment, then abruptly laughed. "You know what? A mistress would be a lot cheaper."

"And a wife a lot more expensive," Janey reminded him.

He held up his hands in mock surrender. "All right, all right. You got me. I'll give you five hundred dollars for the trip. But I expect you to come back looking more beautiful than ever."

"You are a dear." With a smile that produced dimples, she kissed the end of her fingers, then touched them to Richards's lips.

CHAPTER 4

Red Cliff, Colorado Territory

The first thing Smoke did when he arrived in Red Cliff was go to the sheriff's office to let the local lawman know he was in town. "Sheriff Donovan, I'm Deputy U.S. Marshal Smoke Jensen. Marshal Holloway sent me. He said you might need some help."

Donovan was a lean, gray-haired, competent-looking man who had a questioning look in his eyes as he raised his head from the paperwork spread out on his scarred old desk and examined Smoke. "Pardon me for saying this, Deputy, but aren't you just a tad young for the job?"

"I was even younger when I rode with Asa Briggs during the war. Colonel Briggs never questioned me. And neither did the Yankees I fought with."

"I heard of Asa Briggs. Him and Quantrill and Bloody Bill Anderson and Little Archie Clements. So you rode with that bunch, did you?"

"Not with all of 'em. Just with Briggs."

"Well, I wore the blue myself, so I don't cotton to

ever'thing those boys did." Donovan shrugged. "But I reckon if you rode for them, you've got some sand about you. Just how much sand you have is the question."

"I've got enough sand to kill someone who's trying to kill me," Smoke replied.

Sheriff Donovan stroked his chin and studied Smoke for another moment or two, then a smile spread across his face and he stood up and stuck his hand out across his desk. "Do you know what, Deputy? I expect you do. It's good to see you, and I thank you so much for coming out here, all the way from Denver. Did you say your name was Smoke?"

"It's really Kirby, but my friends call me Smoke."

"I know it's quick, but I'd like to consider myself a friend, Smoke. My name is Emerson."

It felt a little odd calling a man that much older than him by his first name, but Smoke nodded. "Emerson, if I understood Marshal Holloway correctly, you're having a problem with cattle rustling."

"Yeah, we are. Big-time. The person behind it is a man by the name of Stan Morgan, though he goes by the moniker of Red. The rustling is so bad that a lot of ranchers are losing their spreads, and it just so happens that Morgan is the one benefiting from it. He's buying up land and cattle at less than half of what they are worth. And the hell of it is, Morgan has half the people in this town believing he's innocent. Why, just last year he was elected president of the Cattlemen's Association."

"Do you know for a fact that he's behind it?"

Donovan opened the middle drawer of his desk. "I've got signed affidavits here from two men up in

Grand County who confess to buying stolen cattle from Morgan."

"They confessed to it?"

"They didn't have much of a choice. The sheriff's deputy up there posed as a dealer and caught them dead to rights."

"If you already have those confessions, why don't you arrest Morgan?"

"We have an election for sheriff coming up soon, and Morgan has already announced that he's running against me. If I arrested him, too many people would think it's just a matter of politics. But since Colorado is just a territory and not a state, you, as a deputy federal marshal, will have jurisdiction anywhere you go, whether he's committed a violation of a federal statute or not."

"Yes, Marshal Holloway explained that to me. Do you have any idea where I might find the man?"

"I saw him and Lucas going into the Ace High Saloon about half an hour ago. I'm sure he's still there."

"Lucas?"

"Lucas Babcock is his right-hand man," Donovan explained. "He also does a lot of his dirty work. When somebody needs to be intimidated, Babcock is generally the one who gets sent to intimidate them." The sheriff hesitated, then went on. "Listen, if Morgan resists arrest, don't push him just yet. As long as I have you to press the federal charges, I can get a couple of my deputies, and we'll help you make the arrest. What I'm saying is that Morgan is very good with a gun, and Babcock is even better. I wouldn't want you to put yourself into an untenable situation."

"Thanks for the warning," Smoke replied, trying to keep a touch of wry humor out of his voice. He pulled the warrant from his pocket, then took a pen from the inkwell on Sheriff Donovan's desk. "What were those names again? Their full names."

"Stanley Morgan and Lucas Babcock," Donovan said.

Smoke wrote them onto the blank space, then blew on the ink to dry it. He put the warrant in his pocket. "It might be a good idea for you to tell me what they look like."

Donovan chuckled. "Yeah, it might at that. They call Morgan Red for a reason. It's not only his hair that's red. He has the reddest skin I've ever seen. You can't miss him. And Babcock has a handlebar mustache, as well as a purple scar that looks somethin' like a fishhook under his left eye."

"What about the people in the saloon? Are they likely to take Morgan's side?"

"There will be a few who generally support him, I reckon, but they would mostly be honest people who just aren't ready to believe that he's a cattle thief. Like I said, he's already announced that he's going to run for sheriff. If it actually comes to a showdown between Morgan and the law, they'll stay out of it. Paul Gordon, the bartender, is a good man, and you can count on him to keep the others honest."

"Thanks." Smoke started to turn around and leave the office, then paused. "Oh, you might want to open a cell door. I wouldn't want Morgan and Babcock to feel unwelcome when I bring them back."

As Smoke walked down the street from the sheriff's office to the saloon, he could hear piano music spilling through the openings above and below the batwing doors.

He stepped into the Ace High and moved quickly to the side and put his back against the wall, a procedure he used every time he entered a saloon. The place wasn't full, but it did have more customers than he would have expected early in the evening.

He studied the others in the saloon. Less than half of them were wearing guns, and less than half of those looked as if they really knew how to use them. From the descriptions Sheriff Donovan had provided, he recognized Morgan and Babcock at the far end of the bar. Unlike most of the men in the saloon, they were wearing their guns in a way that indicated they knew how to use them quite well.

Loosening his pistol in his holster, Smoke walked halfway down the bar, then stopped. "Would you two gentlemen be Stanley Morgan and Lucas Babcock?" The words were loud and authoritative.

Everyone in the saloon stopped talking and looked toward him. Those who were in position to see him from the front saw the star on his shirt. The two men standing at the bar between him and the men he had just called out to moved quickly to get out of the way.

"Who wants to know?" Morgan asked as he turned his head to gaze without much real curiosity at the newcomer.

"Mr. Morgan, I'm Deputy U.S. Marshal Smoke Jensen." Although his name was gaining some recognition, he wasn't all that well-known. Since neither of them reacted to his name, he realized that neither had ever heard of him. That, he knew, was to his advantage.

"What can I do for you, Deputy?" Morgan asked.

"I have a warrant for your arrest, Morgan. And for you as well, Babcock. I stopped by Sheriff Donovan's office before I came overhere and asked him to get a jail cell ready for you. He ought to have it waiting for you by now."

With that announcement, everyone in the saloon got up from the tables and moved out of the way, backing all the way up to the wall.

Out of the corner of his eye, Smoke saw a reflection in the mirror behind the line of whiskey bottles. A man who hadn't moved remained at the end of the bar behind Smoke, staring into his beer mug as if he had no interest in what was going on around him.

"What did you say?" Morgan asked, saying the words in a scoffing, laughing tone of voice. "Did you say that you asked that old fool of a sheriff to get a cell ready for us?"

"That's exactly what I said."

"Now, why would you want to go and do a damn fool thing like that?"

Still standing in the same spot, Smoke answered. "Because, Morgan, I'm arresting you and your friend there for cattle rustling."

"Are you crazy, Deputy?" Morgan threw out his left hand in an annoyed gesture. "What makes you think I have anything to do with all the cattle rustling that's been going on around here?"

"You admit that there has been a lot of cattle rustling going on?"

"Yeah, sure there has. I know about it because I'm the president of the cattlemen's association, but I don't have anything to do with it."

"From what I've heard, your organization is losing members, what with so many ranches being driven out of business by the rustling. I've also heard that you're the one benefiting from their losses."

"Benefiting? I'm helping them. I'm buying them out when they have no place else to go."

"For pennies on the dollar," Smoke pointed out.

"They don't have to sell unless they want to," Morgan responded with a sneer.

Smoke glanced again at the mirrored reflection of the man standing at the bar behind him. Still no movement, not even so much as a glance of curiosity.

Babcock spoke up for the first time. "Didn't you just say that you was a deputy United States marshal?" he asked in a rusty-sounding voice.

"I did."

"Well, even if we was guilty, which I'm sure as hell not saying that we was. But even if we was, it wouldn't be any of your concern. You've got no authority in Summit County."

"Sure I do. As a deputy United States marshal, I've got authority from New York to San Francisco."

"Only for federal cases. Since when is cattle rustling a federal offense, anyway?" Morgan asked.

Smoke smiled as he explained the situation. "Morgan, this is a territory, not a state. I have authorization all over Colorado. I can arrest you for stealing the United States mail or for spitting in the street."

Babcock grunted. "That's a pretty lame charge,

ain't it, Deputy? Are you tellin' us that the whole federal government is comin' down on me an' Mr. Morgan just for spittin' in the street?"

"No. I'm not telling you that the whole federal government is coming down on you, period."

"Well then, what are you tellin' us?" Morgan demanded.

"I'm telling you that *I'm* coming down on you."

"But you're a deputy U.S. marshal," Babcock protested.

"That's right."

"So that means that you do represent the whole federal government."

A broad smile spread across Smoke's face. "Well now, if you're going to put it that way, I suppose you could say that I do represent the whole federal government."

"I'm getting tired of all this palaver," Morgan snapped. "This isn't about spitting in the street, is it?"

"No, it's about stealing cattle," Smoke repeated.

"So you come out here from Denver, just to get involved in a local case?" Morgan asked.

"It's my job."

"Stickin' your nose in somebody else's business isn't much of a job," Morgan said.

"Is that so? Well, right now it's the only job I have, and the truth is, I sort of like it. I especially like it when I can put lowlife people like you in jail."

"Deputy, look out!" the bartender suddenly shouted.

Even as the bartender shouted his warning, Smoke caught sight of movement in the mirror. Spinning around, he saw that the man who had been so studiously nursing his drink at the far end of the bar was pointing a gun at him.

Smoke pulled his own gun, drawing and firing in the same fluid motion, doing it so quickly that the noise of his shot blended with his assailant's shot. They sounded like one gun going off, even though the other man had fired a split second sooner. Smoke felt the bullet fly through the air next to his ear.

"Look out! Babcock and Morgan have drawed on you!" someone else shouted.

Smoke whirled back toward the two men. Remembering that Donovan had told him Babcock was the faster of the two, he took him first.

Even with the gun already in his hand, Babcock was unable to get a shot off before Smoke fired. The bullet slammed into Babcock's chest and threw him against the bar. He bounced off and pitched forward.

In a quick, unbroken action, Smoke shot Morgan as the cattleman was squeezing the trigger. Like the shot of the first man who had tried to kill Smoke, Morgan's bullet whizzed by harmlessly. Smoke, however, was deadly accurate, his bullet catching Morgan between the eyes. It bored through his brain and exploded out the back of his skull in a grisly pink spray. Morgan toppled backward on the sawdust-littered floor. His right arm flopped over onto Babcock's body, the smoking gun still in his hand. Morgan's eyes were open, but a third opening, a small, black hole right at the bridge of his nose, trickled out a small amount of blood. The floor beneath his head was already stained red with the blood that had gushed from the exit wound.

The others in the saloon looked at Morgan's body in shock. It had all happened so fast that for a moment, they could almost believe it hadn't happened at all. Validation of the shooting was the drifting cloud of acrid smoke from the five shots that had been fired in less than a second.

"Are they all dead?" someone asked in awe.

"Yeah," another man answered.

"Huh. He got all three of 'em. I ain't never seen nothin' like that!"

Even as they began to gather around the three bodies in morbid curiosity, Sheriff Donovan came rushing in, gun drawn. He holstered his pistol and walked over to Smoke. "I'll be damned! You did this, Deputy?"

"I didn't have any choice. I explained the situation and tried to arrest them, but they weren't having any of it."

"You should have seen it, Emerson," the bartender said. "All three of 'em drew on this fella first, and he beat 'em all."

"So, Paul, you'd be willin' to sign a statement that Deputy Jensen here was in the right when he shot these three men?"

"It's like he said, Emerson, the deputy didn't have no choice."

"That's right, Sheriff," one of the customers said. "Them other three drawed first. I'll sign any paper you want me to sign sayin' that very thing."

"That won't be necessary," Sheriff Donovan said. "Deputy Jensen was acting in the line of duty. That's all that's required. If you would, Paul, send someone to get Proffer down here to pick up the bodies. Tell him the county will pay for the burial."

"Tyson, there's a free beer in it for you if you go," the bartender said to the nearest customer.

Tyson smiled. "You just have that beer ready when I get back."

CHAPTER 5

"I didn't think Morgan would take too kindly to being arrested, but I didn't figure he would take it this far," Sheriff Donovan said when he and Smoke had returned to the sheriff's office.

"I'm sorry I had to do it. I would like to have brought them in for trial. There would be some satisfaction for the people who were cheated by these men," Smoke said.

"Are you kidding? Don't be silly. There's nothing to be sorry about. As far as I'm concerned, you just saved the county the cost of a trial. And don't you worry about the people gettin' their land and cattle back. We'll put together an arbitration board that will do that very thing."

"I was able to identify Morgan and Babcock. But who was the other man?" Smoke asked.

"That is, or rather that was, Lloyd Winters. He was another of Morgan's men, but I didn't know he was here in town or I would've told you about him, too. I guess the way it turned out, I didn't really have to warn you. You handled things pretty well on your own. I sure feel foolish now for questionin' you about your age and all."

"No need to feel foolish about it, Sheriff. If we both wait long enough, I won't be young anymore."

For a second, Sheriff Donovan looked at Smoke as if he didn't understand the response, then catching the joke, he laughed. "Yeah, I guess that's right, ain't it?"

"What about the rest of Morgan's men? There are more of them, aren't there?" Smoke asked.

"Yes, but with Morgan gone they'll be easy to round up. I expect one or two of them will even turn state's evidence. That will help us do right by all the people Morgan stole from."

"Then you'd say my job here is finished?"

The sheriff nodded. "I would indeed."

"Then I have a favor to ask of you," Smoke said.

"Deputy, if it is something I can grant, I damn sure will do that."

"I'm looking for three men. Wiley Potter, Muley Stratton, and Josh Richards. Have you ever heard of them?"

Sheriff Donovan frowned in thought for a moment, then shook his head. "No, I can't say that I have. Are they wanted men?"

"Well, they're certainly wanted by me," Smoke said. "As to whether there are actually any dodgers out for them, I don't really know."

"Why do you want them? That is, if you don't mind my askin'?"

"I don't mind at all. They killed my pa."

Sheriff Donovan pursed his lips and then nodded.

"That's a good enough reason to want them, all right."

"If you ever hear anything about them, would you let me know? You can send word to Marshal Holloway. He knows I'm looking for them, and he'll get word to me."

"Yes, of course I'll let you know."

"Good. I'll be obliged to you." Smoke reached out to shake the sheriff's hand. "I guess I'll be getting back to Denver now."

"When you get back, please thank Marshal Holloway for sending you down when I asked for help, will you?"

"I'll be glad to," Smoke said.

"Are you hungry?"

"Yeah, I thought I might get a bite to eat before I take the late train back. Do you have a recommendation?"

"I've got more than a recommendation. I've got an offer. Come on over to the City Pig with me and I'll buy your meal."

"Sounds like a good offer to me," Smoke replied with a smile.

As they were eating their dinner, Smoke and the sheriff carried on a conversation which began with no purpose but the pleasant passing of time.

"These men you're looking for," Donovan said. "Were they in the war with you?"

"Not me. I was most always in Missouri or Kansas. These men were in Virginia. I know they were at a place called the Wilderness."

"For the South or the North?"

"For the South, I'm sorry to say."

"I tell you what. As soon as we finish eating our dinner, there's someone I'd like you to meet. He was a colonel in the Confederate Army, and I know he was part of the Wilderness campaign. I've heard him speak of it. He might have some information that would be useful to you. If you want me to, I'll introduce you to him."

"Yes, I would appreciate that very much."

"His name is Colonel Garrison Boyle. He's a rather large man, doesn't get around much," Sheriff Donovan said. "He can no longer sit a horse, so he spends all his time in his house. His wife takes care of him."

After they had finished their meal, the two men walked through the twilight to a neatly kept house on one of Red Cliff's side streets. Donovan led Smoke onto the porch and rapped with a brass knocker mounted on the front door.

"Sheriff Donovan," Mrs. Boyle said, greeting him with a friendly smile as she opened the door. She was a small, pleasant-looking woman with tightly curled dark hair turning gray. "It's always a pleasure to see you."

"Is the colonel receiving today, Mrs. Boyle?"

"Oh, yes, he does enjoy company, and I'm sure he would especially enjoy talking to you and your guest. Please, do come in."

"Thank you." Donovan and Smoke took off their hats as they stepped inside. "We're not interrupting your supper, are we?"

"Not at all."

Mrs. Boyle led them into the small house, into a room that had all the shades pulled so that it was in deep shadow, except for one flickering lamp. A hulking form sat in a chair situated just outside the circle of light.

"Colonel, Sheriff Donovan is here to see you."

"Hello, Emerson," a deep voice rumbled from the shadows. "Come closer."

"How are you doing, Colonel?"

"I'm doing about as well as any three-hundred-and-fifty pound man can expect," Colonel Boyle said. His face was as round as the moon, topped by strands of lank, fair hair.

As Smoke drew closer, he could see that three hundred and fifty pounds wasn't an exaggeration, unless, perhaps, the number was lower than the man's actual weight. He wondered how the chair could even support such weight, but a closer examination showed that the chair was well constructed, with extra bracing.

"Who's your friend, Emerson?"

"He's a deputy United States marshal, name of Smoke Jensen."

"You're the man who took care of Morgan, Babcock, and Winters, aren't you?" Colonel Boyle asked.

"Lord, Colonel, how could you know that?" Sheriff Donovan asked. "It only happened a couple hours ago."

"Word gets around, my boy. Word gets around." Colonel Boyle patted his hand on the arm of the chair. "Even when you are chair bound as I am."

"Colonel, Smoke was in the war on the same side as you, and he'd like to ask you some questions."

Boyle chuckled. "Well, Emerson, you damn Yankee, now you are outnumbered by Rebels. How does that feel?"

"Intimidating," Donovan replied with a little laugh.

"Good, good. Now you know how we felt for the entire war." Boyle turned his attention to Smoke. "Who were you with, son?"

"I was with Briggs."

"Gregg? General Gregg's Brigade? Yes, I knew it well."

"No, sir, Briggs. Asa Briggs."

The smile left Colonel Boyle's face. "Didn't he have an irregular unit with Quantrill?"

"We've been lumped in with Quantrill, but other than the fact that we were an irregular unit not attached to any major command, we were nothing like him."

Colonel Boyle nodded his head. "That is good to know. Some of those irregulars—on both sides— were nothing but butchers."

Smoke surely couldn't argue with that. "Colonel, I'm looking for three men who took part in the Wilderness Campaign."

"On the Southern side?"

"Yes, sir."

"What do you want with them?"

"I want to kill them," Smoke answered frankly.

Colonel Boyle blinked. "Well, that was an honest answer. Unexpected, but honest. Son, let me tell you this. I fought in the Wilderness Campaign with a lot of good men. I don't know who you're looking for or why you're looking for them, but why should I turn over any Confederate soldier to the Yankees?" He held up his hand to forestall any protest from Smoke. "And before you tell me again that you fought for the South, you are now wearing the badge of a deputy U.S. marshal. That means you are working for the federal government, and that means you are a Yankee."

"The men I'm looking for are Wiley Potter, Muley Stratton, and Josh Richards."

"Potter, Stratton, and Richards?" Boyle blew out an explosive breath. "Well, why didn't you say so? Those evil—" The colonel stopped in mid-sentence and squinted at Smoke. "Wait a minute. Jensen? Your last name is Jensen? Would you be any kin to Luke Jensen?"

"I would be. Luke Jensen was my brother."

Colonel Boyle nodded. "Yes, I can see why you're after them. When those deserters stole all that Confederate gold, they shot Luke. Officially, he was reported dead, but we never found his body, so to be honest with you, I never knew whether he was killed or not. Do you know?"

"No, sir, I don't," Smoke replied. "I've had no contact with Luke since he left for the war. But I do know that Stratton, Potter, and Richards killed my pa when he tracked them down after the war. And that's reason enough for me to go after them."

"I wish I could help you, son, I really do. I heard once that they were in New Mexico, but I can't be too sure about that. I just know this. They stole a lot of gold, a lot of it . . . and somebody with that much money is going to spend enough that they're going to get themselves noticed. If you look for them long enough, you will find them."

"That's funny," Smoke said. "That's just what my pa said."

Summit County, Colorado Territory

One hundred and fifty miles east of Red Cliff, three men were standing in the middle of the road, just north of Rush Creek.

"You think three sticks of dynamite are enough, Pete?" Eddie asked.

"Yeah, three sticks are plenty." The man was working with the dynamite.

"Well, let's get it buried and get the fuse laid. The coach is goin' to be here any minute."

"Don't you be rushin' me now, Eddie. You don't want to be too careless when you're messing with dynamite, otherwise you could blow a hand off. You have to be slow and careful."

"Can't you be quick and careful?"

"We're almost there. I've got the sticks buried; all I have to do now is run the detonating wire over to the plunger."

"Hurry, I can hear the coach coming," put in the third man, Merlin, speaking for the first time.

The three men hustled over to the side of the road, then lay down in the ditch. Pete had his hand on the plunger. "Just keep on comin'," he said as he watched for the stagecoach. "Yes, sir, just keep on comin'. I've got a big surprise all laid out for you."

As the six-horse team of the Colorado Springs stage crossed Rush Creek, the hooves of the horses and the turning wheels churned the water, sending splashes into the air where, suspended for a second, they flashed in the late afternoon sun.

"Hyah! Hyah!" the driver shouted, popping the whip over the heads of the team.

Three people were inside—George Thomas, his wife Edith, and their seven-year-old son Billy.

"I do hope we get there before it's too late. I would hate to think that the hotel rooms are all rented and we wouldn't have a place to stay," Edith said.

"We don't have to worry any about that," George said, reassuring her. "Mr. Murphy informed me that he already had a hotel room reserved for us. We can stay there, at his expense, until we find a house of our own."

"Oh, what a wonderful thing for him to do," Edith said.

Every now and then, Billy would lean out the window and point his carved wooden pistol toward the rear of the coach. "Bang, bang, bang!"

"What are you shooting at, Billy?" George asked.

"There's a bunch of stagecoach robbers on horseback and they're trying to catch up with the coach. Bang, bang! I got one."

"Just one? You shot twice," George teased.

"Yes, but one of them I just hit in the shoulder. Bang! Click. Click. Oh, I'm out of bullets."

"Already?"

"Haven't you been counting them, Papa? I've shot six times already, and my gun only holds six bullets."

"You're right," George said, nodding gravely. "I should have been counting them."

"That's all right, Papa. You aren't a famous gun-fighter like I am."

"Oh, so you're a famous gunfighter, are you?"

"Yes, sir, I am. Why, I expect there are books written about me."

George chuckled. "I expect there are, too."

"Mama, will I be going to school in Eureka?" Billy asked, as he "reloaded" bullets into his six-shooter.

"Yes, of course you will, dear. We are moving there."

"But I won't know anyone in that school. All my friends are in Sandborn."

"You'll make new friends in Eureka."

Billy started to pout. "I don't want any new friends. I like my old friends."

"Oh, don't be silly. You'll like your new friends just as much," Edith said with a smile.

"I wish we—"

At that precise moment, the coach was enveloped in a fiery blast as the three sticks of dynamite detonated underneath. The stagecoach blew apart in a brilliant burst of flame.

CHAPTER 6

"Woo, damn! Did you see that?" Merlin asked excitedly. "It went up all fiery-like!" He jumped up from the outlaws' hiding place and danced a little jig as burning pieces of the stagecoach came crashing back to earth in the road.

The three men waited until all the debris had stopped falling, then cautiously approached the devastation. The coach was in several pieces, none too large for two men to pick up. Some of the pieces were still burning.

Lying in the wreckage were five bodies—the driver and shotgun guard, a man, a woman, and a child. They were burned and torn almost beyond recognition as being human.

The two rearmost horses of the six-horse team were dead. The next two horses were bleeding from wounds, and only the front two were uninjured, but they were trapped in the harness, unable to move.

The three outlaws picked through the wreckage until they found the canvas mail pouch.

"How much did we get?" Eddie asked.

Pete cut the bag open and discarded the letters inside it until he came to a bank pouch. "Here it is!"

The bank pouch was opened, then the smiles faded.

"Eighty-seven dollars?" Merlin said after they had counted the money. "All this for eighty-seven dollars?"

"The big guy ain't gonna be pleased," Eddie said.

"What will he have to complain about?" Pete asked. "We done what we was supposed to do. We held up the stage. If eighty-seven dollars was all it had, that ain't our fault. He's the one that picks the jobs out for us."

"How come he don't come with us?" Merlin asked. "We're the ones takin' all the risks. He gets his cut, and he don't do nothin'."

"You want to take that up with him?" Pete asked.

"No," Merlin admitted.

"I didn't think so. There'll be other jobs. Come on, let's get out of here."

Leaving the dead bodies and the nervously whinnying horses behind them, the three men took their paltry proceeds from the brutal robbery and rode off.

Two hours after the three men rode away, Dooley Cooper, owner of the Summit County Stage Line, was one of five men walking around the wreckage. The five bodies had already been loaded onto a wagon, ready to be taken on in to Eureka.

"Boss, them two hurt horses is goin' to have to be

put down," said one of Cooper's men. "I don't know how they lived this long, hurt as bad as they are."

"Yes, Carl, by all means, put them down," Cooper said. "We're going to have to dig a big hole to bury them. We can't leave them here."

"I've got Dewey and Perkins diggin' now," Carl said. "We can use the horses that weren't hurt to pull the others out of the road."

"Take care of those poor beasts."

As Carl walked back over to the bleeding and suffering horses, from which the two lead animals had already been disconnected, Cooper continued to look around what was left of his stagecoach. He saw a wooden pistol lying in the road and bent down to pick it up. A name was carved in the handle.

Billy.

"I don't recall taking on a large money shipment." Fitzsimmons was the clerk of the Summit County Stage Line. Normally he wouldn't have been out in the field, but when the report came in that the coach hadn't just been robbed, but had been completely demolished, Cooper had figured he would need every man in his employ to get the mess cleaned up.

Cooper agreed. "We didn't have a large shipment. Whatever money the coach was carrying had to be less than one hundred dollars, or the bank would have notified us."

"Who would do something like this for less than one hundred dollars?" Fitzsimmons asked.

Cooper showed Fitzsimmons the carved wooden pistol. "This must have belonged to the kid." He shook his head. "What sort of lowlife would blow up a stagecoach and kill everyone in it, for *any* amount of money?"

"Here comes the sheriff." Fitzsimmons pointed to an approaching rider.

"*Now* he gets here," Cooper said in disgust.

Sheriff Jesse Hector was a tall, very thin man with dark hair, a pencil-thin mustache, and a prominent Adam's apple. Dismounting, he tied his horse to the wagon containing the bodies of the five people killed in the stagecoach blast.

"Damn, they did a job on it, didn't they?" Hector said as he approached what was left of the wreckage. Almost half of it had already been cleared away.

"Sheriff, you say that almost in admiration," Cooper said. "There's absolutely nothing about those criminals to admire. They're animals. They killed five human beings, four horses, and destroyed one of my coaches."

"How much money did they get for all this?" Hector asked as he looked over the wreckage.

"I'm not sure. We'll have to wait and see what the bank says. All I know is, they got less than one hundred dollars."

The sheriff jerked around with a surprised look on his face. "Did you say they got less than one hundred dollars?"

"That's right."

"But how can that be? It was my understanding that the bank was going to be transferring ten thousand dollars today."

"Where did you hear that?"

"I don't know. Maybe Scott told me."

Matthew Scott was the president of the bank.

Cooper shook his head. "Well if he was plannin' on shippin' that much money, he must have decided to put it off until later. We have a contract. By contract, anytime he ships more than one hundred dollars, he has to let me know. He hasn't said anything to me about ten thousand dollars, so you better believe it wasn't on this coach."

"Damn," Fitzsimmons said. "Boss, you know what I think? I think that whoever did this must have heard the same information Sheriff Hector heard. They must have thought the bank was shipping a lot of money. Why else would they go to all this trouble and kill all these people?"

"I guess you're right." Cooper raised the wooden pistol up to look at it. "I can't believe anyone is mean enough to dynamite a man and his family. Especially a little kid."

"Boss, there are some mean people in the world. Me and you both know that," Carl put in.

From the *Rocky Mountain News,* October 7, 1870:

SCURRILOUS ATTACK ON STAGECOACH

ALL KILLED

On the fifth, instant, a person or persons unknown planted dynamite in the road over which the Eureka-bound stagecoach of the Summit County Stage Line was required to travel. No doubt activated by some remote means, the dynamite exploded under the coach.

Killed in the attack were the driver, Lloyd "Beans" Crabtree and the shotgun guard Gilbert Wyatt. The passengers, also killed, were George Thomas, his wife Edith, and their seven-year-old son Billy. Thomas was going to Eureka to take a job as a pharmacist for John Murphy, in the Murphy Apothecary of that city.

The Summit County Stage Line lost four horses in the attack, two of which were killed in the explosion and two which sustained injuries so grievous that it was necessary for the poor creatures to be put down.

What is not understood is why the perpetrator or perpetrators chose this particular coach to attack, as, according to the bank's transfer records, it was carrying only eighty-seven dollars.

Sheriff Jesse Hector of Breckenridge in Summit County, where the attack on the stagecoach took place, has stated that he is investigating the crime.

"Eighty-seven dollars? You come here with eighty-seven damn dollars?"

"That's all the stagecoach was a-carryin', I swear," Pete said.

"I know, I know. I read it in the papers. I don't know what happened. I heard that it was going to be carrying a lot more money than that."

"I'm glad you read it in the paper, boss, and ain't

got the idea that maybe me and the others was tryin' to cheat you out of your cut," Merlin said.

The outlaws' employer snorted in contempt. "I don't think any of you are dumb enough to try anything like that."

"Have you got any more jobs in mind for us?" Pete asked.

"I don't have anything yet, but I'll keep my eyes peeled and my ears open, and when I come up with something else, I'll let you know."

Denver

Janey stood on the platform waiting for her luggage to be brought to her. She had already hailed a cab. The driver, leaving his hack tied out front, was standing beside her, waiting to receive the luggage from the baggage claim so he could carry it to the cab.

"Driver, wait here for me, will you? Here is my claim ticket for the luggage. I want to buy a newspaper," Janey said.

"Yes, ma'am," the driver replied.

Richards had given her the five hundred dollars she had asked for, so she needed to plan her buying excursion, which she would take care of as soon as she had the paperwork signed. She figured to start her shopping spree by perusing all the ads in the paper.

Standing nearby on the platform, Smoke watched the pretty woman walk away. For a fleeting moment, he thought there was something familiar about her, but it was for an instant only. He had seen, and met, a lot of women in the past several years.

He stepped closer to the driver. "Is your cab for hire?"

"No, sir, I'm afraid not. I've been hired by that pretty lady over there at the newsstand. You can go ask her if she doesn't mind sharing a cab if you'd like."

"All right, thanks. I believe I will ask her." Smoke started toward the newsstand. The woman might be willing to share the cab with him . . . or she might think he was being a bit forward. At any rate, it wouldn't hurt to ask. Besides, he wanted to get a closer look at her. He couldn't shake the idea that he had seen her somewhere before—not only seen her but had actually met her.

"Smoke!" a man's voice called out to him. "Smoke, over here! It's me, Cephus!"

The man who hailed him was another of Marshal Holloway's deputies, Cephus Prouty.

"Hello, Doodle!" Smoke called back, using the deputy's nickname. Turning away from the woman at the newsstand, he walked toward the deputy marshal.

Janey was just about to buy the paper when she heard the man's voice. Something about it caught her attention. Just a note, but something that tugged at a distant memory, long buried. She turned toward him, but he was walking away from her.

She would have liked to get a closer look, but she was afraid to. What if he was someone she had known in her other life, when she was on the line for Chicago Sue? Or even more dangerous, what if it was someone she had met in Kansas City?

She turned pointedly away. If he was an old client of hers, she didn't want him to recognize her.

"What are you doing here?" Smoke asked Doodle.

"I came to see if you wanted a ride back to the office. Sheriff Donovan sent a telegram to Holloway, telling him what train you would be on."

"Well, that's very nice of you to meet me."

Doodle grinned. "Yeah, well, I want to get on your good side. Sheriff Donovan says you're a hero because of what you done over in Red Cliff."

"Sheriff Donovan exaggerates. But it was nice of him to send word as to what train I would be on." Smoke looked back toward the newsstand where he had seen the woman he thought he had recognized, but she was no longer there.

"What do you say we get a beer first?" Doodle asked.

"Sounds like a good idea to me," Smoke replied.

CHAPTER 7

"Why did you bring these papers here to have them notarized?" the notary clerk asked Janey. "You could have had them done in Salt Lake City."

"That's my fault," she lied. "I talked Mr. Richards into sending the papers here, because I wanted to come to Denver."

The clerk chuckled. "Well, I can't blame you for that. I mean who wouldn't prefer Denver to Salt Lake City? Unless you are one of 'The Saints.'" He examined the papers, then clucked his tongue. "My oh my. This involves quite a bit of land."

"Yes, the PSR is a large operation, one of the largest, if not *the* largest in all of Idaho. But, as you can see, the transfer has been duly signed by all parties concerned."

"Technically, I should witness the signing in order to notarize this."

"You mean I've made this long trip for nothing?" She pouted, looking at the notary with wide, pleading eyes. "I can't go back and tell my bosses that I didn't get these papers notarized. What will I do?"

The notary sighed. "I really shouldn't do this, but I can see that everyone has signed the documents." He chuckled again. "And I certainly would not want to see a pretty young lady like you have to go back empty-handed to your employers. Very well, I'll notarize them."

"Oh, thank you." Janey flashed her most provocative smile. "You are such a dear man."

"I wish you'd tell my wife that," the notary joked.

"Oh, honey, most wives really don't like to see me," she said in a seductive voice.

The notary laughed. "I guess I can understand that."

After getting the papers signed, she stuck them into her reticule and, flashing another coquettish smile toward the notary, left the office to begin her shopping trip. She had a lot to buy, but contrary to what Josh Richards thought, she was buying very little for herself.

Unbidden, she thought of the voice she had heard while buying a newspaper at the stand in the depot. Well aware of the saying, *Curiosity killed the cat* and knowing that she was wanted for murder back in Kansas, she wondered if the voice she'd heard was from Kansas City. What if someone was in Denver looking for her?

That killing hadn't actually been murder, of course. Janey had gunned down an abusive customer in the house where she was working. The man, who had already stabbed another girl, had gone after her with the knife.

The newspaper hadn't reported the story that way. It had called Janey a murderess. All the local lawmen were friends with the man she had shot, who was a member of the City Council, so a murder charge had been a foregone conclusion. Before she could be arrested, she had fled with the help of another customer who had befriended her, and ever since, the bloody incident had hung over her head.

Drawing in a deep breath, Janey put those unpleasant memories behind her and managed to smile at what lay before her. She had all of Denver waiting for her, and the money Richards had given her was burning a hole in her pocketbook.

Her first stop was a ladies' shoe store. She was on a personal quest to find shoes that were pretty and comfortable, and she believed that with five hundred dollars to spend, she could do just that.

Pueblo County, Colorado Territory

At that very moment, not too far away, the driver of a stagecoach saw something in the road ahead which required his immediate attention. "Whoa, whoa!" He hauled back on the reins.

Up ahead, a log was lying across the road, blocking it enough that the coach couldn't get around. A man wearing a long duster and a broad-brimmed brown hat stood calmly just in front of the log.

"What the hell happened here?" the driver asked.

"Oh, you mean this log?"

"Yeah. How did it get here?"

"I put it here."

The driver stared. "What? Why in Sam Hill would you do a thing like that?"

"Because I wanted you to stop, and I didn't figure you would if all I did was try and wave you down." Moving fast, the man pulled his pistol and pointed it toward the driver and the shotgun guard. "I believe you're carrying fifteen hundred dollars, aren't you?"

"How in blazes did you know that?"

The man smiled. "Thank you for confirming my belief. It is my intention to take that money from you."

Slowly, almost imperceptibly, the guard started moving his hand toward the shotgun, which was leaning up against the front right corner of the footrest.

The man in the road fired his pistol. The sudden blast made both men on the seat jump as the bullet hit the shotgun, knocking it over. It fell flat into the bottom of the footrest.

"You don't want to do that," warned the man on the road. "In fact, why don't you just go ahead and put your arms up? I know it'll be a little uncomfortable for you to hold them up that way until my partners and I conclude our business here, and I apologize for that, but it just might save your life."

"What partners would that be?" the driver asked. "You're the only one I see."

The gunman nodded. "Yes, we planned it that way." He hollered, "Boys, keep an eye on them. If anyone tries to be a hero . . . shoot him."

"Where are they?" the shotgun guard asked, looking around nervously.

"You ask too many questions. How many passengers are you carrying?"

"Two men and two women."

"Ladies and gents in the coach, for your own safety, I'm going to ask that you come on out now. Stand to the side of the road where I can keep an eye on you."

Two men exited the stage first, one of them quite elderly. The two women followed. One was also quite elderly.

"I'm sorry to inconvenience you," said the surprisingly well-spoken robber. "But if you will just have a little patience with me, this will all be over in just a moment."

The older woman immediately put her hand across a brooch she was wearing.

The stagecoach robber chuckled. "You don't have to be worried, ma'am. I'm not going to be taking anything from any of you nice folks." He looked back up at the driver and the guard. "Now if you would, please, just go ahead and throw that money shipment down."

The driver picked up a canvas pouch.

"Wait a minute," the road agent snapped. "Is that the mail pouch?"

"Yes, it is."

"I don't want any of the mail. We wouldn't want all the grandmas and grandpas not to be able to write to, or hear from, their grandchildren now, would we? Just open it up and take the money out."

"The pouch is locked, and I don't have a key," the driver protested.

Quick as a wink, the man on the ground took a knife from his belt and threw it toward the driver and the shotgun guard. The blade flashed in the sunlight, then stuck in the back of the seat, exactly between them.

"Yow!" the shotgun guard shouted in shock.

"Good Lord, mister," the driver added shakily.

"Cut it open, then toss the money down," the man ordered. "I'm sure that the money is all in nice, neatly bound stacks."

The driver did as he was told, then tossed three bound stacks of currency down to the ground.

"Ah, yes, see what I mean? And now if you would, please return my knife. Carefully."

Again the driver complied, leaning down from the seat to hand the knife to the robber.

"All right. You and the guard can climb down from there and move the log off the road. It only took two of us to drag it out here, so I'm sure you won't have any trouble with it."

The robber stood by watching until the log was moved and the driver and guard had climbed back up onto the box.

"Ladies, gents, if you would, please, get back into the coach now, and do have a pleasant trip."

"You are such a nice, polite young man," the older of the two women said. "Why are you robbing stagecoaches? You know your mother wouldn't approve of such a thing."

"No, ma'am, I don't suppose she would."

"Can we go now?" the driver asked after the passengers had reboarded.

"Yes, by all means. Bye now."

"Good-bye, young man," the elderly woman called back, waving through the window of the coach.

The highwayman watched until the coach was some distance away, then he walked around to the other side of a line of rocks where his horse had been tethered for the entire time. He swung into the saddle and rode away.

Denver

Janey had so many packages that she had to hire a buckboard to take her to the depot to catch the train back to Bury, Idaho. She made arrangements for all the packages to be shipped, then she settled down in the lobby to wait for the train.

As she sat there she saw at least half a dozen families who were also waiting, husbands and their wives, and the children. They were all a part of "the other life"—how she referred to those people who lived normal, respectable lives—working fathers and mothers who stayed at home keeping house for husband and children.

Most of the time, Janey was perfectly content with her life. She had more money than she would ever spend. She had a private carriage that had been built for her in Paris and a uniformed black driver. She even had bodyguards who often accompanied her whenever she went into town.

She was certain the bodyguards were not as much for her personal protection as they were to intimidate anyone who might want to get closer to her. Especially any man who might want to speak with her.

Sometimes she would slip away, not in the ostentatious carriage with the resplendently dressed driver, but in a simple surrey. She had done it a few nights ago in order to play cards with her friends at the Pink House.

But for all the money and elegance, there were times when she watched the interplay between mothers and their children, that she felt as if something might be missing in her life. She thought of her own family, her father Emmett and her brothers Luke and Kirby. Were they still alive? And if they were still alive, where were they?

What was she being so melancholy about? She had a family—Flora, Emma, and all the other girls at the Pink House. Like her, the other girls had no family, or the family had turned their backs on the girls when they had entered the profession.

People who were drawn together by such mutual experiences were closer than normal families anyway. There was no such thing as sibling rivalry.

CHAPTER 8

Hermitage, Colorado Territory

Clell Dawson stood at the bar of the Yellow Dog Saloon, staring down into his mug of beer. The bar, the saloon, and the town were all parts of his life, even though he had never been there before. Rough towns and rougher saloons had become part of his heritage, and he couldn't deny it without denying his own existence.

Clell had noticed the young man when he first came into the bar, a slick-looking dandy, all dressed out in black and silver. Black trousers, black shirt, a silver belt buckle, his black holster decorated with silver conchos, a silver bolo tie, and a silver band around his black hat.

Clell knew who he was. He didn't actually know the man's name, but he knew who he was. For the last three or four years, he had encountered men like him all through the West.

Clell sometimes hired out his guns, but he wasn't

without scruples and sold his talent only to people who had need for a paladin to right wrongs for them. However, on those occasions when he found himself in need of money, he wasn't totally averse to out and out breaking the law by holding up a stagecoach, or a bank, or even a train.

As a result of such activities, there was paper out on him, and from time to time a bounty hunter would recognize him and try to collect. But it wasn't only bounty hunters he had to be aware of. There were others who also hired out their guns . . . with somewhat less scruples than even his rather loose adherence to principles. If they could add to their résumé the accomplishment of having beaten Clell Dawson to the draw, it would not only get rid of some of the competition, it would also increase their asking price.

Clell was sure that the dandy in black and silver was just such a man.

"Hey, you," the dandy called out.

Clell made no response, continuing to stare into his glass of beer.

"Mister, when I'm talkin' to you, you damn well better quit broodin' into your beer and pay attention to me." The young man's voice was harsh, causing the other customers in the saloon to interrupt their own activities and conversations and follow what was developing before them. They knew the young man in black. His real name was Steve Blake, but he called himself The Concho Kid. He had proven his skill with a pistol many times. At least three times right in the Yellow Dog Saloon.

Clell looked over toward him. "Well now, by all means, I do want to be well-advised. So I suppose I had better be looking at you."

"When's the last time you had a bath?" The Concho Kid asked.

In fact, Clell had taken a bath quite recently, so the only thing he had on him was some trail dust, which he intended to get off yet that night. He'd wanted a beer to get some of the trail dust out of his mouth first.

"I can't rightly say," Clell replied, purposely baiting the young man. "I don't know. Last year, I guess."

"Last year? You haven't had a bath since last year?"

"Maybe the year before. Why do you ask?"

"You're stinkin' up the place. You need a bath."

"Well now, I admit that you're a fine-looking young man. I mean, what with wearing that black outfit with all those silver geegaws and all. But if you're looking for some man to get naked and take a bath with, I have to tell you that I'm just not your type. I'm afraid you're gonna have to look somewhere else, because I'm not interested."

At the unexpected reply from the man who was being challenged by The Concho Kid, the others in the saloon laughed. At an angry glare from the gunfighter, they choked their laughs off.

Concho turned his attention back to Clell. "Mister, that smart mouth of yours may have just bit off more than you want to chew. Do you know who you're talkin' to?"

"Yes, of course I know who I'm talking to," Clell said.

A proud smile spread across Concho's face.

"I've run into people like you from Laramie to Laredo—young punks who think they can draw fast and shoot straight and who want to run up a reputation by adding another notch to the handle of their gun. How many notches do you have now?"

"Twelve," The Concho Kid replied with a sneer.

"Twelve. My oh my, that's just awfully impressive. Maybe they'll put that on your tombstone. Here lies . . . what *is* your name?"

"They call me The Concho Kid."

"You mean you don't have a regular name like everyone else in the world?"

"I'm The Concho Kid, damnit! That's all you need to know. Are you tryin' to tell me that you've never heard of me?"

"Can't say as I have," Clell replied with a wry smile. He had heard of The Kid, but he had no intention of giving the young punk the satisfaction of knowing that. "But if that's the name you want on your tombstone, I imagine you can be obliged."

Clell held his hand out, as if gesturing toward a tombstone. "Here lies The Concho Kid. He had twelve notches on his gun when he was killed. It's rather ironic, don't you think, that you'd get killed on your thirteenth try?"

A collective gasp of surprise erupted from the others in the saloon. Did the stranger in the dirty clothes really not know who he was talking to?

The arrogant smile left Concho's face. "What? What did you say?"

"You heard what I said, sonny. Of course, if you want to shut up now, and mind your own business, you might live long enough to get another notch someday. But I can guarantee you, boy, you aren't going to be putting another notch on that gun today. Not here, anyway."

"Mister, I was just goin' to fun with you a little bit," The Concho Kid said. "But now, I think I'm going to kill you. What's *your* name, anyway? I wouldn't want to kill somebody without even knowing their name."

Clell's smile broadened, and that smile unnerved Concho, who was used to seeing fear in the faces of the men he faced.

"Well, I'm afraid I don't have a fancy name like yours. My name is—"

"Draw!" The Concho Kid shouted, his hand already dipping toward his pistol as he shouted the challenge.

His gun didn't even clear leather before a pistol appeared in Clell's hand, his draw so fast it was a blur. Clell fired once, the bullet hitting The Concho Kid in the middle of his chest.

With an expression of surprise on his face, he took a step back, dropped his own gun, then slapped his hand over the wound. Blood streamed through his fingers. "How?" he asked with a pained expression on his face. "Who?"

"Well now, Concho, that's two different questions," Clell replied. "Which one do you want me to answer?"

It didn't matter which one he answered. The Concho Kid had crumpled to the sawdust-covered floor and lay there dead.

"What's your name, mister?" the bartender asked, shocked at what he had just seen.

"Dawson. Clell Dawson." He put his pistol away.

Again, there was a collective gasp from the saloon patrons, for *Clell Dawson* was a name known all through the West.

"Damn," the bartender said. "If The Kid had known that, he would have never drawn on you."

"Yeah, he would have. That boy had a need to prove himself stuck in his craw, and he would have drawn on me if I had been his own brother." Finishing his beer, Clell nodded at the bartender, then left the saloon, walked next door, and checked in to the hotel.

Bury

"Janey, you shouldn't have bought me this," Sally said, looking at the dress spread out on the bed in her small house. "I mean, why would you do such a thing?"

"Because you're my friend, and when I saw this dress while I was in Denver, I just knew it would look so good on you. Your eyes are such a beautiful color, and this dress will make them stand out. Do try it on."

"I really shouldn't. I mean, I've never given you anything. I feel like such a—"

"Nonsense. You *have* given me something. You've given me your friendship. That's something none of the other . . . ladies . . . of Bury have done." Janey set the word *ladies* apart from the rest of the sentence as if questioning whether there really were any ladies in Bury.

"And why shouldn't I?" Sally said with a broad

smile. "After all, you did save my life the first day I arrived in town."

"Yes," Janey said, returning the smile. "I did, didn't I?"

"How was your trip to Denver? You were gone for two weeks."

"I very much enjoyed it. I got to see a play . . . *Around the World in Eighty Days* it was called . . . and oh, it was so delightful. And I saw a musical revue. I know you're from the Northeast and you're used to big cities, but for a Missouri girl like me, it was all just wonderful and fascinating. I bought so many beautiful things, not only for you, but for Flora and Emma, too, and all the other girls."

"You are a valuable friend to have, Janey, in more ways than one," Sally said. "I will have to do something for you, someday."

"Like I told you, Sally, you're my friend. You know who I am and what I am, but still, you're my friend. You've already done a lot for me. Let's go so I can give away the other things."

They walked down to the Pink House, where Janey presented her gifts to Flora and the others.

"You really shouldn't have spent so much of your money on us," Flora protested.

Janey laughed. "It wasn't my money, it was Josh Richards's money. I told him that if he wanted me to get some papers signed for him in Denver, it was going to cost him five hundred dollars."

"What papers did he want signed?" Flora asked.

"They were deeds of transfer—probably illegal. They probably made him ten times as much money as I made him give me."

"Janey, why do you stay with him?" Flora wanted to know. "By your own admission, he is a crook. Someday someone is going to catch up with him."

"I'm sure they will, someday. But for now, I intend to ride that horse for as long as it has a saddle."

Flora laughed. "I like that, riding a horse for as long as it has a saddle."

"I have a gift, too," Emma announced. "I made a blackberry cobbler."

Flora's girls squealed with delight as she began cutting it up.

"Oh, this is so good!" one of the girls said as she took a bite.

"My mother used to make blackberry cobbler," Janey said. "My younger brother loved them. He could probably eat this whole thing by himself."

"Your brother? You've never mentioned that you had a brother," Flora said.

"Actually I have two of them. I think. I haven't seen either one of them in a very long time, and I have no idea where either one of them are right now, or, to be honest, even if they are still alive."

"Oh, I'm sorry."

"Yes, well, I'm not sure Kirby would want to see me, even if he is alive." Janey recalled taking all the money when she left the farm. She hadn't stolen the money, at least, not in her eyes. It was supposed to have been an investment. Garner had sworn to her that he would double, even triple the money, and it had been her intention to return the money to Kirby, with interest.

But of course, that hadn't happened.

Denver

"Smoke, didn't you say when you were in Red Cliff that you met someone who told you the men you were looking for were in New Mexico?" Marshal Holloway asked.

"He didn't say that it was definite they were in New Mexico," Smoke replied with a shrug. "He said he had heard that they might be down there."

"Then I've got another job lined up that might work out well for you. I had intended to send Doodle, but when I recalled what you told me about meeting that Confederate colonel, I decided to send you. I want you to go to Salcedo. That's a little town on the Colorado and New Mexico border. After you take care of a little incident that happened there a couple days ago, you might want to take a look around to see if you can find those three men."

Smoke smiled. "I appreciate that, Marshal. Thanks for giving me the opportunity. What is the incident you want me to take care of?"

"Well, it might a little more than just an *incident*. A few days ago a group of men broke a Mexican out of jail, then they lynched him."

Smoke frowned. "What about the local law?"

Marshal Holloway shook his head. "Well, now, that might be a part of the problem, you see. The only thing they have for local law is a couple city marshals, and this morning I got a telegram from one of the local citizens by the name of Leroy Peyton.

"It so happens that I know Peyton. He was a judge back in Kansas before he moved out here. He had to be careful with the way he worded the telegram, but he sort of suggests that Bradford and Cassidy might have been in on it. If Peyton believes that, I'd be willing to say there might be something to it."

Smoke had never heard of them. "Bradford and Cassidy?"

"They're the city marshals."

"What about the county sheriff?"

"The county sheriff is more of a political position than anything else. Right now the sheriff is Roy Beck, but he's well into his seventies. There's no way he can handle this. That's why I'm sending you."

Smoke nodded. "All right. I'll see what I can do."

"Handle it any way you want, Smoke. Then, when it's done, you can take some time off to go into New Mexico and look around."

"Thank you, Marshal. I appreciate that."

CHAPTER 9

Salcedo, New Mexico Territory

As Smoke rode near the town a week later, he didn't have to stop and inquire as to whether or not a man had been recently lynched. The truth was profanely and arrogantly displayed just outside town. A man's body was hanging from a high, horizontal limb of a large cottonwood tree.

With winter only a month away, the weather was chilly, but despite that, hanging from the tree limb for days had not been good for the corpse. The body was displaying considerable damage left by vultures. In addition, the face had been blackened by prolonged exposure and deterioration. A crudely lettered sign told the story.

THIS MEXICAN
Was hung for murder
Leave his carcass here for the buzzards

Smoke removed the marshal's star from his shirt and dropped it into his pocket before he continued his ride into Salcedo. He passed through the main part of town without stopping, going all the way to the far end of the town into the Mexican section. He stopped in front of a building with the sign CARLOS BUSTAMANTE, MORTUORIO painted on it.

Smoke didn't actually speak Spanish, but he understood enough to know that the sign meant Bustamante was the undertaker for the Mexicans. Tying Seven off in front of the building, he stepped inside, where he was greeted by a man dressed all in black.

"*Sí, señor?*"

"You're the undertaker?" Smoke asked.

"*Sí,* for the Mexicanos, I am the undertaker," Bustamante said. "The Americano undertaker is back up the street several blocks."

"I'm askin' about a Mexican." Smoke's voice was grim as he went on. "He's hanging from a tree just outside of town."

"*Sí,* that is Juan Montoya, *Dios sea con él,*" Bustamante said with a sigh as he crossed himself. "He was hanged because they say he killed an Americano *puta.* But he did not kill her."

"How do you know he didn't kill her?"

"Señora Echeverria works at the *casa de putas* as a maid. She saw Señor Quinncannon coming from the room of Señorita Fannie. He had blood on his hands, and when Señora Echeverria went into the room, Señorita Fannie . . . ah, she was dead."

"Why didn't Señora Echeverria go to the law?"

"She did, señor. She told Marshal Bradford and Marshal Cassidy what she had seen, but they did not believe her. And then, Señor Quinncannon and some others said that Montoya was the one who murdered the puta."

"Why would they choose Montoya?"

"He worked in the casa as a cook. But he was not even there, then. He was home. His neighbors saw him. When Señor Quinncannon and the others came for Montoya, the neighbors told them that he had been at home all night, but they would not listen." Bustamante shook his head solemnly. "Instead, they took him out of town and hung him from a cotton-wood tree."

"Señor Bustamante, I don't understand. If you're the undertaker for your people, why do you let the corpse of Juan Montoya hang from a tree for many days?"

"Señor, perhaps you did not see the sign. The sign said that Juan Montoya, may he rest in peace, must be left hanging there."

"You say may he rest in peace. But it doesn't seem to me that he can rest in peace with the buzzards picking at him. I want you to go get him, bring him in, and bury him."

"Señor, I am afraid of Quinncannon. He is a *muy malo hombre.*"

Smoke nodded. "All right, I suppose I can understand that. Do you have a wagon and a horse to pull it?"

"I have a wagon and a mule."

"Hitch the mule to the wagon. I'll go cut Montoya down and bring him to you."

Bustamante's eyes widened. "If you do that, you will be killed, señor."

"You let me worry about that."

Fifteen minutes later, Smoke came back into town a second time. He was driving the undertaker's wagon, and in the back of the vehicle, conspicuously visible, was the vulture-picked and deteriorating body of Juan Montoya.

"Look," he heard someone exclaim. "Ain't that Montoya's body in the back of that wagon?"

"That's the Mex undertaker's wagon, ain't it?" another man asked.

"I don't know, but that sure ain't no Mex drivin' the wagon."

"Mister?" the first man called out to Smoke. "Can't you read? Quinncannon said that Mexican's body was s'posed to stay out yonder where it was danglin' from a tree limb."

Smoke kept the wagon moving steadily, paying no attention to any of the shouts directed toward him.

"What the hell? Do you think maybe that fella is deaf?"

Several more in the Anglo section of town turned out along both sides of the street, most of them staring in fearful curiosity. They believed they might see the young driver shot at any moment. None of them followed him.

His passage was also watched by the Mexican citizenry once he entered their part of town, but none were hostile, and many crossed themselves as the wagon went by.

Smoke stopped the wagon in front of the Mexican mortuary and jumped down as the undertaker exited the building. "Here he is, Señor Bustamante. Do I need to pay you anything to bury his body?"

"No, Señor. The people will pay to bury him. *Gracias.* I fear now, for your life, but *gracias.*"

Smoke nodded, turned, and remounted Seven. He rode back into town, stopping in front of what appeared to be the only saloon in Salcedo. He entered it as he entered all saloons, by stepping in and quickly pressing his back against the wall until he had made a thorough observation of everyone present.

"Hey, you!" someone called to Smoke. "Are you the man who cut down that Mex body, and brung him into town?" The questioner had close-set eyes, a beak-like nose, and a projecting chin so turned up it looked like his nose and chin might actually touch.

"I am." Smoke's response to the challenging question was calm, as if he were blissfully unaware of the hostile nature in the tone of the questioner's voice. He turned to the bartender. "I'd like a beer, please."

"Didn't you see my sign saying to leave that Mex hangin' there?"

"You must be Mr. Quinncannon," Smoke said, extending his hand.

Quincannon ignored the hand but smiled briefly, surprised but obviously pleased to be recognized. "Heard of me, have you?"

"Yes, I have."

"Well, if you've heard of me, you should damn well know better than to cut that body down. You can read, can't you? 'Cause if you can read, you shoulda been able to read the sign I posted. The sign that warned anyone against doin' that."

"So you admit to posting the sign. Are you also the one who lynched him?"

"You're damn right I am," Quinncannon said.

Smoke kept up the calm demeanor. "The sign said you lynched him because he was a murderer. Who did he murder?"

"He murdered a harlot," Quinncannon replied.

"Would the woman you say he murdered be named Fannie?"

"Yeah."

"How do you know he murdered her?"

"How do I know? 'Cause he worked there . . . in the house where she worked. I think he must have asked her to be with him, but she wouldn't do it, 'cause of him bein' Mex an' all. So when she turned him down, he killed her."

"So you decided to kill Montoya yourself, is that it?" Smoke asked.

"You're damn right I—" Quinncannon stopped abruptly mid-sentence when he saw Smoke take the badge from his pocket and pin it onto his shirt. After that second of surprise, he demanded, "Who are you, and what are you doing here?"

"My name is Smoke Jensen, Quinncannon, and I'm a deputy U.S. marshal. You know what I think? I think you killed Fannie, and to cover it up, you accused Montoya, then you lynched him. I'm going to put you in jail for the murder of both of them. I expect you will stay there for about three days."

"Three days," Quinncannon snorted. "And what's going to happen in three days?"

"There'll be another hanging," Smoke replied. "Only it's going to be legal."

"Who do you think you're kidding?" Quinncannon asked. "You ain't goin' to be able to put together a jury in this town that will hang me for what I done. Hell, half of 'em was out there, eggin' me on!"

"Then I'll take you back to Denver with me. Either way, you're going to hang."

"The hell I am!" Quinncannon shouted. He clawed at his gun, even as he yelled his defiance.

Smoke drew faster than the eye could follow. His Colt roared before Quinncannon even cleared his holster. Smoke's bullet crashed into Quinncannon's heart, killing him so quickly that he was dead before he hit the floor.

"Drop your gun, mister!" a loud voice called.

Looking into the mirror, Smoke saw two men. Both were wearing stars and both were holding shotguns pointed at him. He turned toward them. *Bradford and Cassidy*, he thought.

"You can lower your guns," Smoke told them. "I'm a deputy United States marshal. I came here to arrest Quinncannon for murder."

"Yeah?" one of the men said in a harsh, angry voice. "Well, you didn't arrest him, did you? You shot him. Not even a United States marshal can shoot a man down in cold blood."

"I didn't shoot him in cold blood. He drew on me."

"What do you mean, he drew on you? Look at him. His gun is still in the holster."

What the city marshal said was true. Quinncannon had started his draw, but Smoke was so fast that he drew and shot before Quinncannon could even clear leather. As a result, the pistol dropped straight back down into the holster.

"Unbuckle your gun belt and let it fall to the floor," one of them said.

Smoke looked directly at the speaker. "Which one are you? Bradford or Cassidy?"

"I'm Cassidy."

"Tell me, Cassidy, where were you two officers of the law when Quinncannon lynched Montoya?"

"We was right there watchin' him do it," Bradford put in. "Far as I'm concerned he just saved the county the cost of a legal hangin'. He was right. Montoya was the one that kilt the girl."

Smoke kept up his questioning. "Isn't it true that an eyewitness came to you two and told you that she had seen Quinncannon coming from Fannie's room with blood on his hands? And when she went into the room, she found Fannie dead?"

"Bradford, is that true?" the bartender asked.

"You never said nothin' about any eyewitness tellin' you Quinncannon done this," exclaimed one of the saloon patrons.

"Yeah, well, you know who it was that told us that, don't you?" Bradford glared around at the people in the room. "It was a Mexican maid that worked there, and she was just takin' up for Montoya. Who are you goin' to believe, some damn Mexican or an American?"

"Well, if Quinncannon is the one who actually done it, you know damn well he was goin' to lie about it," pointed out one of the others in the saloon. "Don't you think this is somethin' that maybe the rest of us shoulda knowed about?"

"Don't let this man get ever'one all confused now," Cassidy said. "Can't you see that he's just tryin' to make trouble? Montoya is the one that done it."

"Don't you think that should have been decided by a trial?" Smoke asked coolly.

"If he was a white man, maybe. But he wasn't no white man, was he? He was just a greaser."

"You know what, Bradford? I think we should throw this guy in jail," Cassidy said. "Don't you think it would be funny to have a U.S. marshal in a city jail?"

"Nah. Some damn federal judge would just let 'im out. I think we should just kill 'im and be done with it."

Even as Bradford made the suggestion, he was pulling the trigger of his shotgun. Flame erupted from the weapon's right-hand barrel. But instead of hitting Smoke, the double-ought buckshot chewed splinters from the corner of the bar.

Smoke had anticipated, to the split second, when Bradford was going to fire and dove out of the way, grabbing his pistol on the way down. He landed on the floor and rolled to his left just as Cassidy loosed a load of buckshot at him. The deadly charge gouged a hole in the floor a couple feet from Smoke.

Both men had one shot remaining.

Smoke returned the fire, snapping off two quick shots, both of which found their marks. Bradford and Cassidy staggered back as the slugs ripped through them. They collapsed just as Smoke surged to his feet. Still holding the gun in his hand, he swung around to see if anyone else was up to the challenge.

No one was. They were all stunned by the deafening blasts and could only stare dumbly through the drifting shreds of powder smoke.

"Bartender," Smoke said into the hush that followed the gun thunder.

"Y-yes sir?" the bartender replied, stuttering in his fear.

"Do you know a man named LeRoy Peyton?"

"You mean the judge? Yes, sir, I know him."

"Send someone after him. Bring him here to me."

The bartender didn't have to say anything. Several men practically tripped over their own feet as they hurried out to follow the order.

In the time it took to round up LeRoy Peyton, almost a dozen men came over to Smoke to thank him for ridding their town of such an outlaw element as Quinncannon and the two city marshals. Most claimed they had had nothing to do with the lynching, and never believed Montoya was guilty in the first place. A few of the more honest ones admitted that they actually did think Montoya had killed the girl and had been present for the lynching, though they took no personal part in it.

Half an hour later, LeRoy Peyton, a tall, silver-haired and dignified looking man in a sober dark suit, arrived at the saloon. By that time, the three men Smoke had killed had been dragged out onto the front porch to await the mortician—the *American* mortician.

Smoke was sitting alone at a table in the back corner of the room.

"You must be the man Marshal Holloway sent," Peyton said as he came up to the table.

"I am. Have a seat, Your Honor."

Peyton chuckled. "It's been a while since I've been addressed that way."

"How would you like to be addressed that way again?"

"What do you mean?"

"I'm going to appoint you as a federal judge."

Peyton looked surprised. "Hold on there, Deputy. I was just a state judge, but I know that a deputy U.S. marshal can't appoint a federal judge. Only the President can do that."

"Really?" Smoke smiled faintly as he leaned forward and lowered his voice. "How many people in Salcedo know that? Besides, maybe Marshal Holloway can pull some strings and turn it into the real thing."

"You know, you may have something there," Peyton said slowly as he frowned in thought. "I don't think even Holloway has enough connections to get me appointed as a federal judge, but he just might be able to get me appointed as a magistrate. You're right. If I just assume the position until it's made official, nobody here will be the wiser."

"You're going to have a lot of work cut out for you if you take the job," Smoke said.

"I know. But I was getting tired of retirement, anyway."

Smoke stood up, drew his pistol, and pounded it on the table loudly enough to get everyone's attention. "Folks, I have brought with me an appointment for His Honor, LeRoy Peyton, as a judge of the territorial court. Would everyone please stand for this solemn occasion?"

Without question or hesitation, everyone did so.

"And now, Your Honor, would you hold up your right hand and let me swear you in?"

Peyton did so and was "sworn in" by Smoke.

Afterward, Peyton addressed the others. "I am going to appoint new, *and honest,* city marshals. With the help of the good citizens of this town, we are going to make Salcedo a safe and law-abiding place in which to live."

Peyton's announcement was met with enthusiastic applause and the bartender calling out that drinks were on the house.

Maybe there is something to be said for wearing a badge after all, Smoke thought as he watched the celebration.

CHAPTER 10

Risco, New Mexico Territory

Smoke wandered around in northern New Mexico for several weeks, as the season changed to winter. The weather was cold, but the snows had held off so far. Smoke just drifted, thinking it wouldn't be good for him to go too far south. He owed it to Marshal Holloway to keep himself fairly close. The town of Risco seemed to just come up out of the desert in front of him, the buildings the same color as the ground from which they rose. He was greeted by an optimistic sign as he rode into town.

RISCO, NEW MEXICO
379 INDUSTRIOUS PEOPLE
Come Grow With Us

Tying his horse in front of the only saloon in town, Smoke swatted some of the trail dust from his clothes, then went inside. After looking around for a moment, he stepped up to the bar and ordered a beer.

"You're new in town," the bartender said. It wasn't a question.

"I'm not actually *in* town," Smoke said. "I'm just passing through. Thought I'd have a couple drinks, eat some food that isn't trail-cooked, and maybe get a room for the night."

"What brings you to this neck of the woods?" the barkeep asked as he drew the beer.

"To be honest, I'm looking for someone," Smoke said.

"Who are you lookin' for?"

Smoke gave the same answer as always. "Three men named Wiley Potter, Muley Stratton, and Josh Richards." He was not wearing his deputy U.S. marshal's star. He wanted to do this on his own . . . at least the initial search.

"Nope, can't say as I've heard of 'em."

"They came into a lot of money some time ago and they're probably really big spenders, unless they've already spent it all." Smoke slid a coin across the hardwood to pay for his beer, then lifted the mug to his lips. Taking a swallow, he wiped his mouth with the back of his hand. "Is there a place to eat in this town?"

"You might try Kathy's Place just down the street."

"Kathy's Place?"

"That's what it's called. You'll see the sign out front. She don't serve nothin' fancy, but the food is good."

A voice spoke up from Smoke's left. "Hey, mister, what makes you think you can just come in here an' start askin' questions? What do you think we are, a liberry?"

Smoke turned to look at the man standing at the bar. The hombre had a scraggly black beard and was wearing a dirty shirt and a sweat-stained hat. He glared darkly at Smoke.

"Well, you don't get answers if you don't ask questions," Smoke said, trying to ease the sudden tension with a smile.

It didn't work. The black-bearded man poked the air. "Yeah? Well, we don't like folks comin' in here, askin' a bunch of fool questions."

"Barkeep"—Smoke nodded toward his antagonist—"this gentleman and I seem to have gotten off on the wrong foot here. Give my new friend a drink, on me."

The bartender poured a couple fingers of whiskey in a glass and set it in front of the bearded man. "Here you go, Miles. Compliments of the gentleman."

Miles pushed the glass away so hard that it fell off the bar on the other side.

The bartender stepped back quickly to keep the spilled whiskey from splashing on him. "Damn it, Miles, you had no call to do that," the apron said angrily. He picked up the glass. "You coulda broke the glass."

Miles turned toward Smoke again. "I don't like you, mister. I don't like you at all."

"Really? And here, I thought you and I were getting along so well."

The others in the saloon laughed at Smoke's dry comment.

"Miles, this fella is doin' all he can do to be friendly," a man said.

"What's put the burr under your saddle?" one of the others in the saloon asked.

"Because he's nosy, and I don't drink with nosy folks."

"Let me get this straight," Smoke said. "You don't drink with just anybody? Or you just don't drink with nosy anybodies?"

Again, others in the saloon laughed.

"Miles, seems to me like this feller is just a little too quick for you," someone said.

That was the last straw. Miles, his face flushed red with anger and embarrassment, charged toward Smoke with a loud yell.

"Look out, mister! He's got a knife!" someone shouted, and Smoke saw a silver blade flashing toward him.

Smoke jerked to one side as adroitly as a matador avoiding a charging bull. He palmed his pistol from his holster and brought it down hard on Miles's head.

Miles went down.

Smoke pouched the iron, drained the rest of his beer, put the glass down, and slapped another coin on the bar beside it. "I'll have another."

"Them three fellas you was askin' about? Stratton, Potter, and Richards?" the bartender said as he placed a second mug of beer in front of Smoke.

"Yes?"

"They was here for a while. They started 'em a saloon and gamblin' house down at the other end of the street, but a cowboy got kilt one night, and the next mornin' they was all three gone."

"They killed the cowboy?"

"Some say Richards is the one who done it, others

say it was Potter. It's pretty much for sure that one of 'em done it. Anyhow, they was all three gone the next day."

"Do you have any idea where they went?"

The barkeep shook his head. "No, sir, I don't have no idea at all."

"Well, thanks for the information."

"Miles, there, worked for them. He had a pretty good job throwin' out drunks and people that got out of hand. The story was that if someone started winnin' money at buckin' the tiger or blackjack, he'd throw them out, too. What set him off, I reckon, is when he heard you askin' about 'em. I don't know why he feels any loyalty to them three. They left him behind like they did ever'one else that worked for 'em. You know these fellas, do you?"

Smoke shook his head. "I've never met them."

"Why are you lookin' for 'em? Are you a bounty hunter?"

"No, it's personal."

The bartender nodded. That was all the information he needed. Out on the frontier, nobody pried too much into another man's business.

Miles groaned, then slowly got to his feet, rubbing the bump on his head. "What happened?" he asked as he looked around groggily.

"You fell off the bar rail," the bartender replied.

"What? How did I do that?"

"I don't know, but that's what you done. Maybe you had too much to drink. I think you should go home and sleep it off."

"Yeah," Miles said, still rubbing the bump on top of his head. He looked at Smoke. "Who are you?"

"Just someone who stopped in for a beer," Smoke replied.

Miles saw his knife lying on the floor. "I must have dropped that." Picking it up, he put it back in its sheath, then stumbled out the door.

"Damn, he didn't remember a thing about what happened to him!" exclaimed one of the patrons in the saloon.

"Yeah, sometimes when folks get knocked out like that, they don't remember nothin' afterward," another said.

"I wanted him to know that someone took him down," a third man said. "He had it comin', the way he used to treat folks when he worked in that other place."

"It'll come to 'im, eventually, I reckon." The bartender gave Smoke a meaningful look. "Might be better if you were out of town by then, mister. Better for Miles, I mean. You took it easy on him this time. Not so sure you'd do it again."

"Neither am I," Smoke said, now that he knew the man had worked for the three lowdown murderers he was looking for.

Ten minutes later, Smoke had removed the star from his packet, pinned it onto his shirt, and stepped into the sheriff's office.

The balding, walrus-mustached lawman was sitting in his chair with his feet propped up on his desk, drinking coffee. He didn't get up. "What can I do for you?"

"Sheriff, I'm Deputy United States Marshal Smoke

Jensen, and I'd like to talk to you about some men who, I understand, lived here for a while."

The sheriff sat up, stirred from his casual pose by the revelation that Smoke was a federal star packer. "I'm Sheriff Murchison, Deputy, and I'll be glad to help you if I can. Who are the men?"

"Wiley Potter, Muley Stratton, and Josh Richards."

A big smile spread across the sheriff's face. "You've found them!"

"No, but I am looking for them. And you can help me."

The sheriff shook his head. "If you're askin' me where they are, I'm afraid there's nothing I can do to help you. I don't have any idea. I heard from someone that they had been seen up in Wyoming, and I sent a telegram to a sheriff up there, sayin' they was wanted for murder, but I never got no reply."

"So they are wanted men?"

"You're damn right they are. I want 'em," Sheriff Murchison said.

Smoke smiled. "Then, if you would, please, Sheriff, write out a request for help from the U.S. marshal's office. That will give me the authority I need to look for them."

The sheriff got a confused look on his face. "I thought you was already lookin' for 'em."

"Yes, but that was for a personal reason. If I have a request from you, it'll be official."

Sheriff Murchison pulled open the middle drawer of his desk and took out a piece of paper. "You're damn right I'll write out a request," he said, taking the pen from the inkwell.

Preacher's cabin, Colorado Territory

On his ride back to Colorado, Smoke had decided to spend some time with Preacher. He pulled up to the cabin weary and cold, and dismounted. Gray clouds filled the winter sky overhead.

Preacher heard him ride in and met him at the door. He noticed the star pinned to Smoke's shirt right away. "So, you've got yourself a full-time job, do you boy?"

"Yeah, I do. I tried to turn in my badge, but Marshal Holloway talked me into keeping it. Only now I'm getting paid for it."

"How much?"

"Forty dollars a month, plus travel expenses."

"I reckon that's a goodly amount of money, all right. Since the market for plews is 'bout all dried up, I don't keep up with money much anymore. I see you stopped at Schemerhorn's Tradin' Post. What have you got there?"

"Oh, I picked us up some flour, beans, bacon, corn-meal, sugar, coffee, that sort of thing," Smoke replied as he lifted the sack of supplies he had carried into the cabin.

"What'd you go and waste your money on sugar for? You know damn well I got me a couple beehives, and in my way of thinkin', honey's better'n sugar any day."

"Oh, honey is fine all right. And don't get me wrong, Preacher, I like rabbit and squirrel, and dove and quail and duck . . ."

"And don't forget beaver and possum, and deer

and bear meat," Preacher added. "And chickens. Remember, I got me some chickens now, and they ain't just for eatin'. Truth is, them chickens is givin' me eggs. I'd near 'bout forgot what a likin' I had for eggs. I shoulda got me some chickens a long time ago."

"Aren't you glad I talked you into it?" Smoke asked, grinning.

"Yeah, but I was afixin' to get me some chickens anyway. You just happened to remind me of it, is all."

"Yes, well, I'm glad I thought to remind you. But speaking of eggs, wouldn't you like some bacon and biscuits to go with them? And later, maybe some cornbread and beans?"

"Yeah, that wouldn't be bad," Preacher said. "Hey, and I know where there's some wild greens to go with them beans and cornbread."

"I knew you'd appreciate that. I got some coffee too."

"Yeah. Now, coffee, that is somethin' you got to go down to Schemerhorn's for. Coffee and a beer ever now an' ag'in is about the only thing they is in civilization that's worth a little more'n a bucket of warm piss."

Preacher had come out to the mountains when he was fourteen years old, after leaving the family farm in Ohio. During the first part of his journey, he had freed a slave girl who was three quarters white, fought river pirates on the Mississippi, ridden a raft down the river where, even though still a boy, he had taken part in the Battle of New Orleans with Andrew Jackson.

Shortly after arriving in the Rocky Mountains,

he'd killed a bear with only a knife, but was badly mauled. He was taken in by a couple trappers named Pierre Garneau and Clyde Barnes. Those two old mountain men not only saved his life, they taught him everything he needed to know about trapping beaver and living alone in the High Lonesome.

In the time he had been in these mountains, he had seen an era come and go, and had attended rendezvouses with men like Grizzly Adams and Jim Beckworth. He had once spent the winter with Kit Carson. He had seen more things and had more adventures than most men could cram into a lifetime . . . and he was just getting started.

When Smoke had come along, Preacher took him under his wing, teaching him as much as he knew. It was just as Pierre Garneau and Clyde Barnes had done for him, more than half a century earlier. Smoke had never known a finer man than Preacher, nor a truer friend.

"Seein' as you got yourself a job, I don't reckon you'll be spendin' that much time with me now, will you?" Although Preacher tried to say the words teasingly, there was a hint of melancholy in his voice. He had never been married long enough to have children of his own, and ever since Smoke's father Emmett had been killed, Preacher regarded Smoke as his own son.

"Just long enough to eat up all the store-bought food I brought," Smoke replied with a laugh. "And maybe long enough to take you down to Schemerhorn's to spend some of this newly earned money on a couple of those beers you were talking about."

The talk about the money Smoke had earned as a

deputy marshal was just that, talk. What only Preacher and Smoke knew was that Smoke's father lay buried in a place called Brown's Hole, up in the northwest corner of Colorado, near the Idaho line. And buried right beside him was a veritable fortune, several thousand dollars in gold that had once belonged to the Confederacy.

Initially stolen by Potter, Stratton, and Richards, Emmett had recovered some of the gold. By that time, the Confederacy was no more, and Emmett had fought too long, too hard, and had lost too many close friends in the war to give that money to the Yankees. He was dead, and the money belonged to Smoke. He was a very wealthy man, though he didn't show it in the way he lived.

Despite his youth, Smoke already knew there were a lot of things that money just couldn't buy.

CHAPTER 11

For the next few weeks, it was like old times as the two men hunted and fished. Preacher still ran a trapline just to keep his hand in, but he had only a few traps out and most of the beaver skins he took, he used himself, making caps and muffs to ward off the winter cold.

"Hey, old man," Smoke said one day when the weather had thawed a bit and after they had eaten most of the bacon and beans and used up all the flour and cornmeal. "What do you say we go down to Schemerhorn's so you can get reprovisioned?"

"Boy, you've done got yourself all citified on me, ain't you? You already tired of game? I'll have you know I lived here for years before Schemerhorn ever built that tradin' post of his."

"I thought we might get a couple beers, too," Smoke added with a smile.

"Well, damn! Why didn't you say so? Let me get my cap."

It took them an hour to ride down from the mountains to what was the semblance of civilization nearest to Preacher's cabin. They tied up their animals in front of a building constructed of notched logs. It was of a fairly substantial size with a sign hanging down from the eaves.

SCHEMERHORN'S TRADING POST
DRY GOODS, GROCERIES, AMMUNITION,
GUN POWDER, LIQUOR, AND TOBACCO
Seamus Schemerhorn, Proprietor

Stepping inside the building, they were assailed with a dozen different comforting fragrances—cured wood, smoked meat, tobacco, flour, and various spices. Seamus Schemerhorn—a tall, bald man with a full mustache, a hawk-like nose, and wire-rimmed spectacles—was sweeping the floor. There were no other customers in the store.

It was relatively dark inside, the principal illumination being the bars of sunlight, filled with dancing dust motes, that stabbed down from the narrow windows at the top of the walls. A lantern sat at the end of the counter augmenting the dim light, the burning wick adding the smell of kerosene to the other fragrances.

Schemerhorn looked up at the two as they came in stomping snow off their boots and smiled at them in recognition. "Hello, Preacher, hello, Smoke. Preacher, I haven't seen you in so long that I swear I was about to send someone up to your cabin to bury you," he teased.

"You send someone up to my cabin that I ain't expectin', and it'll more'n likely be me buryin' them," Preacher said.

Schemerhorn laughed. "Damn, I hadn't even thought about that. You might just be right. You need some provisions, do you?"

"Yes," Smoke said. "But first we thought we might have a couple beers."

Schemerhorn went around behind the counter, which, on an occasion such as this, could double as a bar. He drew two beers and put one in front of each of the two men. Smoke reached over to the beer Schemerhorn had put in front of Preacher and pulled it to himself. "These are mine. Let that old man order his own beer."

Schemerhorn chuckled. "I guess I just wasn't reckonin' on that much of a thirst. Two beers for you as well, Preacher?"

"Do I look like some kinda drunk to you, Schemerhorn?" Preacher asked. "One beer is plenty for me, thank you most to death."

"Oh, I'm sorry," Schemerhorn said, holding up his hands, open palms facing Preacher. "One beer it is."

Schemerhorn drew another beer and set the mug in front of Preacher.

"With a shot of whiskey chaser," Preacher added.

With another chuckle, Schemerhorn poured the shot.

"While we're drinking, you might fill this order," Smoke said, passing a list over to the merchant.

"I'll be glad to."

"I'll not be riding back up to the cabin with you," Smoke said to Preacher a moment later as Schemerhorn was moving about the store, gathering the supplies on Smoke's list.

"I figured as much," Preacher replied.

"It's just that, if I'm going to deputy for Marshal Holloway, I don't think I should be taking too much time away."

"Tell the old coot I said hello when you get back there."

"Old coot?" Smoke laughed, then took a swallow of his beer. "Funny, that's just what he called you."

PSR Ranch, office, near Bury

"Governor of the Territory of Idaho," Wiley Potter said. "How does that sound?"

"Do you think Governor Bennett is going to just step aside and let you be the governor?" Stratton asked.

"I know he's plannin' on givin' it up. That means there will have to be a new governor."

"You forget, governors of territories ain't elected," Richards said. "They are appointed by the President, and Grant is the President. There ain't no Yankee general gonna give an appointment like that to someone who fought for the South."

Potter chuckled. "We wasn't exactly what you would call loyal to the South. Besides which, ever'one knows that his brother-in-law, Corbin, can get anything from Grant you want, if you pay him enough."

"How much is enough?" Stratton asked.

"I don't know, but however much it is, it'll be worth it. Just think about what I can do for all our business enterprises if I'm the governor."

"He has a point, Muley," Richards said.

They heard someone come into the house.

"Janey, is that you?" Richards called.

She stepped into the ranch office to join Richards and the others. "Yes."

"Janey, pour the four of us a drink," Richards said, pointing to the liquor cabinet. "We're celebrating."

"What are we celebrating?"

"Wiley, here, is going to be our new governor," Stratton said.

Janey smiled. "Really? When did that happen?"

Richards shrugged. "It hasn't happened yet. But it's going to happen."

"Well then, why don't we drink to it when it does happen?" she suggested.

Stratton laughed. "Josh, this woman sure has control over you, doesn't she?"

"I don't know," Richards answered. "Do you have control over me, Janey?"

She walked over to him, then leaned into him and kissed him. "What do you think, my sweet?"

"Boys, I think maybe Janey is right. We'll drink to Wiley being governor when he has the presidential appointment in hand."

Hearing the laughter behind her, Janey walked up the stairs to her room. More than a room, it was a suite, almost a private apartment. She had a bedroom, a sitting room, a private bathing room with running water and a wood-burning stove to heat water for her bath. Financially, she had it better than she had ever had it at any time in her entire life. But there was more to living than just being financially secure.

She thought of the families she had seen during

her recent trip to Denver. Men and women, happily married, with children. Even as she thought of it, she realized that it was something she would never have.

She knew that Richards would marry her—he had suggested it more than once—but somewhere in the back of her mind was the idea that one should be in love before getting married. She loved the luxury Josh Richards was able to provide for her, but she didn't love *him.*

Also, she knew that if they did get married the relationship between them would change, drastically, and not for the better. As his wife, Richards would have authority over her, and she had no doubt that he would exercise that authority absolutely, and if necessary, cruelly. She would never give him that power.

She couldn't help but wonder, though, what her life would be like if she could find a man who really did love her, and who she could love.

Denver, late January 1871

"Hello, Miss Wilson," Smoke said as he stepped into the United States Marshal's office a few days later.

"Hello, Deputy," Annie Wilson replied.

"And how is the most beautiful girl in Denver?"

Annie laughed. "Smoke Jensen, I'm almost old enough to be your mama. Well, maybe not quite, but certainly old enough to be your big sister. You ought to be ashamed of yourself."

"I'm older than you think I am."

"You forget, I keep the records of all our deputies. I know exactly how old you are."

"Ah, but that's only in years. Surely experience counts for something, doesn't it?"

"You may have a point there, Deputy. I've also seen a file of some of your . . . uh . . . exploits. Some people could live a hundred years and not experience the life you've already lived."

"Maybe. But it's also true that some of the events in my life I would just as soon have not experienced. Is the marshal in?"

"He's with the governor right now. It'll be just a moment. There's some issues of the *Rocky Mountain News*, if you care to look at them while you wait."

"Thanks," Smoke said, picking up a paper and taking a chair to read it. One story quickly caught his attention, even though it was a couple of months old.

GENTLEMAN BANDIT STRIKES

Fifteen Hundred Dollars Taken

Nobody Hurt

"He was just absolutely one of the nicest gentlemen one would ever hope to meet," was the way Mrs. Ethel Joyce described the man who stopped a stagecoach in Pueblo County last week, relieving the driver and shotgun guard of the fifteen-hundred-dollar bank transfer the coach was carrying.

According to the driver, the robber, who didn't wear a mask, knew in advance not only that the coach was carrying a money shipment, but knew to the penny how much the shipment was.

The coach was stopped by means of blocking the road with a log. And although the robber made reference to a partner, or perhaps partners, neither the driver, his guard, nor any of the stagecoach passengers saw anyone except the highwayman himself.

It is not the purpose of this newspaper, dear readers, to bestow accolades upon a felon, but one cannot help but draw a comparison between the gentlemanly, almost courtly, manner in which the robber performed his illegal activities with the brutal and cowardly dynamite attack two weeks previous, in which five people, including a child and a young woman, were killed.

At present there are no clues as to who may have perpetrated either of the two robberies.

The door to Marshal Holloway's office opened, and he and the territorial governor stepped out. Governor McCook had reached the rank of brigadier general during the war and still carried himself with a military bearing. He had a full mustache that curled down to either side of his mouth, but he didn't have a beard.

Holloway said, "Governor, this is my newest deputy, Kirby Jensen. Though he is better known as Smoke."

"Smoke, is it? Well, Smoke, Marshal Holloway has been saying good things about you. Keep up the good work."

"I'll do my best, Governor," Smoke replied as he dropped the newspaper back on the table where he had gotten it.

"I'm glad to see that you're back," Marshal Holloway said to Smoke after the governor left. "I want to send you to the town of Running Creek. The sheriff there, Frank Tanner, has asked for help."

"What does he need?"

"To be honest with you, Smoke, I don't know what he needs because he didn't say. But I know Frank. He's a good man, and he wouldn't ask for help unless he really needed it. How soon can you be ready to go?"

"About as long as it takes me to walk from here to my horse," Smoke replied.

Marshal Holloway laughed. "Then apparently I'm keeping you from your work by standing here talking to you. Go, go. Don't let me detain you."

CHAPTER 12

Running Creek, Colorado Territory

When bounty hunter Crack Kingsley walked into the Black Jack Saloon it was busy, but he found a place by the end of the bar nearest the door. He ordered a beer, then took out a flyer and examined it. The name on the flyer was Val Holder, and the reward was $2,500.

The line drawing of Holder wasn't as effective as a photo, but it was close enough that Kingsley was certain the man standing at the other end of the bar was the one he was looking for. He was helped along in the belief by having heard that Holder had taken up residence in Running Creek.

Having developed sort of a sixth sense about men like Kingsley, Holder had noticed him the moment he walked in. The dark-haired, dark-eyed man tossed his whiskey down, then ran his finger across the full mustache that curved around his mouth like the horns on a Texas steer and called out, "Mister bounty hunter."

Kingsley was shocked to hear himself addressed that way. His effectiveness as a bounty hunter depended upon an element of surprise. If he had been recognized, that element was gone.

"Mister bounty hunter!" Holder called again, loud and authoritatively. "What's the matter? Have you gone deaf? Answer me."

Everyone in the saloon recognized the challenge implied in its timbre. All other conversations ceased, and the drinkers at the bar backed away so nothing but clear space was between Holder and Kingsley. Even the bartender left his position behind the hardwood.

Kingsley looked up from his beer. "I'm sorry, mister. Do I know you?"

"You should. Isn't it your job to know me?" Holder asked. "You *are* a bounty hunter, aren't you?"

It hadn't started out so well, but Kingsley had to keep his nerve. "What makes you think that?"

"I know a bounty hunter when I see one. No, I know a bounty hunter when I *smell* one. And mister, I see and smell a bounty hunter."

"I'm afraid you've got me mixed up with somebody else."

"No, I don't think so," Holder said confidently. "My name is Val Holder. I expect I'm the one you're looking for."

"That name don't mean nothin' to me." Kingsley lifted his mug to take a drink, hoping Holder didn't see that his hand was shaking.

"Well, let me tell you what it means. It means I am the law in this town."

"You're the law? I don't see a badge."

"I don't need a badge. I'm the law, simply because I say I'm the law. And I'm tellin' you now to ride on out."

"Why should I?"

"Let's just say I don't like bounty hunters."

"And if I choose to stay?"

Holder smirked. "You'd be makin' a big mistake."

Kingsley had lost the advantage of surprise, but he had been in the business too long to be buffaloed out of a prize so big. No way was he going to turn away from $2,500. He wiped the foam from his lips with the back of his hand. "All right, Holder. You're right. I am a bounty hunter. My name is Crack Kingsley."

A few sharp intakes of breath came from the saloon patrons. Kingsley's name was well-known. It was also known that he specialized in going after "Dead or Alive" outlaws, and took none of them in alive.

"The thing is, Holder, you've got a pretty fair amount of money posted on you right now," Kingsley went on. "And I don't intend to leave this town without claimin' my bounty."

Holder raised an eyebrow. "Is that a fact? Well, Mr. Bounty Hunter, you won't be collecting any bounty on me."

"And how do you propose to prevent me from doing that?"

"I propose to kill you," Holder said easily.

More than a few quick intakes of breath could be heard. They were collective, creating quite an audible gasp from those who were intently watching the drama being played out before them.

Kingsley set his beer mug down, stepped away from

the bar, and flipped his duster back so that his gun was exposed. He was wearing it low and kicked out, the way a man wears a gun when he knows how to use it. "You talk too much, Holder."

Holder stepped away from the bar. He wore his gun low and kicked out, too. He smiled a cold, evil smile. "Well, Mr. Kingsley, you brought me to the ball, so . . ."

Although Kingsley had lost the advantage of surprise, he had been in shoot-outs before and he was fast. In fact, he was very fast, especially if he had the edge of drawing first. Without another word he made his move, pulling his pistol in the blink of an eye.

But Holder, whether reacting to Kingsley's draw or anticipating it, had his own pistol out just a split second faster, pulling the hammer back and firing in one fluid motion. In the close confines of the barroom, the gunshot sounded like a clap of thunder.

Kingsley's eyes grew wide with surprise at how fast Holder had his gun up and firing. He tried hard to beat the bullet with his own draw but he couldn't do it. Holder's shot caught Kingsley in the chest and the bounty hunter's eyes glazed over even as he staggered backward, crashing through the batwing doors and falling flat on his back on the boardwalk in front of the saloon. His gun arm was thrown to one side and the still unfired pistol was in his hand.

There was a moment of silence, then one of the patrons nearest the door ventured a peek over the top of the batwings. He turned and shouted back to the others, "He's dead, folks. He's deader than a doornail."

"Bartender," Holder said.

"Yes, sir, Mr. Holder?"

"Set up drinks for the house."

"Yes, sir, Mr. Holder."

With a happy shout, everyone in the saloon rushed to the bar to give their order.

It was close to eleven o'clock that same night when Smoke arrived in town. Unlike his trip to Red Cliff, which had been by train, he had ridden on horseback to Running Creek after riding from Preacher's cabin to Schemerhorn's Trading Post, then from the trading post to Denver, and from Denver to Running Creek. In addition, he had risen at sunrise, which had occurred at about five o'clock. It had been one very long day.

He didn't make an attempt to contact the sheriff; he would look him up in the morning. All he wanted was a drink and a bed. A beer wouldn't do it. He wanted a stiff drink.

The Black Jack was the most substantial looking saloon in a row of saloons. He tied his horse at the hitch rail in front, stepped over a drunk who was passed out on the steps in front of the place, and went inside.

Stepping immediately to the side as usual, he looked around. The chimneys of all the lanterns were covered with soot, making the light dingy and filtered through drifting smoke. The place smelled of whiskey, stale beer, pungent tobacco, and unwashed bodies. A long bar on the left had dirty towels hanging on hooks about every five feet along the front. A large mirror was behind the bar, but like everything else in the saloon, it was so dirty Smoke could scarcely see any images in it. What he could see was distorted by imperfections in the glass.

Against the back wall, near the foot of the stairs, a baldheaded musician was playing a cigar-scarred and beer-stained upright piano. In the center of the saloon were eight or ten tables, nearly all of them occupied. A half dozen or so soiled doves were flitting about, pushing drinks and promising more if the price was right. A few card games were in progress, but most of the patrons were just drinking and talking. The subject of their conversation was the gunfight that had taken place in the saloon earlier in the day.

Most had heard of the gunfight in Red Cliff a few weeks ago. The killing that afternoon had roused speculation as to which of the two gunfighters was best.

"In my mind there ain't no doubt," said one of the men at a table. "This feller Smoke Jensen took on three men at the same time, and he kilt all three of 'em. You can't compare that with what Holder done just killin' one man."

"The hell you can't," another man contended. "Them three wasn't gunfighters. They was just cattle rustlers. They thought because there was three of 'em they could take 'im on. Holder called Kingsley out and stood up to 'im, face-to-face. And did you see Holder's draw? Faster'n greased lightnin' it was. Why, it was so quick I never seen nothin' more'n a jump of his shoulder and the gun was in his hand. In his hand and blazin', it was, and Kingsley was graspin' his chest and fallin' back through the door without gettin' off even one shot."

"Still, three to one," one of the others said, and the argument continued.

"You're both forgettin' the one who's the fastest of 'em all. Faster than Holder or Jensen."

"Who would that be? You ain't goin' to say Hickok are you? 'Cause I seen him oncet, and I don't think he could hold a candle to either Jensen or Holder."

"Clell Dawson, that's who. He kilt The Concho Kid, and The Concho Kid was maybe faster than either Jensen or Holder."

"I heard o' him."

"I'd sure like to see a couple o' them fellas go up ag'in each other," another said, putting voice to what all were thinking.

"Whoowee! Wouldn't that be somethin' pure-dee, though?"

The bartender was pouring the residue from abandoned whiskey glasses back into a bottle when Smoke stepped up to the bar. The barkeep pulled a soggy cigar butt from one glass, laid the butt aside, then poured the whiskey back into the bottle without qualms.

Smoke held up his finger.

"Yeah?" the bartender responded.

"Whiskey."

The bartender picked up the bottle he had just poured whiskey into.

"Not that bottle. A clean bottle."

"You're some kind of particular, ain't you?" the bartender asked.

"If I want a cigar I'll smoke it, not drink it," Smoke replied.

The bartender chuckled. "Most of the drinkers in

here don't never even notice I'm here, let alone what I'm doin'. But since you called me out on it, I'll get you another bottle."

The bartender took a bottle from one of the glass shelves behind him, pulled the cork, poured a drink, and handed it to Smoke, who examined the liquor for any possible residue before he paid for it.

"Go ahead. Check it out if you want. This here is a clean bottle," the bartender said.

Smoke tossed the drink down without answering, then wiped the back of his hand across his lips. "I didn't see a hotel when I rode in."

"That's 'cause the onliest one we had burnt down a couple months ago. We got rooms upstairs, though."

"All right. I'll take one."

"With or without."

Smoke frowned. "With or without what?"

The bartender looked up in surprise. "Are you kiddin' me, mister? With or without a woman."

"Without."

"Six bits."

"Six bits? Isn't that a little expensive?"

"If we left it empty so the girls could use it for their customers, we could make three, maybe four times that," the bartender said. "Six bits, take it or leave it."

Smoke had been in the saddle a long time. Six bits? *Hell,* he thought, *I'd pay six bucks to get a little sleep.* "Here." He slapped the coins on the bar. "Tell your girls and their customers not to come into my room by mistake. If they do, they just might get shot."

"Mister, I don't know who the hell you are, but it ain't healthy to go around making threats you can't back up," the bartender growled. He picked up the silver and took it over to the money box, then reached for a key. "Here you go. It's Room Two, right at the top of the stairs. You'll have a good view of the street from there."

"Thanks." Smoke picked up his key.

"Yes, sir," he heard someone behind him say as he started up the stairs. "Dawson, Holder, and Jensen, goin' at one another. That would be somethin' to behold. Folks would come from miles around to see somethin' like that."

When he got to Room Two he lit the lamp, then had a look around. The room had one high-sprung, cast-iron bed, a chest, and a small table with a pitcher and basin.On the wall was a neatly lettered sign. Do NOT SPIT ON THE FLOOR. GENTLEMEN, PLEASE REMOVE SPURS WHILE IN BED.

CHAPTER 13

Snyder, Summit County

As Smoke crawled into bed that night, some fifty miles away, three men sat astride their horses on a hill, looking down to the town. The breath of men and horses alike frosted in the cold air. A cloud passed over the moon, then moved away, bathing in silver the little town that rose up like a ghost before them. A big white house stood at the outer edge on the near side of town. The edifice was resplendent with cupolas, dormers, balconies, porches, and gingerbread trim, all shining brightly in the moonlight. The property was surrounded by a white picket fence which enclosed not only the house, but a carriage house and stable, as well.

"There it is," Pete said, pointing to the house.

"You sure that's where the banker lives?" Eddie asked.

"You see any house in town that's any bigger than that one? Hell, there ain't even no buildin' that is bigger than that house." Pete's declaration was accu-

114

rate, for not even the hotel was as large as the house he had pointed out to the others.

Neither Eddie nor Merlin challenged his statement.

"All right. Come on, then. We'll leave the horses in the stable at the back of the property. That way no one will notice any strange horses hangin' around the house." Pete headed down the hill.

The three men rode slowly into town, the hoof-beats sounding exceptionally loud in the quiet of the night. They avoided the main street and followed one of the back streets. Approaching that way gave them an angle least likely to be noticed in the event that someone in town was actually awake.

The high-pitched yap of a dog came from somewhere nearby, and his bark was answered by another dog some distance away. A baby, perhaps awakened by the barking dogs, began to cry. A wind came up, and as it passed over a loose piece of tin on the roof of the small house they were passing, it made a clanking sound.

"What's that?" Eddie asked, startled. He twisted around in the saddle to search for the source.

"Quiet. It's nothing. Just the wind," Pete told him.

Closer to the big white house, they turned their horses into the alley and rode up behind the banker's carriage house. There, they dismounted.

"Lookie here at this brougham," Merlin said, pointing to the elegant carriage. "This sum'bitch must do pretty well."

One of the stabled horses snorted as if questioning the uninvited guests, but the interrogation died with one whicker.

Pistols drawn, the three men moved from the shadows of the stable across the backyard and up onto the back porch. The locked back door did nothing to impede their entry into the house. The door opened into the kitchen with the faint but still discernable aroma of the pork that had been the family's supper.

The outlaws moved through a spill of moonlight to the bottom of the stairs, then climbed them quietly, stepping on the carpet at the center to silence their approach. At the top of the stairs, they moved toward the nearest bedroom, the carpet muffling any sound.

Pete slowly opened the door. The same splash of moonlight illuminating the parlor also lit up the bedroom where a man and woman were sleeping. The man was snoring.

Pete put his pistol away and pulled a knife, while at the same time clamping his hand over the woman's mouth. Startled, she opened her eyes but was unable to cry out.

"Woman, if you scream I'm going to cut your throat." He showed her the knife in the moonlight.

She looked up at him with her eyes open wide in terror.

"Damn. What does it take to wake that guy up?" Pete asked, looking toward the sleeping man. "Wake 'im up, Merlin."

"Hey you. Wake up."

The snoring continued.

"I said wake up!" Merlin's admonition was much louder and was accompanied by a rough shaking of the man's shoulder. The effort was successful.

"What is this?" The man gasped, sitting up quickly.

"Just sit still till we tell you to move." Pete's warning was augmented by the pistol Merlin was holding just inches from the man's head.

"Who are you and what are you doing in my house?" The man tried to muster a little bravado in his voice as he made the demand, but he failed miserably.

"We're arranging a little loan," Pete said, adding with a chuckle, "Only we ain't never gonna pay it back." He sheathed the knife, then drew his gun and pointed it toward the woman's head.

"If you don't want to see your woman's brains scattered all over the bed, you'll rattle your hocks down there to your bank, take out one hundred thousand dollars, and bring it here."

"Mommy? Daddy? Who are these men?"

At that unexpected question, Eddie exclaimed, "Son of a—" and twisted around, thrusting his revolver out in front of him ready to shoot. His finger was taut on the trigger, but he managed not to fire when he realized the questioner was a little girl, no older than four or five, standing in the doorway of the bedroom holding a rag doll.

The woman in the bed struggled to sit up and tried to let out a terrified scream, but Pete still had his hand over her mouth.

He pushed her back down and said between clenched teeth to Eddie, "Grab that kid and bring her here so we're all together."

Eddie didn't look happy about the order. He was already shaken because he had almost shot the little girl. He knew from reading stories in the newspaper about the stagecoach robbery that a kid had been killed in that explosion, but that wasn't quite the same as shooting an innocent little girl standing just a few feet away from him.

He knew he had to do what Pete told him. Jamming his gun back in its holster, he leaped toward the girl, who whirled around, yelled in fright, and tried to run. Eddie snagged the back of her nightdress, jerked her toward him, and swept her up in his arms. He clamped a hand over her mouth to keep her from screaming.

"And now you, Mister Banker," Pete said in a satisfied voice. "You go get us that hundred thousand dollars like I told you to."

The man shook his head. "I can't do as you ask. We don't have a hundred thousand dollars in the bank right now."

"How much do you have?"

"Just over thirty thousand."

"Well then, go get the thirty thousand and bring it back. And don't get any idea 'bout goin' to the law or anything. The only person I want to see here is you, and you had better be carrying a bag of money. If anyone besides you shows up, we kill the woman and kid. And if you ain't back in half an hour, we kill the woman and the kid, anyway." Pete took his hand away from the woman's mouth and urged, "You better make sure your husband knows we ain't foolin'."

"Filbert, please. For heavens' sake, just do it." Her voice quavered with terror.

"Don't be so alarmed, Beth." Obviously, he was trying to summon up some courage again. "I don't believe they really mean you any harm."

Pete nipped that in the bud. "Tell you what. Just to

show you we're serious, if you ain't back in twenty minutes, me an' my friends here are gonna start havin' a little fun with your wife, if you know what I mean. Then, after we've had our fun with her, if you still ain't back with the money, we're gonna kill her and the little girl."

"All right, all right," the banker said. "Please don't hurt anyone. I'll get the money."

"Now you're gettin' smart."

Quickly, the banker got dressed, then started toward the door.

"Remember, be back here with the money before twenty minutes is up, or we start on your woman." Pete reached over to grab one of Beth's breasts, squeezing it hard enough for her to gasp with pain. "This is just to show you that we're serious."

"I beg of you, don't do anything to hurt my family," the banker pleaded, thoroughly cowed. "I'll do what you say."

The little girl had become quite heavy. Since she had stopped struggling, Eddie set her down.

She immediately ran over to hit Pete on the leg. "Don't you hurt my mommy!" she demanded.

"Ha," Merlin said. "Your little girl has more courage than either of you."

"Suzie, come here!" Beth called.

The girl crawled into the bed and huddled next to her.

After the banker left, the three men stared at Beth. Her eyes reflected her terror, but she was fighting hard to keep herself under control.

"How come you ain't cryin'?" Eddie asked. "Most women would be cryin'."

"Would it do me any good to cry?" Beth replied.

Eddie laughed and shook his head. "I reckon you've got a point there. No, it wouldn't do you no good to cry."

"Why don't we just all go down into the parlor and have a seat?" Pete suggested. "It'll be more comfortable, and there ain't no sense in us gettin' tired while we're waitin', now is there?"

"Suzie should go back to bed. She's just a little girl."

"Maybe she can find a place to sleep down there. Surely somebody as rich as you folks are have a sofa."

"Yes, we have a sofa."

"Then let's just all go down there and relax while we wait."

They went downstairs and into the moonlit parlor. Beth started over toward one of the tables.

"What are you doin'?" Pete asked.

"I'm going to light a lamp."

"No, you ain't. We don't want anyone comin' over wonderin' why there's a light on at this time of night."

"Why don't you let 'er light one, Pete?" Eddie asked. "I'll bet she's one fine-lookin' woman, and I'd like to get me a good look."

"You can see her good enough."

Suddenly there was a *whirr*, then a *gong*.

"What the hell was that?" Merlin asked.

Pete laughed. "Damn, Merlin. You're so jumpy that a clock scares you? That was just the half hour chime, is all."

"Yeah, I knew that," Merlin said, trying to recover some of his composure.

Pete made conversation to pass the time. "I tell

you what, Beth, your husband . . . what's his name? . . . Filbert?"

Beth nodded, but gave no audible reply.

"Yes, well ole' Filbert better be back here before the clock strikes again."

"He'll be back," Beth said.

"Mommy, I'm scared," Suzie said.

Beth put her arm around her daughter's shoulders. "Don't be afraid. Daddy will be back soon, then these men will leave."

"I want them to leave now. I don't like them."

Merlin laughed. "Now that just breaks my heart that you don't like me."

As they were waiting, Eddie wandered around the room, picking up pieces for a closer examination, then putting them back down. He picked up a porcelain doll. "What's this?"

"Oh, please do be careful with that, it is very"— Beth started to say *expensive*, for indeed it was, having come from the Song Dynasty in twelfth-century China, but she amended her comment—"dear to me. My mother gave it to me when I was a little girl."

"Don't worry. I ain't goin' to play with no dolls," Eddie said.

"Look at all this stuff," Merlin said. "You people must be filthy rich to have all this."

Beth didn't reply.

He smiled. "We're gonna be rich, too, if your husband does what we told him to do."

"Here he is, comin' back," Eddie said.

"Is he carrying anything?" Pete asked.

"He's carryin' a big sack."

Merlin smiled broadly. "That's our money! Hey Pete. His idea worked!"

The banker came into the house, and not glancing toward the parlor, started up the stairs.

"We're in here," Pete called to him.

"I have the money," Filbert said.

"How much did you get?"

"I got every cent that was in the bank, just like you told me. Thirty thousand, one hundred and seventeen dollars."

PSR ranch house

With a sigh of frustration, Josh Richards sat up. He was on the edge of the bed in Janey's room, having failed again in his attempt to have sex with her. His periods of impotence had started over a year ago. At first they were intermittent, but over the last six months he had become totally impotent. "I'm sorry, I couldn't do it."

"Don't be sorry, darling," Janey said, reaching out to put her hand on his. "Believe me, you don't need to prove yourself to me."

Though she didn't show it, Janey was glad Richards was impotent. She very much appreciated the economic benefits of living with him and was willing to make her bed available to him as part of the price she had to pay for the luxury she enjoyed, but she had always done so out of a sense of obligation, never for pleasure.

"Don't you ever tell anyone about this," Richards warned. "Do you hear me? Don't you tell Wiley or Muley, and especially, don't you tell any of your friends down at the Pink House. If I ever hear tell that you've told anyone, I'll beat the hell out of you."

"No, you mean you'll kill me."

"I wouldn't go that far but—"

"You'd have to go that far," Janey interrupted coolly.

"Why do you say that?"

"Because, Josh, dear, if you ever hit me, and leave me alive, I'll kill you."

Richards laughed out loud. "You know what? I believe you would."

"Oh, you can count on that." There was no laughter in her voice.

CHAPTER 14

Running Creek

The next morning Smoke walked over to the sheriff's office to introduce himself. He found the man behind a desk, which was where most star packers who were half lawman, half politician tended to spend a lot of their time.

"Sheriff Tanner? I'm Smoke Jensen."

The sheriff sprouted a big smile as he stood up, then came around from behind his desk with his hand extended. He was a silver-haired man with a weathered face and the beginnings of a paunch.

Probably a capable lawman at one time, thought Smoke, *but nearing the end of his run.*

"Deputy Jensen, welcome to Running Creek. And am I glad to see you. I hope your trip here was without incident."

"It was. Marshal Holloway said you needed some help."

"He didn't tell you what I needed, did he?"

"He said he didn't know."

"That's right, I didn't tell him, did I? Well, to tell you the truth, Deputy, I was afraid that if I told him what I needed, he might not be able to get a deputy to come. Have you ever heard of a man named Holder? Val Holder?"

"Yes, I've heard of him." Smoke thought about the conversation he had overheard in the saloon last night, in which Holder's name was mentioned. But that wasn't the first time he had heard of him. Holder was said to be extremely fast with a gun, and even quicker to use it.

"He's wanted for murder up in Wyoming, and he's killed a few people here in Colorado. In fact he killed a man yesterday, right here in Running Creek."

"You arrested him?"

Tanner looked uncomfortable. "Well . . . no, I didn't. All the eyewitnesses said it was a fair fight. And to be honest, I don't think I can arrest him."

"You mean you don't have anything on him?"

"No, I mean I don't think I can arrest him. If he decided to resist arrest, I . . . well, I'm no match for him. I don't know if Marshal Holloway told you, but I asked for you by name."

"Oh?"

"Yes. I heard what you did in Red Cliff, and frankly, it would take someone who could do something like that to go up against Holder and have any hope of surviving."

"What charge do you have against him?"

"I don't have any charge against him, but like I said, there is a warrant on him from Wyoming. You, being a federal marshal, could serve that on him.

Frankly, Deputy, I just want to be rid of him. Since he came to town last month, he has pretty much taken over. He knows that I won't, or can't, do anything to stop him, so he's got the whole town afraid of him.

"I figure if you arrest him, once I've got him in jail, I can hold him until Wyoming sends someone down for him. In jail and without a gun, he'll be just another prisoner."

"Do you think he'll come along peaceable-like?"

"No, I don't think he will. I think he'll challenge you, and you're going to wind up having to kill him. Or . . ."

Sheriff Tanner's voice trailed off in mid-sentence as he realized he had almost said more than he intended to say.

"Or be killed by him?" Smoke replied, smiling faintly at the sheriff's discomfort.

"Yes," the sheriff admitted. He took his hat off and ran his hand through his hair. "Look, Deputy, if you want to turn around and go back to Denver, I understand. I . . . uh . . . have no right to ask you to risk your life like this."

"Sure you do," Smoke replied without hesitation. "I'm a deputy U.S. marshal, and that's what we do. But I tell you what, Sheriff. Why don't we both go see this man Holder? You make the arrest; that'll send a message to everyone that you're the one in charge here. And I'll be right there with you to back your play if need be."

A broad smile spread across the sheriff's face. "Yes. Now, that is a great idea."

* * *

Even as Smoke and Sheriff Tanner were discussing Holder, Holder was in the Black Jack Saloon having a similar discussion with a man named Vince Jarrett.

"Smoke Jensen?" Holder asked. "Are you sure Smoke Jensen is in town?"

"Yeah, he's here all right. He had a drink right here in this very hotel last night. I recognized him right off." Fox-faced Jarrett had been a petty criminal and owlhoot his entire life. He and another local ne'er-do-well named Eric Reid had joined up with Val Holder.

"What's he doin' here?"

"He's a deputy U.S.marshal, you know. I heard that the sheriff called him in to arrest you."

"Did he, now?" Holder asked, smirking.

"Ha! I'm lookin' forward to seein' him try to do that," Reid said. "You'll shoot him down just like you done Kingsley."

Holder shook his head. "Yeah, well, it ain't goin' to be quite that way."

Reid frowned. "What do you mean?"

"I've heard of Jensen. He's good. He's damn good. I don't plan to go up against him without an edge."

"What kind of edge?" Jarrett asked.

"You two will be my edge. There will be the three of us against the one of him."

"Wait a minute!" Jarrett said, putting his hands out. "Maybe you didn't hear about what happened over in Red Cliff. They was three men that went up ag'in him there, too, and he kilt all three. One of 'em was Lucas Babcock. Babcock was damn good with a gun, but that didn't matter. Jensen got all three of 'em."

"Yeah, I heard about that. But them three men was stupid because they tried to face him in the open," Holder said. "It ain't goin' to be that way with us. Jarrett, you're gonna be up on the second-floor landing. Reid, you'll be sittin' over there at that table behind the piano. The both of you will shoot him just before the play starts. After it's all over, Jensen will be dead, and there won't nobody but the three of us who'll know what really happened."

"How will we know when to shoot?" Reid asked.

"You'll hear me say 'it looks like me and you is goin' to have a little dance.' You two be ready, 'cause just as soon as I say the word *dance . . .* that's the signal for both of you to start shootin'."

"That's a pretty long shot from over there behind the piano. What if I miss?" Reid asked.

"It won't make any difference whether you miss or not. That'll be enough of a distraction to give me the edge I need."

"Yeah," Jarrett said. "Yeah, that's a damn good idea!"

"Reid, you go over there and stand in the doorway now," Holder ordered. "I want you to keep a lookout and let us know if you see Jensen coming. That'll give us a chance to get into position."

"All right," Reid said.

"You, Treacher," Holder called to a man sitting at a nearby table, listening in on the conversation. "Give me your pistol."

"What?"

"You heard me. I said give me your pistol."

"Why should I do that?"

"Because I'll kill you if you don't."

Frightened by the threat, Treacher pulled his pistol and handed it over.

With Treacher's pistol in hand, Holder walked down to where the bar curved and stretched to put the gun into the small lip under the overhang.

"Here he comes," Reid called. "I'll be damned. He's got the sheriff with him!"

"All right, Reid, you and Jarrett get to your places—Jarrett, you upstairs, and Reid, you behind the piano," Holder ordered.

Holder didn't move. He put his hand on the bar, just above where he had secreted the pistol.

Sheriff Tanner and Smoke Jensen came into the saloon.

"Holder, I've got a warrant for your arrest that came from Wyoming," Tanner said. "And I'm here to serve it on you now."

The gunman smirked. "Since when can you arrest me on paper from Wyoming?"

"I asked him to," Smoke said. "I'm a federal officer, and that means that it could be Wyoming, Colorado, or Texas. Anywhere in the U.S., it makes no difference to me."

"So, you're the one who's gonna arrest me, are you, Sheriff?" Holder asked with a contemptuous grin.

"Yes, I am, so I'd be obliged if you would unbuckle that gun belt and let it drop to the floor."

"I have no intention of obligin' you, Sheriff. So it looks like me and you is goin' to have a little *dance*."

At that cue, Jarrett stepped to the upstairs railing and aimed his gun at Tanner.

"Sheriff, there's a man on the landing with the drop on you." The warning shout came from Treacher.

Angry that his ambush plans were spoiled by the yell, Holder grabbed the gun he had hidden, but as he tried to bring it up, he hit his hand on the end of the bar, slowing his draw.

Jarrett fired from the balcony and missed, the bullet slamming into the glass mirror behind the bar. The mirror shattered and fell, leaving only a few jagged shards hanging in place to reflect in distorted images the scene playing before it.

Jarrett didn't get off a second shot, Smoke drew and fired, his bullet finding its mark. Jarrett dropped his pistol and grabbed his throat, standing for just a moment, clutching his neck as bright red blood welled between his fingers. His eyes rolled up in their sockets and he fell forward, toppling over the railing.

Even as Jarrett was flipping in midair, Smoke heard the roar of two more Colts. Though it seemed to him that time had stilled, the truth was that the battle between Holder and the sheriff had taken place almost simultaneously with his own fight. And because Holder's draw had been slowed when he hit his hand on the bar, Sheriff Tanner managed to get his shot off first, putting his bullet in the middle of Holder's chest. Holder's shot was reflexive, and all it did was punch a hole in the floor.

"There's another one over behind the piano." Treacher pointed toward Reid.

Reid, seeing that things were going against them, had not even joined the fight. He stepped from behind the piano and thrust his hands in the air. His pistol was still in its holster. "No, no, don't shoot! Don't shoot!" he shouted in panic. "I ain't a part o' this! I ain't in it at all!"

"Shuck your belt," the sheriff ordered.

"I'm adoin' it, I'm adoin' it." Reid used his left hand to unfasten his belt buckle. The gun belt dropped to the floor with a clatter.

The sheriff looked at Reid for a long moment, and Smoke almost believed he was going to shoot anyway.

Finally Tanner sighed and made a waving motion with his pistol. "Get out of here, Reid. Leave town and don't ever come back. If I ever see you in town again, I'll throw you in jail and you'll rot there. If I don't kill you first."

"But this here is where I live," Reid whined. "I got me a room over at Miss Blum's roomin' house."

"I'll give you one hour to get packed and be gone," Sheriff Tanner said.

"All right. I'm agoin', I'm agoin'." Reid walked out the door.

"Damn, did you see that?" someone said. "The sheriff took Holder."

"The sheriff is a good man. I've always said that," Treacher said.

"Sheriff Tanner, I have to agree with these men. You did a good job. No, you did an outstanding job," Smoke said, noticing an unmistakable look of pride on the sheriff's face.

"I couldn't have done it without you."

"Don't sell yourself short."

The sheriff looked at Smoke, then up toward the top of the stairs where Jarrett had been when he'd tried to ambush them, then back to Smoke. "That was one hell of a shot, Deputy. I'd make that better'n sixty feet, easy."

"More like eighty, maybe even ninety feet," Treacher said.

"Treacher," Sheriff Tanner said. "I want to thank you for the warning."

"Yeah, well, Holder took my gun," Treacher said, reaching down for it.

"Boys," the bartender said. "Holder ran roughshod around here long enough. Step up to the bar. There's one free round on the house."

The men cheered, then hurried toward the bar.

"Hey, Kelly, what about the women? Are they free too?" someone asked.

"We'll drink one drink with you," said one of the soiled doves. "But that's as free as it gets."

"Aw, Belle, don't you love me no more?" another cowboy asked.

"Of course I love you, honey." Belle put her hand on her hip and thrust it out provocatively. "I love all you boys. As long as you've got money."

"Sheriff, I'd like to ask you a question," Smoke said when they'd returned to the sheriff's office.

"Deputy, ask anything you want," the sheriff said with a broad smile.

Smoke asked the question he had asked so many times it came out automatically, flat toned, as if he had no personal interest in the reply. "I'm looking for three men—Wiley Potter, Muley Stratton, and Josh Richards. Have you ever heard of them?"

"No, I don't think so. Are they wanted men?"

"Yes, they committed a murder down in New Mexico. The sheriff down there thinks they might have gone to Wyoming, and if they did, they would have had to come through here."

"What do they look like?"

Smoke had been asked that question many times during his quest, and he was no more able to answer it now than he had been the first time the question was asked. "I don't know what they look like, but I expect they're using their real names."

Tanner frowned. "Why would they do that?"

"Because they are arrogant and wealthy. It's more than likely they settled someplace where there isn't any law . . . or they have bought the law."

"I hate men like that. I hate them almost as much as I hate the lawman who can be bought. I've never heard the names, but you can be very sure that if I ever do hear anything about them, I'll let you know."

"Thanks. I appreciate that."

CHAPTER 15

O n his way back to Denver that night, Smoke camped out just twenty miles east of where Clell Dawson was camping. The two men were far enough apart to not run into each other and traveling along trails that wouldn't cross. Even if they had met on the trail there would have been nothing more than a nod between them. While Smoke had heard of Clell Dawson, and Clell had heard of Smoke Jensen, neither would recognize the other on sight.

The next morning, Clell made coffee by putting a few coffee beans he had chewed up into a tin cup of water, which he then heated. That and a piece of jerky was his breakfast. As he sat there, he wondered how far it was to the next town. Going from town to town and settling down in none of them was vastly different from the life he had planned when he'd studied medicine.

He had become a doctor because he'd once thought that he had a genuine desire to help people. Then came the war, where he had been a surgeon on the battlefield. That experience had changed, forever, how he looked at the profession of medicine.

He stared into the fire, remembering.

Near Franklin, Tennessee in 1865 the battle was pitched with guns roaring, shells bursting, and men screaming.

It was the latter, the men screaming, that dominated the sounds. Clell was at the first-aid station set up behind the lines, which was a joke. Earlier, a nearby bursting shell had killed one of his medical aides. Clell had his sleeves rolled up. Blood covered his hands and arms all the way up to his elbows. He was holding a bone saw in his hand as a wounded soldier was put on the table in front of him.

"Here's another one, Doc," said one of the two men carrying the wounded soldier.

"How many more out there?" Clell asked.

"I don't know, thirty, forty maybe. It don't make much difference 'cause there's more comin' all the time, and lots of those that's waitin' dies. The number ain't never the same from one minute to another."

The wounded soldier looked over to his right and saw a pile of amputated legs and arms. "No, Doc! No!" he screamed. "Don't cut off my leg! Don't cut off my leg!"

"Soldier, the cannonball has already just about done that. All I'm doing is cleaning it up."

"But you're a doctor! Can't you do somethin'?" the man pleaded.

Clell shuddered. He wasn't a doctor any longer. The war had turned him into little more than a butcher.

Standing up next to his campfire, Clell tossed out the last dregs of his coffee, and with that action closed the door to his memories. Over the years he had developed the skill of being able to dip into those memories when he wished and shut them off when they became too painful.

Not all veterans of that terrible war were so skilled.

The brutal, bloody struggle between North and South had ended when Lee surrendered to Grant at Appomattox, Virginia, but for many, the surrender was just the beginning of a much more personal conflict. Young men who had lived their lives on the edge of death for four years found it nearly impossible to return home and take up the plow, or go back to work in a store, repair wagons, or any of the other things that were a necessary part of becoming whole again.

Some found nothing to come home to. Many who had fought for the South returned to burned-out homes, farms gone to seed or, worse, taken for taxes. Those men became the dispossessed. Unable to settle down, they became wanderers. Many of them went West, where there would be less civilized encroachment upon their chosen way of life.

Some took up the outlaw trail, continuing to practice the skills they had learned during the war. But most were innocent wanderers with all bridges to their past burned and the paths to their future uncharted.

Clell Dawson was such a man. Finding that he no longer felt a calling for medicine he, too, had nothing to come home to.

But there was another, darker side to Clell. The same deft touch and dexterity that had made him a great surgeon also made him exceptionally good with a gun. Never, in all his wanderings, did he openly seek trouble. But neither did he back away from it.

"All right, Dan. What do you say we get going?" Like many men who rode the lonely trails, he had gotten into the habit of talking to his only real companion—his horse. "We've got another long day ahead of us."

Dan snorted, then stood quietly as Clell extinguished the fire and threw on the saddle. He mounted and resumed his wandering, with no particular destination in mind and no need to go back to anyplace he had been before.

It was mid-afternoon when Dan stepped into an unseen prairie dog hole. With a sharp whinny of pain, his right foreleg folded, he went down, and Clell was tossed over his head.

Getting up, Clell hurried back to Dan.

Dan was lying on his side, looking up at Clell as if his big, brown eyes were begging the man to do something for him. A bloody, jagged end of bone was sticking out through the skin of Dan's leg.

"Oh no," Clell said, shaking his head. He closed his eyes for a moment, but when he opened them, the terrible damage hadn't gone away. "No no no."

He stroked Dan's face for a moment, talking quietly to him. "We'll meet again someday, Dan. I know damn well we will. But you're going to have to go on ahead of me."

Clell took out his pistol and aimed it right between the horse's eyes. Dan continued to look at him, and he knew that Dan knew what was about to happen. Closing his eyes, Clell pulled the trigger.

* * *

Late that afternoon, Clell dropped his saddle with a sigh of relief. Climbing up the ballast–covered berm, he stood for a moment on the crossties between the twin ribbons of iron. He looked first toward the distant and empty horizon to the east, then he turned toward the purple mountains to the west. For the moment, the empty tracks offered no more comfort than the empty prairie or the foreboding mountains. He knew that a train would be passing that way sometime before sundown, whether going west or east, he wasn't sure. It didn't matter.

It had been a long, hard walk to the railroad, but he hadn't wanted to leave his saddle behind. Climbing back down from the berm, he lay down beside the tracks, making a pillow of the saddle.

He waited for the train for just over an hour, and when first he saw it, it was coming from the east. Against the great panorama of the plains, the train seemed puny, and even the smoke that poured from its diamond-shaped stack made but a tiny scar against the deepening blue of the eastern sky. He could hear the train quite clearly, the sound of its puffing engine carrying across the wide, flat ground—the way sound travels across water.

It was a freight. He had been hoping for a passenger train. He believed he would have been able to flag it down and pay for passage to the next town. He sighed. The only way he was going to get a ride on this train was to hop onto one of the cars, and because he was carrying his saddle, he would have to choose a car with an open door. He sighed again. He knew it wasn't always possible to find a car with an open door on a cross-country freight.

He caught a break as the train approached. It had started up a long, gradual grade, slowing down to no faster than a brisk walk.

Clell waited in a little gully until the engine passed. He didn't want the engineer, the fireman, or the brakeman to see him. After the engine and tender had passed, he looked down the row of cars until he saw one with an open door. Picking up his saddle, he climbed up the berm and began running alongside the train, not quite matching his speed to it, so the car with the open door caught up to him. Matching its speed, he tossed the saddle in through the open door, and was about to grab hold, when a hand stuck out from the darkened interior of the car.

"Grab ahold, friend, and I'll jerk you up here!" a voice called.

For a second, Clell was hesitant to trust the offer, but he figured if it wasn't genuine, he could always jerk the man down from the car. The man didn't try any tricks, though, and with the stranger's help, Clell half climbed and was half pulled into the car.

The man in the car appeared to be in his late forties or early fifties. He had long white hair and a scraggly white beard.

"Thanks," Clell said. "That was decent of you."

"Yes, sir, well, I've been pulled onto a few trains myself, from time to time. You're new at this, ain't ya?"

"Yes, how did you know?"

The old man chuckled. "You don't see a lot of boes carrying saddles."

"Boes?"

"Hoboes," the man said. "That's what I am, and I'm proud to claim it. The name is Nick." He stuck his hand out.

"Clell," he said, taking the man's hand.

"Somethin' happen to your horse?"

"Stepped in a prairie dog hole and busted his leg. I had to put him down."

Nick shook his head. "Sorry to hear that. I hate to see any creature have to be put down. I had me a dog that used to travel with me for a while, but he jumped down afore he was supposed to one day, and got runned over by the train. Sure pained me when that happened. I don't mind tellin' you, it plumb brung me to tears. Where you headin'?"

"To the next town."

"Do you know what the next town is?" Nick asked.

Clell shook his head. "I don't know, and I don't particularly care."

Nick laughed again. "Clell, you may not know it, but if you are of that kind of a mind, why then, you're a bo, same as the rest of us. But just so that you know, the next town will be Kremmling. It's about another hour or so, I reckon. We're 'bout to go through Kremmling Pass. If you got a interest in it, we can climb up on top of the car and you can get a real good view of the pass as we go through."

"That sounds good to me," Clell said.

"Wait till we go around the next curve, then climb up on the near side of the car to the curve. If you climb up on the out side, why it'll purt' nigh throw you off, for some reason. But if you're on the inside, what it does is, it throws you against the side of the car, and that helps you to hold on as you're aclimbin'."

"Centrifugal force," Clell said.

"Beg pardon."

"Centrifugal force," Clell repeated. "It's the force that tends to throw a body away from the center of rotation."

"You don't say. Well, whatever it is, it's a good thing to keep it in mind when you're outside on a train while it's agoin' around a curve. Get ready, we got one comin' up, now."

The long string of freight cars bumped and rattled on the uneven tracks and filled the pass with thunder as steam gushed from the drive cylinders of the laboring engine. The two men climbed to the top and perched on the forward end of the car. Their legs dangled over the edge in such a way that they could look down between their feet and gauge the speed of the train by watching the passing of the cross ties and the ballast. Not long after, it grew so dark they could no longer see the ground.

No matter how the train lurched and jerked over the rough roadbed, though, the two were sitting as securely in their places as birds on a swaying tree limb. The two men, who had never met until Clell decided to jump the freight, were sitting elbow to elbow, engaged in measured conversation. Clell had learned long ago that it wasn't good to give away too much information to strangers.

"I tell you what," Nick said. "When we get to the very top of this pass, if you'll look to the right, just between the V of the tops of the hills, you'll see the lights of Kremmling. It looks just real purty out there on the valley floor, all lit up like that."

"Have you ever been to Kremmling or do you always just pass through?" Clell asked.

"Oh, from time to time I've stopped there. Sometimes you can find a hobo camp just out of town, down by Muddy Creek. There's most always some folks there, and most always a pot of stew goin', but they like for you to bring somethin' to throw in it, like taters or carrots or some such thing." Nick laughed. "This time o' night, I can generally snatch me up a chicken somewhere and use that to buy my way in. By the time whoever I steal the chicken from discovers it missin' and goes to the sheriff about it, why it's too late, the chicken's done been throwed into the pot and et, so there ain't nothin' nobody can do about it. I got me some taters in a sack down in the car, though. There ain't no need for me to steal nothin' tonight. You're welcome to come to the camp with me if you want. My taters will get us both in."

"Well, I appreciate the offer, Nick, but I'm not sure I would feel comfortable going in there, carryin' my saddle."

Nick chuckled. "I know what you mean. We'd better climb back down into the car now. We'll need to jump off before the train comes into the depot. Like as not, they'll have railroad bulls lookin' for us. And they ain't pleasant men to be around."

Fifteen minutes later, both men were sitting in the open door of the car.

Nick said, "I'll tell you when to jump. And do it as soon as I say so, 'cause if you wait any longer, you'll wind up on the rocks."

Clell picked up his saddle and was holding it so he could toss it out when he got the word.

"Now!" Nick said, and with Clell tossing the saddle even as he jumped, the two men leaped from the car, hit soft dirt, and rolled a few feet before coming to a stop.

"This here is the only soft dirt on this part of the road," Nick said.

"You picked a good spot," Clell replied. "It was almost like jumping into a featherbed."

Nick laughed. "I'll have to 'member that."

They waited until the end of the train passed, then Clell picked up his saddle and started across the track heading for the lights of the town.

"This here is where I'll leave you." Nick stuck his hand out. "You've been good company."

"Wait," Clell said, reaching down into his pocket. "Here, take this."

"What is it?" Nick asked.

"It's a ten-dollar bill. I figure I owe you that, for pulling me into the car."

"Lord o' mercy. Ten dollars?" Nick's voice reflected his awe. "I ain't seen ten whole dollars this entire year!"

"Enjoy it," Clell said, shifting the saddle to his shoulder and heading toward the town. He looked around a few minutes later, and saw Nick still standing there, trying to make out the bill in the dark.

He smiled at Nick's reaction to the money. He could have given him one hundred dollars, since he had the money. But one hundred dollars might cause Nick to ask too many questions. And the truth was, he seemed just as pleased with ten as he would have been with a hundred. Besides, if someone else knew that Nick had a hundred dollars, it could be danger-ous.

Clell was quite sure that if Nick had it, he would not be able to keep secret the fact that he was carry-ing one hundred dollars.

CHAPTER 16

Kremmling, Colorado Territory

"What are you doin' sleepin' here in one of my stalls?" The man gave a harder than necessary kick to the bottom of Clell's foot.

Clell sat up fast, a gun instantly appearing in his hand. He eared back the hammer, the cocking sound having a chilling effect.

The man put both hands up and jumped back. "Hold on there, mister, hold on!" he shouted, fear coloring his voice. "I didn't mean nothin' by it. I was just wakin' you up, is all."

Clell stood up, then returned his gun to its holster. "To answer your question, I slept here because I didn't want to leave my saddle unguarded. I had to put my horse down, and I need another one."

"You . . . you're stealin' a horse from me?"

"What?" Clell frowned. "No. Who said anything about stealing a horse? I said I *needed* a horse. I want to buy one from you, if you have one for sale. If you don't have one for sale, I'd appreciate it if you would tell me where I might buy one."

"Oh. Well, you don't have to go nowhere else," the liveryman said, smiling at the prospect of a sale. "I've got some of the best horseflesh you ever laid your eyes on."

"Really? I've seen some pretty good horses in my day," Clell replied.

"Well, they, uh, might not be the best you've ever seen"—the stableman paused in mid-sentence—"but they're damn good. How much money are you lookin' to spend?"

"As much as it takes to get the horse I want."

Again, the stableman was all smiles. "Come out back with me, and I'll show you what I've got."

Looking at the available horses, Clell had a sharp intake of breath when he spotted Dan. That was impossible, of course, but the horse was the spitting image of Dan. He walked over to him. "I want this horse."

"Mister, I could tell you lies about how good that horse is, but the truth is, he's at least seven or eight years old. If you look around, I'm sure you can find a younger horse, and one that would suit you better."

"This is the horse I want," Clell declared. His tone made it clear he wasn't going to change his mind.

"All right, you're the one paying for it. If that's the horse you want, you can certainly have him. His name is Blackie."

"No, it isn't."

"Sure it is. That's the name that was on the paper when I bought him."

"His name is Dan," Clell said.

Three quarters of an hour later Clell, mounted once more, was riding out of town. He passed by a gulley near a stream of water—he believed he remembered Nick referring to it as Muddy Creek—when he heard a voice that he recognized.

Nick was telling a small group of raggedy men about "the feller I had to pull onto the train or he woulda been runned over for sure."

Clell smiled as he rode on.

Denver

"I don't know what you did or said to my friend Frank Tanner while you were there," Marshal Holloway said. "But he sent me a telegram singing your praises. That telegram was so long it musta cost him five dollars to send it. To spend five dollars on a telegram takes some kind of motivation."

"The truth is, Sheriff Tanner did it himself," Smoke said. "He's the one who faced Holder down, and when Holder drew on him, he's the one who shot him."

"Yeah, he said something about you backing him up and helping him regain some face in that town." Holloway cocked his head to one side. "Boy, you got a lot more smarts in you than most people your age. I don't know how long you plan on bein' my deputy, but I want you to know that I am right proud to have you with me for as long as you plan to hang on to that badge."

"Thanks. I've made no secret of the fact that I'm looking for the men who killed my pa. I figure that having this badge can only help. I mean, it helped me find the men who killed my ma."

Holloway nodded. "I understand. I don't like the idea of using a badge just for vengeance, but I certainly can't complain about the way you've treated the job so far. You've been more than willing to take on any task I set for you. Anyway, since Sheriff Murchison has asked for our help in finding those same men that you're looking for, we can't exactly call it vengeance, can we?"

Smoke smiled. "No, sir, I guess we can't."

"I've been thinking about this, and I almost hate to offer it to you, for fear you'll take me up on it. But you've certainly earned the right. How would you like to be a deputy emeritus?" Marshal Holloway suggested.

"A deputy what?"

"A deputy emeritus. Emeritus is what you call somebody who is retired, but has maintained the title and the authority. I think something like that is used mostly for college professors, but I don't know why I can't use it for you."

"I'll be. I've never heard of that word."

"I think it would fit your situation perfectly. Basically, what it will do is give you the freedom to go or do what you want, while keeping your badge, and if I ever have anything specific that I want you to do, I'll find some way to get in touch with you."

"Wait a minute, are you telling me that I don't have to report to you, but I can still have the authority of being a deputy U.S. marshal?"

"Yes. That is exactly what I'm telling you. That is, if you would like to do that."

Smoke gave it only a moment's thought. "Yes. I think I would very much like to do that."

"The only thing about this kind of position, Smoke, is that you would no longer be on the payroll except when you are actually engaged in an official and specific operation."

"That would be fine by me, Marshal. I appreciate you doing this for me."

"Where do you plan to go first?"

"I'll probably go back and check in with Preacher. Maybe stay around for a year or so."

"You mean you're going to give up looking for those three men you've been searching for?"

"I'm not giving up, exactly, I figure they'll still be out there when I'm ready to start looking for them again. But Preacher isn't getting any younger, and truth to tell, I don't know how much longer he's going to be around. He's the closest thing to family I've got. And I'm more than likely the only family he's ever had, so I'd like to spend some time with him. I'll never let him know that, though. He'd be so embarrassed he'd probably run me off."

"I wouldn't doubt that for a minute," Holloway said with a little laugh. "All right, take a year, eighteen months, two years if need be. The badge is yours to keep, and anytime you're ready, come on back and I'll find something for you to do. You take care of that old man now, you hear? He's as much a part of this territory as the Rocky Mountains themselves."

"I will, Marshal. And thanks again for doing this for me."

Bury

Sally Reynolds sat primly in a chair at a meeting of the school board.

"It has been reported, Miss Reynolds, that you have been seen keeping company with Janey Garner and Flora Yancey," the president of the school board said with an ominous frown.

Sally nodded and said simply, "Yes."

"Yes?" The school board president's eyebrows climbed up his forehead like a pair of bushy worms. "You mean you don't deny it?"

"Why should I deny it?"

"Do you not feel a sense of *shame* for keeping company with those people?"

"No, why should I feel shame? Miss Garner and Miss Yancey are both friends of mine."

"But surely you can see the impropriety of that," Mrs. Pinknell said, leaning forward and staring at her through a pair of pince-nez wire-rim glasses.

"No, I cannot see any impropriety in that," Sally said. "Janey and Flora are my friends. There are not that many women in Bury with whom I can be friends, and I feel very lucky to have encountered some unmarried women who are near my age, and whose company I find to be entertaining."

"It has also been reported that you have been seen going into, and leaving, the Pink House," declared one of the male members of the Board of Education.

"I sometimes go there to play whist with my friends."

"Miss Reynolds," Mrs. Pinknell said. "Are you totally unaware of the profession followed by the young women who reside in the Pink House?"

"I have been given to believe that they are prostitutes." Sally raised an eyebrow. "Have I erred in that belief?"

Sally's frankness was totally unexpected by the members of the board, as they had thought she would dissemble and obfuscate.

"Uh, yes, that is what they are. Do you see nothing wrong with that?" the board president said.

"Well, it isn't an occupation that I would care to follow," Sally said with a slight shrug. "But then, neither would I want to be a lawyer, or a horse trader, or a pawnbroker." She smiled, knowing she had named the occupations of at least three of the board members.

Mrs. Pinknell glared at her and said, "I'm afraid that you are going to have to give up your friendship with these women or we will be forced to remove you from your position as a schoolteacher."

"All right," Sally said.

Mrs. Pinknell smiled triumphantly. "I'm glad you see it our way. Then we can be assured that you will no longer keep company with those women?"

"No," Sally replied. "When I said all right, I meant you can go ahead and remove me from my position as schoolteacher. I have no intention of turning my back on my friends."

"What?" Mrs. Pinknell gasped. "Miss Reynolds, you can't be serious."

"Oh, but I'm quite serious. And, as I shall no longer be employed by the school board, I understand that I shall have to give up my quarters, so I will look for a new apartment immediately."

"Wait, now. Let's not be too hasty here." The president of the board held up his hand. "Give us a moment of deliberation, would you?"

"Yes, of course." Sally stepped out of the room for a moment.

"We can't ask her to step down," he said to the others. "There is no way we could get a new schoolteacher for next year at this late date. It's already March."

"But she has been seen in a brothel!" objected one of the others.

The president frowned. "Who would know this, except habitués of such an establishment? I hardly think their opinion is valid. I say we let the whole thing drop."

"Well I, for one, am opposed to letting it drop," Mrs. Pinknell said.

The president sighed. "You're only one vote. I say she stays, and I say we vote now."

An immediate vote was taken, and the outcome of the vote was to retain Sally Reynolds as teacher for the Bury Grammar School.

Janey laughed about it as she and Sally shared dinner that evening at the Gold Nugget Restaurant. "I would love to have seen the expression on that old biddy Hortense Pinknell's face when the board voted to keep you on as teacher."

"Would you? Well, I can show you the expression." Sally pursed her lips, squinted her eyes, and made wrinkles appear around her nose.

"Stop!" Janey said, laughing even harder. "You should go on the stage. You mimicked her perfectly."

"You know Mrs. Pinknell, do you?"

"Oh, indeed I do," Janey said. "Sometimes I'll have Mr. Jefferies drive down the street by Mrs. Pinknell, even if it is out of the way . . . just so I can see her stick her nose in the air. One of these days, she's doing to do that and a bird is going to drop a little bird turd right in one of her nostrils."

Sally had just lifted a fork, but she had to drop it, she laughed so loud at Janey's comment. "Oh, Janey, hush. You're going to make me laugh so hard that the manager will come kick us out of here."

"No, he won't. The PSR owns this restaurant. Laugh all you want."

CHAPTER 17

Preacher's cabin

The old man dressed in buckskin met Smoke at the door. "Damn, boy, this is the second time in the last three months you've showed up here. Are you tellin' me I ain't rid of you yet? I raised me a wolf oncet. Found 'im when he was a pup, I did. And when he growed big enough to take care of hisself, I set 'im free, but damn if he didn't keep comin' back. You ain't no different from that wolf, 'ceptin' at least there come a time when that critter quit comin' around. When is that goin' to happen to you?"

Smoke chuckled. In the old man's eyes and the tone of his voice, he could read the pleasure Preacher felt at having him back.

"I figure I have to keep an eye on you, Preacher. You're getting so old, I'm not sure you can even feed yourself, anymore."

"Don't you worry about me feedin' myself. If I have to, I'll take a fish out of a grizzly's hand, and you know I can do it," Preacher said, continuing the banter.

"I know that, old man. That's why all the grizzlies steer well clear of you."

"What brings you back? Did you get fired?"

"Sort of."

"How the blazes can you get *sort of* fired?"

"I'm a deputy emeritus."

"Boy, how am I gonna know what the Sam Hill you're talkin' about, if you don't speak English?"

Smoke laughed. "Are you telling me that you don't know what the word *emeritus* means?"

"Yeah, that's what I'm tellin' you. I don't have no idea what that word means."

Smoke shook his head. "Why, I thought everybody knew what that word meant." He had to laugh as Preacher glared at his joshing. He defined the word, then explained, as Marshal Holloway had explained to him, how it meant he could keep the badge but was free to do things on his own.

"Good, good. You got back just in time," Preacher said.

"Just in time for what?"

"Just in time to move these half-broke horses we been gatherin' to someplace where we can sell 'em. Especially since you ain't gettin' paid for wearin' that tin star no more."

"What were you going to do with them if I hadn't come back when I did?" Smoke asked.

"I was gonna shoot 'em," Preacher said.

Smoke laughed. "Preacher, you can go to hell for lying as well as stealing, you know."

"Well, in that case, I'll be among friends. I don't

hardly know no mountain man, from Jim Bridger to Pierre Gardeau to Kit Carson, who ain't turned the air blue with their lies. Or did they turn it blue with their cussin'? I never could get that straight."

"Are we going to round up the horses or are you just going to stand here all day with your jaw flapping?" Smoke asked.

"You're the one doin' all the talkin', boy. Come on. Let's get with it." Preacher led the way.

It had been Smoke who, some time ago, got Preacher interested in raising and selling horses. With the beaver pelt business no longer profitable, it hadn't been that hard to talk the old mountain man into the idea. Since most of the horses were wild mustangs they had captured and penned, there had been very little financial investment in the business.

Smoke had thought that the hardest thing would be finding and capturing them, but that proved to be less difficult than breaking them.

"You don't want to break 'em all the way now," Preacher said one spring day as Smoke got up painfully and started back toward the horse that had just thrown him. "You got to leave some spirit in 'em or they won't be worth a damn."

"Yeah? Well, I'll try and keep that in mind," Smoke said with a grin that was more of a grimace as he returned to his task.

Their first trip to market a couple weeks later wasn't nearly as much of a chore as he had assumed. They kept the number of mounts they were moving relatively small, no more than thirty, and the horses considered it more desirable to stay with their own, rather than wander off.

Several weeks later, Smoke and Preacher were pushing nineteen head of half-broken mustangs and sixteen head of Appaloosa south into the wild country. They crossed the Colorado River, then cut southeast.

A few miles from the Dolores River the wind changed.

Smoke lifted his head. "Smell's like somethin's burning."

Preacher brought them to a halt and stood up in his stirrups to sniff the air. "Yeah, somethin' is burnin', and there is more to it than wood. Take a sniff of that air, boy, and tell me what you smell."

Smoke tried to identify the mixture of strange odors as he bunched the horses. "You're right, it's more than wood. Leather and burnt cloth maybe? And . . . something else . . . something I can't figure out."

Preacher's reply was grim. "It's burnt hair and flesh, that's what it is. What do you say we put the horses in that box canyon over yonder, then go take us a look-see?"

"All right," Smoke agreed.

After securing the open end of the canyon with brush and rope, the men rode slowly and carefully toward the smell of charred flesh, the odor becoming thicker as they rode. At the base of a small hill, they left their horses and crawled up to the crest.

From there, they were able to look down on a scene reflecting the tragedy that had befallen the occupants of two partially burned wagons below.

Tied by his ankles from a limb, and hanging head down over a small fire, was a naked man. Even from the distance, Smoke and Preacher could see that his head, face, and shoulders were little more than blackened meat. The mutilated bodies of two other men were sprawled out on the ground, and a third was tied to the wheel of one of the burned wagons. Like the man hanging by his ankles, all had died hard.

"You said you heard gunfire about two hours ago," Preacher whispered. "Turns out you was right. It was the damn Apache."

"Apache, up here? Isn't this a bit north of their territory?"

"Oh, they come up this far ever' now and again. Most of the time so's they can raid the Utes."

Appalled, Smoke whispered, "What were these people doing here in the first place? And how the hell did they get the wagons this far? There's no road and very little open ground to speak of."

"Sheer stubbornness, I reckon. But I sure hope they warn't no women with 'em. If so, God help 'em."

"I wonder if the Indians are gone." Smoke looked around.

"Yeah, they're gone. If they warn't I'd be able to smell 'em," Preacher said.

Smoke wasn't sure whether Preacher meant they really could smell them or if that was just his colorful way of saying he would feel it if they were present, but knowing Preacher as well as he did, he was ready to believe that Preacher actually could smell the Apaches.

"I think we should go down there and poke around some, then give those hombres a Christian burial. Maybe after we plant 'em, we can say a word or two." Preacher spat on the ground. "Damn heathens."

They slid down the hill to the charred wagons.

On the ground beside one, Smoke found a shovel with its handle intact. Taking turns, they dug a long, shallow grave, burying the remains of the men in one common grave. That done, they walked around picking rocks to cover the mound so as to keep wolves and coyotes from digging up the bodies and eating them. Preacher took off his battered old hat and stood alongside the grave. Smoke followed suit.

Preacher began speaking. "Lord, from seein' what's left of a Bible that was here in one of the wagons, I know the fellers that was travelin' in 'em was most likely good Christian folk. There ain't nothin' more we can do for 'em now, other than turn 'em over to you. Amen." He put his hat back on and looked over at Smoke. "That'll do it, I reckon." He turned and walked the area, cutting sign, trying to determine if anyone got away.

Smoke rummaged through what was left of the wagons and found what he didn't want to find. "Preacher!" he called.

The mountain man turned back. Smoke held up a dress, then another, smaller than the first.

Preacher shook his shaggy head as he walked back. "You found any women's bodies?"

"No."

"God have mercy on their souls, that means the Injuns musta took'em," Preacher said, fingering the gingham. "They won't kill 'em, but it's goin' to be a hard life for 'em. Any man that would bring a woman down here to this part of the country is a damn fool."

"Maybe the women got away," Smoke said hopefully.

"It ain't likely. But we'll take a good look."

Almost on the verge of giving up after an hour of looking, Smoke made one more sweep of the area. He saw shoe prints mixed in with marks and tracks. The prints were small—a child or a woman. He pointed them out to Preacher.

"Good Lord! Them is women's tracks! Mayhap she got clear and run away." Preacher circled the tracks until he got them separated. "Don't seem like they was followin' her. Get the horses, son. If she's gonna have any chance o' survivin', we got to find her before dark."

It didn't take them long to track the woman who got away. They found her hiding behind some brush at the mouth of a canyon. Try as she could to be still, she gave away her position. Some of the branches of the bush where she was hiding showed movement.

"Girl," Preacher called to her. "You can come out now. You're among friends."

Smoke could see one high-top button shoe. "Please come on out now. We're not going to hurt you."

There was no response from whomever was in the bush.

"Reason we're tryin' to get you to come out is we just seen a rattler crawlin' in there with you," Preacher lied.

With a little gasp of alarm, a young woman bolted

from behind the bush and straight into Smoke's arms.

Smoke had expected it to be a young girl, perhaps no more than eleven or twelve, but she was a young woman, at least eighteen or twenty. Her eyes were light blue, set in a heart-shaped face, framed with hair the color of wheat.

She was, Smoke realized, an exceptionally pretty woman.

They stood for several long heartbeats, gazing at each other, neither of them speaking.

"What's your name?" he finally asked.

"Nicole. Nicole Woodward. Are they . . . is everyone dead?"

"I'm afraid so." Smoke knew the news was harsh, but he spoke as softly as he could, trying to break it to her gently.

Nicole put her face in her small hands and began crying. "I don't know what to do. I don't have any family to go back to. I don't have anyone."

Smoke put his arms around her and pulled her to him. He quickly became aware of two things—he felt intensely protective of her, and she felt soft and vulnerable in his arms. "Sure you do, Nicole. You have us."

She pulled away after a long moment of being in his embrace and saw the deputy marshal's star on his chest. "You're a sheriff? Where were you? Why weren't you here before? Why weren't you here when we needed you?"

"I'm not a sheriff. I'm a deputy U.S. marshal. And believe me, Nicole, I would give anything to have been here earlier when you needed me."

Preacher cleared his throat. "We best be gettin' a move on."

She shook her head at Smoke. "I'm sorry I yelled at you. I'm just so . . . so—" She was unable to finish the sentence.

"I know," Smoke said. "You don't have to apologize. Come on. Let's go back to the wagons and see what we can find for you."

"Are they . . . I mean . . ." Nicole put her hands over her eyes. "I don't want to see anyone."

"You won't," Preacher promised. "We already buried 'em. Come on. Nothing to see now but burned wagons and scattered goods."

Rummaging around in the debris, Smoke found a few garments, including a lace corset, which a red-faced Nicole quickly snatched from him. He also found a saddle that had suffered only minor damage. Everything else was lost.

"You can ride Seven," Smoke said. "He'll be gentle with you if I tell him. I'll throw this saddle on one of our trade mounts."

"Now, how you figure she's gonna set that saddle?" Preacher demanded. "What with all them skirts and pretty thingees she's more'n likely wearin' underneath?"

"She won't be wearin' that. She found a pair of men's trousers that belonged to her uncle. She can put them on and ride astride."

"Ridin' astride ain't fittin' for no decent woman to do. Nobody except a soiled dove would do that."

"Well, Preacher, just what the hell do you suggest we do with her? Build a travois and drag her?" Smoke grumbled.

Preacher walked away muttering to himself as the girl came to Smoke's side.

"I can sit a saddle. I rode as a child in Illinois."

"Is that what you're from?"

"No. I'm from Boston. My parents died when I was just a little girl, and I moved to Illinois to live with my uncle and aunt. What's your name?"

"Smoke." He jerked his thumb. "That's Preacher. Don't pay him any never-mind. He always talks gruff, but he doesn't really mean it."

"I already had that figured out." She smiled.

Smoke swallowed. She was beautiful.

"Your name is Smoke?"

"That's what I'm called."

"At the trading post, we heard talk of a gunfighter called Smoke. Is that you?"

"I guess so."

"They say you killed fifty men." There was no fear in her eyes as she said it.

Smoke laughed. "I reckon I've killed more than my share, but I don't think I've killed fifty. And the ones I did kill were all trying to kill me. They were fair fights."

"You've had a lot of people try to kill you?"

"Yes."

"You must piss a lot of people off."

The answer was so unexpected that Smoke laughed out loud. He laughed so hard that his sides began to ache.

"What in Sam Hill is so damn funny?" Preacher asked, coming back to them.

"Nothing," Smoke said, still laughing. "There's nothing funny at all."

"Well?" Nicole asked, innocently unaware of how funny her response had been. "Do you?"

"I seem to have a habit of running into people who are doing things they shouldn't be doing, especially since I've put on this badge." Smoke indicated the star on his shirt. "People like that do tend to get angry with me, and then they try to shoot me. I've been fortunate enough to be faster and more accurate than them."

"You don't look like a gunfighter."

Smoke frowned. "I don't?"

"No, not at all."

"What does a gunfighter look like?"

"Mean and menacing, like this." Nicole squinted her eyes, and turned the corner of her lips down, trying to snarl, but she couldn't hold it and broke into a laugh.

She was joined by Smoke.

"I swear, the way you two is carryin' on is like a couple o' schoolkids," Preacher said. "Come on, let's get out of here. I don't expect the Injuns to come back, but I got no desire to test that thought out, neither."

CHAPTER 18

"Now that you found her, what do you aim to do with her?" Preacher asked later, when he and Smoke were alone for the moment beside their campfire.

Nicole was nearby in the bushes tending to personal business, close enough to sing out if anything—or anybody—bothered her.

"Well, I thought maybe we'd take her back to the cabin after we deliver these horses," Smoke said.

Preacher shook his head. "That cabin ain't fittin' for no woman, and you know it."

"Well then, what do you propose?"

"I think we should build a cabin for the two of you," Preacher said.

Smoke looked startled. "The two of us?"

"Yeah, the two of you. You don't plan on just leavin' her in a cabin all by her lonesome, do you?"

"No, but—"

"Don't get yourself all in a fret. I'll help you build

the cabin, and I'll stay there with the both of you till things gets comfortable betwixt the two of you."

"What do you mean by *get comfortable?*"

"Boy, here I think I've larnt you near 'bout all I can larn you, and the next thing I know you up and say somethin' so damn foolish I figure I ain't larnt you near 'bout nothin' at all."

"What about the horses?" Smoke asked.

"What about 'em? We won't sell 'em just yet. They're all yourn now. You'll need somethin' to get your ranch started, won't you?"

Gradually, Smoke began to realize what Preacher was saying to him. "Yeah," he mused. "Yeah, I reckon I will."

"Well, then let's get started and find a good place. You'll want the cabin all built up and chinked in, and a goodly supply of wood afore the winter sets in. And that ain't goin' to be too much longer."

High in the mountains, Colorado Territory

The house they built was of adobe and logs and rocks, with rough planking and sod for a roof. Smoke wouldn't settle for a dirt floor. He carefully smoothed and shaped logs, which had to be dragged from the forest. Nicole joined in with the construction and proved to be a very good worker.

The work was hard and backbreaking, but no one complained except for Preacher, who crabbed all the time about almost everything, just on general principles. Neither Smoke nor Nicole paid any attention to him, knowing it was his way and he was not going to change.

Nicole never spoke of leaving, and Smoke never brought it up.

Preacher just grinned at them both.

They finished the house just before the first snowfall, then Smoke and Preacher spent some time hunting for food and carving and curing the meat for the harsh winter ahead of them. It had been too late to start a garden, but they found some cattail, wild asparagus, dandelion, fireweed, and edible mushrooms to augment the meat.

With the house up and food to last the winter, Preacher saddled his horse one morning and readied the packhorse. "I'm headin' east," he told them. "Over to the Springs, maybe. Maybe beyond. I'll prob'ly winter in the mountains with some old cronies that's still up there, so more'n likely I won't be back until spring. See you younguns then."

He rode off, well aware that he was leaving a young man and a young woman alone together in a snug cabin during a long, cold winter. He had decided the young folks needed some time to themselves and was giving it to them.

Nicole touched Smoke's arm. "When will he be back?"

"When he feels like it. With Preacher, there's just no telling."

"Why did he leave like that? Without even a fare-thee-well?"

"Lots of reasons. He knows he doesn't have that many winters left, and he wants to be alone some. That's the way he's lived all his life. And he wants us to have some time alone together."

Nicole smiled self-consciously at Smoke. "Doesn't he know that we've found the time to be . . . alone?"

Smoke put his hand under her chin and tipped her face up toward him, raising her lips to his. "I reckon he knows," he mumbled as he closed the distance between them with a kiss.

Spring 1872

One day, Nicole told Smoke that they needed to talk.

Smoke chuckled. "What do you mean, we need to talk? We talk all the time."

"We don't just talk *all the time*," Nicole said with a twinkle in her eye. "And that's what we have to talk about."

"I swear, Nicole, you aren't making any sense at all."

"We've got to get married, Smoke."

Smoke chuckled. "You don't have to propose to me, Nicole. I've already proposed to you, remember? We're going to be married as soon as Preacher comes back, don't you remember?"

"We can't wait."

"What?"

Nicole smiled at him. "We can't wait, Papa."

"Papa?"

"Smoke, are you that thickheaded? What I'm saying is, I'm going to have a baby. No, *we* are going to have a baby."

Smoke sat stunned in one of the chairs at the rough-hewn table. "Nicole, you can't have a baby! Don't you know we're better than a hundred miles from the nearest doctor?"

Nicole laughed again. "Darling, you can't just say I can't have a baby as if I can change my mind. It's already started. We're going to have a baby, but don't worry about a doctor. I went to nursing school, and believe me, the baby is going to get here, with or without a doctor. All I want is for us to be married. I want the baby to have a legal name."

"Preacher told me there was a little settlement of Mormons a ways west of here over in Utah territory. We can probably find someone to marry us there. But it will be nearly a week there and a week back. Can you stand the ride?"

She smiled and kissed him. "You just watch."

On the eighth day of their travel, Smoke figured they were in Utah territory, probably had been all day. The settlement of Mormons should be in sight. But all they found were rotting, tumbledown cabins, and no signs of life.

"Preacher said they were here in fifty-five," Smoke said. "I wonder where they went?"

Nicole's laughter rang out over the deserted collection of falling down cabins. "Honey, that was almost twenty years ago." Her eyes swept the land, spotting an old graveyard overgrown with weeds. "Let's look over there."

They examined all the rotting markers, and the latest date they could find was fourteen years old.

"There is no preacher, and I don't have any idea

where one might be from here," Nicole said, obviously disappointed.

"We're going to be married today, Nicole," Smoke declared, "preacher or no preacher."

"How?"

"I'll show you."

Smoke built a fire and spent an hour heating and hammering a nail into a perfect circle. When it was cooled, he slipped it on her third finger, left hand. "Before God, I take you, Nicole Woodward, as my wife."

Nicole looked into his eyes. "Before God, I take you, Smoke Jensen, as my husband."

Smoke kissed her then smiled. "Now let me ask you something. Would you feel any more married if a preacher that neither of us had ever met had married us?"

Nicole smiled. "Not at all. As far as I'm concerned, we are married. Come on, husband, let's go home."

Smoke's cabin

Preacher was sitting on the rough bench in front of their cabin when Smoke and his new bride rode into the yard. He was spitting tobacco juice and whittling on a piece of wood. "Howdy." He greeted them as if he had been gone only a day instead of months. "Where you two been?"

"What do you mean where have we been?" Smoke replied. "You're the one that rode off. Where have you been?"

"I've been around," Preacher replied as if that was

all the answer that was needed. "I told you I'd be back, come spring."

"We got married," Nicole said proudly, showing him her ring.

"You with child, girl?"

"Yes, sir."

"I figured if I left you two alone, you'd get into mischief."

Nicole grinned. "I'll go fix supper." She left the two men alone.

When she had closed the door to the cabin, Preacher turned to Smoke. "You can't be going looking for those men anymore, boy. You're married now, and you've got responsibilities to that woman who is carrying your child."

"If they leave me alone, I'll leave them alone."

"It ain't goin' to work that way, though."

"What do you mean?"

"I figure they already know that you've been after 'em, and more 'n likely they found some people who will come after you. They'll be payin' them to do it, bounty hunters mostly, because a damn bounty hunter don't really care who he's after as long as he gets his blood money."

"I'm through with all that now, Preacher. I'm hanging up my guns. I want to raise horses, maybe run some cattle. You, me, and Nicole. We're going to raise a family and our children will need a grandfather. That's where you come in, you old goat."

"Much obliged. Reckon that's the nicest thing you said to me in months."

"I haven't seen you in months," Smoke pointed

out, but Preacher's grin told him the old mountain man already knew that.

Preacher grew solemn again as he asked, "When is the girl gonna give birth?"

"November, she thinks."

"Just like a woman. Don't never know nothin' for sure."

The summer passed uneventfully with Smoke tending to their large garden and looking after his growing herd of horses. He also hunted for game, curing some of the meat, making pemmican out of the rest. Nicole had sent him down to Schemerhorn's to get canning jars, and soon she had canned enough beans, corn, okra, tomatoes, and beets to last them through the winter.

The baby was born just after the first snow, and Smoke enjoyed sitting in front of the fireplace in one of the two rocking chairs he had made, warm and content as he watched Nicole nurse little Art.

"What do you mean you named him after me?" Preacher asked. "You mean you're gonna call him Preacher?"

Smoke and Nicole laughed.

"No, we're naming him Arthur and we're going to call him Art. That is your name, isn't it?" Smoke asked.

Preacher frowned. "Oh. Yeah, I guess you're right. My name is Art, only I ain't been called that by nobody in so long I sometimes near 'bout forget. Seems to me like I been called Preacher near 'bout my whole life."

PSR Ranch, office, Spring 1873

Richards, Stratton, and Potter sat in chairs surrounded by killers. Felter, Poker, and Canning were on the sofa. Stoner and Evans had each found a hard-bottom, straight-back chair, while Clark, Grissom, and Austin were sitting on the fireplace hearth.

"We'll give you eight thousand dollars," Richards said. "There are eight of you, so that works out to a thousand dollars apiece."

"You're givin' the eight of us a thousand dollars apiece, to kill one man?" Felter asked.

"Yeah, well, he's not just any man, and I want to be sure the job is done," Richards said. "I've been followin' him for some time now. I don't know how the hell he ever found out that we was the ones that kilt his ol' man, but he ain't let up since then. Word has reached me that he's askin' ever'where about us. If he keeps at it long enough, he's goin' to find out where we are."

"There are three of you," Felter said. "Are you saying that one man is better than all three of you put together?"

"No, I'm not saying that," Richards replied. "But there's somethin' you've got to understand. Muley, Wiley, and I are important people in this town. Hell, we are important people all over the West now. It wouldn't do for us to get involved in some shooting scrape with Smoke Jensen. Even if we killed him, and I'm sure we would, it wouldn't look good for us. That's why we're hiring the eight of you to do it. Eight of you to kill one man. It shouldn't be that hard."

"Do you know where he is?" Felter asked.

Richards smiled. "I know exactly where he is. He's down in Colorado, livin' with some woman he found out on the trail. Word is that she's whelped by now, and that should give you men an edge. Not that you would need one."

"A thousand dollars apiece?" Felter said.

"That's a lot of money. I expect you to produce."

"We want half of it now," Felter said.

"I figured you would. Before my woman went into town, I had her write out eight bank drafts. You can cash them at the bank in Bury before you leave."

Richards nodded at Stratton, who walked over to the desk and picked them up from where Janey had left them.

As the eight men were leaving, an elegant carriage arrived, driven by a liveried black man. Stopping the carriage and setting the brake, the driver hopped down to help a very well-dressed and exceptionally attractive woman into the carriage.

"Lord a'mighty, who is that?" Stoner asked.

"That's somebody you don't want to look at twice," Potter said. "That's Richards's woman."

"I'm goin' to get me a woman like that, soon as we finish this job and I've got the money," Stoner said.

"Stoner, if you were getting ten times as much money, you could never get a woman like that," Potter said.

On that beautiful spring day, the woman didn't so much as glance toward them as she climbed into the carriage.

"Mr. Jefferies, do you know who those men were?" Janey asked her driver as the carriage rolled down the long drive from the house to the road into town.

"No, ma'am, I don't. I truly don't," Jefferies replied.

She had written eight bank drafts for five hundred dollars apiece earlier that morning. Eight men were leaving the house as she did. For some reason, the thoughts going through her head were very troubling.

CHAPTER 19

"I have no idea who they were or what it was all about," Janey told Sally as the two women shared breakfast. "But I know they are up to no good. You don't just give eight men five hundred dollars apiece unless you expect them to do something for you. In this case, I know whatever it is, is something illegal."

"Janey, why do you stay with that man?" Sally asked.

"He pays well," Janey replied with a wry smile.

"You are much too intelligent to waste your life with him. I know you could find something better to do."

"The only other thing I would be qualified for is to work for Flora. I've done that enough to know I don't want to do it again. I've made my bed, Sally. Now I must sleep in it."

Smoke's cabin

Now that Smoke had a wife and a baby to support, he had given up his search for Richards and the other two men. He still wore the badge of a marshal emeritus, but he had promised Nicole that sometime in the summer, he would take her and the baby to Denver, and he would turn in the badge. He was not only through with hunting for Potter, Stratton and Richards, he was through with the deputy marshal business. He still wore his gun, but it was more an act of habit, rather than necessity.

Nicole had recently asked how long it would be before they went to Denver. She had never seen the city and was excited over the prospect of visiting it. Smoke knew that being all alone, so far from anyone else, was probably hard on her, though she had never mouthed so much as one complaint. She seemed perfectly satisfied and happy with her little mountain home, her husband, and her child.

They weren't entirely alone, of course. Preacher was a frequent guest, even though he had to ride some ten miles to get from his place to theirs. He often told them it was foolish to name a baby after an old man, but Smoke and Nicole knew he was pleased by it. They were also tickled to see how taken with the boy he was.

"The kid knows me," Preacher said late one morning. "You see the way his face gets all lit up, ever'time I come over and he sees me?"

"Of course he knows you, Preacher," Nicole said. "He thinks you're part of the family. And why shouldn't he think that? You are a part of the family."

"You think maybe when the kid gets old enough that . . . maybe . . . he could call me Granpa? I mean, I know I'm not, but—"

"Oh, but you are his grandpa," Nicole said. "In every way that counts, you are Little Art's grandpa."

"You know what I'm gonna do when the boy gets old enough? I'm gonna teach him to hunt and fish. And I'm gonna start early on him, too. I ain't gonna wait until he's half growed, so's I have to unlearn him a bunch of things, like I had to do with Smoke," Preacher said, happily anticipating being a part of the child's life. "You know what I'm gonna do? I'm gonna ride to the closest town and get some geegaws for you and that youngun."

After a quick lunch, Preacher spent the afternoon riding the dozen miles into town. A group of men were gathered in front of the saloon. Most were local men, but he saw two of them appeared to be gun-hands. He actually recognized one—a man he knew only as Felter.

A former cavalryman, Felter had been publicly flogged and then dishonorably discharged for deser-tion in the face of the enemy, the enemy being the Cheyenne up in the northern part of the territory. After his humiliation and discharge from the army, he had turned bounty hunter, selling his gun to the highest bidder.

Preacher rode on past the saloon down to the store, where he bought some ribbon for Nicole and a silver cup for the baby. "Can you sort of scratch his name on that cup?"

"Sure, I can engrave his name," the storekeeper said. "What is it?"

"Same as mine," Preacher said with a broad grin.

The merchant frowned. "The baby's name is Preacher?"

The question irritated him. "No, it ain't Preacher. It's Art, dadgum it."

"I'll be damned. I ain't never heard you called nothin' but Preacher."

The old mountain man waited around until the engraving was done, then, with his purchases secured in the saddlebag of his horse, he decided to stop into the saloon for a drink before he headed back.

As he stepped up onto the porch, a young man wearing a red checkered shirt, dark trousers tucked into polished boots, and a pair of pearl-handled revolvers grinned at him. "Hey, Grandpa! Ain't you too old to be walking around without someone to look after you? You're likely to forget your way back home."

Preacher glanced at the young man and without breaking stride or even giving him a second look, drove the butt of his Henry into the loudmouth's stomach. The young smartmouth doubled over, vomiting in the street.

Preacher reached down and pulled out both of the young gunman's pistols, then dropped then in the watering trough. "Maybe you better run along on home now, sonny. When you've got yourself full growed, why maybe you can come on back and play with the adults."

Aware of Felter's uncompromising gaze, Preacher pushed on into the dark shadows of the saloon and stepped up to the bar. "Give me a beer and a shot of whiskey."

Just as the drinks were delivered, the city marshal came inside. "Any trouble out there, Preacher?"

"Nothing I couldn't handle."

The marshal chuckled. "That young fellow you doubled over calls himself Kid Austin. He thinks he's quite a hand with those fancy guns." The marshal stepped up to the bar and ordered a beer, then waited until the bartender stepped away. He turned toward Preacher and spoke quietly. "I haven't seen Smoke around for a while."

"That's 'cause he ain't been around for a while."

"You in touch with him?"

"Sometimes I am and sometimes I ain't."

"Sometime when you are in touch with him, you might let him know there's some bounty hunters after 'im."

"What for? Smoke ain't got the law after him."

The marshal shook his head. "This don't have nothin' to do with the law. From what I've heard, it's money bein' put out by three men who want your friend dead."

"Potter, Stratton, and Richards," Preacher muttered.

Surprised, the marshal asked, "You know about 'em?"

"I've heard of 'em," Preacher said without giving out any more information.

"Yes, sir, that's the ones all right. Kid Austin is one of the bounty hunters. Those other two out on the porch are called Felter and Canning. All three of 'em are workin' for Potter, Stratton, and Richards. From what I hear, there's five more of 'em, hardcases they are, that's ridin' with 'em. They're camped out just north of town. When you leave, and I hope it's soon, ride out easy and cover your trail."

Preacher nodded. "Thanks."

* * *

The bullet that almost took him out of the saddle hit him in the left shoulder, driving out his back. Preacher slammed his heels to the side of his horse, and keeping low in the saddle, headed for a hole in the mountains. Through his pain, he could hear men yelling off to his right.

Felter hollered, "Get him alive! Don't kill him. He knows where Jensen is."

Getting Preacher took more doing than the men chasing him had. Another rifle barked and the slug hit him in the leg, deflecting off bone and angling upward, ripping a hole when it exited out his hip, taking a piece of bone with it.

Preacher leveled his Henry. He intended to blow the lights out of all three varmints, but his injury threw his aim off. The shots that erupted from the rifle all went low and struck the horses instead. The men crashed to the ground as their mounts collapsed.

Preacher wheeled his horse and urged it into a run. Behind him, the men leaped to their feet, yelling curses as they futilely emptied their six-guns after him.

The racket was lost in the background as he slipped away from them. He was losing a lot of blood, and it was all he could do to stay in the saddle throughout the late afternoon as he rode, barely conscious, until he reached a small lake, where he stopped for the night. He wrapped his hip and shoulder the best he could, in spite of knowing that he was close to death.

He lived through the night, then mounted his horse, and continued his ride. Through sheer iron will, stubbornness, and hardheaded determination, he finished the long journey to Smoke's cabin.

Nicole was out front when he rode up.

"Howdy, pretty thing," Preacher said, then he toppled from his pony.

"Smoke! Come quick!" Nicole cried. "Preacher's here. He's dying!"

"No, I ain't," Preacher rasped as Smoke rushed out of the cabin to kneel beside him. "I didn't come . . . this far, to up . . . and die on you. Give me a week or two . . . of restin' and eatin' . . . and I'll be ready to go back to my own place . . . and leave you folks be." Too hurt to say more, Preacher closed his eyes.

Together, Smoke and Nicole dragged him inside.

True to his prediction, Preacher made a remarkable recovery over the next few weeks as the weather warmed and April turned into May. When the time came for him to leave, Smoke helped him load up his packhorse.

After telling Nicole and the baby good-bye, Preacher went out front to mount up. Smoke followed him.

"Smoke," the old mountain man said. "Them people that put the bullets in me is lookin' for you. I don't think they got no idea 'bout where at you are alivin' now, but you might want to keep an eye open all the same. I know you wasn't goin' to look for 'em no more, but that don't mean they ain't lookin' for you. So be careful."

"I will be," Smoke promised.

As Smoke watched Preacher ride off, he couldn't

help but wonder if he could ever live in peace. That ever-present speculation haunted him, especially considering that he had a wife and son.

In a nearby settlement

After losing their horses to Preacher's rifle, the three bounty hunters had spent a few very long and very unpleasant hours on foot, finally arriving back in town. They'd managed to acquire horses before the gang had moved on to yet another small town.

They were a quarrelsome bunch while they waited for their opportunity.

Kid Austin was quick with a pistol—uncommonly fast—perhaps the quickest of them all. The others left him alone.

Because the man they were hunting was a friend of the old mountain man who had humiliated him in front of the saloon, Kid Austin had a particular hatred for Smoke. He dreamed of killing him, of facing him down in the street, beating him to the draw, and watching him die hard in the dirt, crying and begging for mercy, while men stood on the boardwalks and feared the man called Kid Austin, and women stood and wanted him.

Felter was much more patient and shared none of the Kid's dreams. Felter didn't know exactly how many white men he had killed—around twenty-five or so—but none of them in a face-to-face shoot-out. Unlike Kid Austin, he didn't consider killing a sport. He killed when it made things easier for him to do whatever he had in mind doing. Or if he got paid for it.

He spun the cylinder of his Colt and said to the

others, "They got to be in that valley, somewhere southwest of here. Everything points in that direction."

"Do you remember that old Indian we talked to?" Canning asked. "He said something about a blond-haired woman that was the only white woman down in that valley. Richards said that Jensen has took him a wife and has a kid. That blond-haired woman the Indian was talkin' about has to be his."

"More'n likely," Poker said.

Canning grinned. "You boys can have the gun-fighter; I'll take me a taste of his wife. I'd like to have me a white woman."

"I tell you what, Canning, you can have all the squaws you take a mind to," the bounty hunter named Grissom told him. "There don't nobody give a damn about them. But you do that to a white woman, and you're going to wind up gettin' yourself hung."

Canning's grin spread across his unshaven face. "Not if I don't leave her alive to tell any tales, I won't."

"What about the kid?" Poker asked.

"We'll kill the kid, too," Canning said. "Hell, it don't make no mind to me. Besides, we don't want to leave a young sprout around to grow up and get mean, then come lookin' for us when we're old men, do we?"

To a man, the bounty hunters agreed that made sense. They would pleasure themselves with the woman, then kill her and the kid.

"I want Smoke Jensen for my own self," Kid Austin put in. "I want to face him straight on so I can beat him at his own game. The rest of you can just watch me."

"Yeah, Kid,"said the man called Poker. "You're a real grizzly, you are."

Austin pointed his gun as he closed one eye. "I just need one chance."

Felter grinned. "That's good, Kid, 'cause one chance is all you're likely to get."

CHAPTER 20

Near Smoke's cabin

Aware of the new "responsibilities" Preacher had charged him with, Smoke worked long hours in the summer, gathering his precious herd of horses, putting them in a blind canyon where they could be held while he searched for others. He'd also found a cow and an old brindle steer that had wandered up with her. Probably the only survivors of an Indian attack on a wagon train. He figured having milk would be good for the baby.

During the late afternoon of a day out, he thought he heard the faint sounds of gunfire carrying on the wind, blowing from the north, but he couldn't be certain. He listened intently for several moments but could hear nothing except the wind sighing from a long way off, far in the mountains. He returned to his work, picking out a young colt that he was going to raise and gentle for Little Art.

Smoke wasn't much of a daydreamer, but he enjoyed picturing his son on that horse, first as a young child, then as a teen-aged boy, and finally as a young man, riding at Smoke's side. He would teach him to ride and to shoot. Maybe, he thought, the day would come when he would resume his quest for the men who had killed his father . . . and Art would be there with him.

Smoke didn't realize that, even as he was gathering his herd of horses, the eight men Richards had hired were at his house. At least, six and a half were. They weren't having an easy time of it. Nicole fought well. One of the attackers was lying out front, dead, and another, Clark, had a bad arm wound.

He was sitting in a chair cursing as he attempted, without help from any of the others, to bandage his bloody arm. "That damn woman can shoot. She damn near tore my arm off. Somebody see if you can find a bottle of laudanum."

Felter's eyes found the body of Stoner lying in front of the cabin. "Yeah, she sure can shoot. Just ask Stoner."

"How we gonna do that?" Poker asked. "She done shot Stoner dead."

"Yeah, well, you have to say this about her. She is one damn fine-lookin' woman," Canning said, looking at Nicole sprawled semiconscious on the floor. His eyes lingered on her bare breasts and legs exposed to the lustful gaze of the hired killers. The bodice of her dress had been ripped open and her dress had slipped all the way up to her thighs when she'd been knocked to the floor.

Canning licked his lips and repeated, "Yes, sir, she is just real fine."

"Yeah, well, let's find Jensen's gold," Felter snapped. "Then you can buy yourself a dozen women like that."

It wasn't until after they had started their pursuit of Smoke that they'd heard he had tens of thousands of dollars in gold, stolen from the Confederacy at the end of the war. That would be a much greater reward than the eight thousand dollars Richards, Potter, and Stratton had promised them. They didn't know if the three wealthy ranchers even knew about the gold or not, but the gunman had no intention of sharing it with them.

Soon the interior of the cabin was in shambles. They had literally destroyed it in their search for the gold that wasn't there.

"Drag Stoner's body out of sight," Felter ordered. "We don't want to spook Jensen when he comes ridin' up. And hide your horses so he can't see 'em. We'll grab him when he comes in."

"What do you mean we'll grab him when he comes in? You mean we'll shoot 'im, don't you?" Austin asked.

"No, I want to take him alive."

"Why the hell would you want to do that?" Clark asked.

"We ain't found the gold yet, so I figure that, more than likely, it ain't nowhere in this house," Felter replied. "What I aim to do is torture him till he tells us where the gold is."

Canning knelt down beside Nicole, his hands busy on her body. The baby began crying.

"Will somebody shut that kid up before I shoot the little snot?" Felter snarled.

"I'll shut the brat up." Grissom picked up a blanket and walked over to the cradle. Folding it over, he held it over the baby's face for a long time. . . .

On the morning of his third day out, Smoke began to have a prickly awareness of something being wrong. A feeling of dread was building up within him, and some primitive warning called on him to cut the roundup short. He left the cow, the steer, and the horses, which for the last two days had been so important to him, and headed for home, pushing Seven as fast as he dared.

As he came closer to the cabin he made a wide circle, staying in the timber on the opposite side of the creek that ran behind the house. If anyone was there who shouldn't be, he could slip up on them, unseen.

If Smoke had come one day earlier, he might have been able to save his wife, but he was too late.

Nicole was dead.

He ground tethered Seven. Taking the big Sharps buffalo rifle that Preacher had carried for years, Smoke crept closer. Seeing no one, he cautiously made his way to the woodpile.

Inside the cabin, the brutality that was still going on made Kid Austin sick to his stomach. He raced out the back door, stopping quickly and turning left to puke on the ground.

At least one, Smoke thought as he turned quietly around the back corner of the cabin.

Grissom walked out the front door of the cabin, sure Smoke would return from the south—the same direction his tracks had indicated when the gunmen first arrived. And why not? He had no reason to suspect that anything was amiss.

But even as Grissom stood there in the front doorway, he began to feel a little uneasy. His years on the owlhoot trail told him that something was wrong. "Felter?" he called over his shoulder.

Felter was rolling a quirly and stepped outside. "Yeah?"

"I got me a feelin' there's somethin' here that ain't quite right."

"Yeah. I got me that feelin', too. But what is it?"

"I don't know, but I do have this feelin'."

Felter stepped back into the house and looked at the dead woman lying on a blood-soaked bed. He wished she wasn't dead. He had enjoyed his times with her, and if they hadn't killed her, he could be with her again.

Grissom's feeling that something was wrong intensified, and the hair stood up on the back of his neck. He started to call out for Felter again, when he sensed a movement behind him. Even as he was turning, he reached for his pistol and saw the tall young man standing at the corner of the cabin, Colt in hand.

The young man fired, and Grissom felt a numbing blow in his chest. Hearing the pistol shot, Felter ran from the cabin, firing at the corner.

But Smoke was gone.

"Behind the house!" Felter yelled. Gun in hand, he ducked behind the water trough.

Smoke dived behind the woodpile.

In the outhouse, Poker made the foolish mistake of opening the door to see what was going on. Smoke shot him twice, leaving him to die on the outhouse floor.

Still leaning against the back of the cabin, Kid Austin, who had insisted many times over that he wanted to face Smoke down, ran for the banks of the creek, panic driving his legs. Smoke shot at him, the ball hitting him in the right buttock and traveling through the left cheek, tearing out a sizable hunk of flesh. Austin screamed, then fainted from the pain, falling into a rolling sprawl.

The men in the cabin were firing wildly in all directions.

"Where the hell is he?" Evans shouted.

"I don't know!" Canning cried.

"Well, keep looking!"Clark ordered.

The shooting stopped, and moments ticked by in silence. Smoke wiped the sweat from his face and waited, knowing without having to be told that Nicole was dead. He also knew that, for the moment, he had the advantage.

Something came sailing out the back door to bounce on the grass, and when he saw it, he fought back the urge to vomit from pure anger. It was the body of his son, and the boy had been dead for some time.

"You want to see what's left of your woman?" Canning called from near the back door. "I got her hair hangin' on my belt. If you'd like, I'll throw it out to you, just so's you can have a keepsake.

"I'll tell you this! She sure was a good one all right, near 'bout the best I ever had. We all took a time or two with her. And you know what? I think she liked it. No, I don't just *think* she liked, I *know* she liked it. Why do you think that was, Jensen? You think maybe that was because you wasn't man enough for her? You wasn't able to take care of her like a man should?"

Rage charged through Smoke, but he remained still behind the thick pile of wood, forcing himself to control his fury. It wasn't by happenstance that when he left the corner of the house he had taken shelter behind the woodpile. Before the shooting started, he'd left Preacher's buffalo rifle behind the woodpile. It could drop a two-thousand-pound buffalo from six hundred yards away. It could also punch a hole through a small log.

The voices from the cabin continued to call out, mocking him, trying to draw him out. But Smoke remained quiet, refusing to give in to the urge to hurl curses at them. He looked around. To his right was the meadow, which was totally devoid of cover. To his left was the shed. He knew it was empty of men because it was still barred from the outside. The man he shot in the butt was to his right, and the man in the outhouse was either dead or passed out and dying, because his screaming had ceased.

Smoke aimed the Sharps at a chink in the log wall where he thought he had seen a man move, just to the left of the rear window. He squeezed the trigger and the weapon boomed, the planking shattered, and a man began screaming in pain.

Canning ran out the front door of the cabin, sliding down beside Felter behind the water trough.

"This ain't working out," Canning panted. "Grissom, Stoner, and Poker are dead, Clark is wounded, and Evans is either dead or dying. The slug from that buffalo gun 'bout blew his arm off."

Felter had been thinking the same thing. "Let's get the hell out of here."

"What about Austin?" Canning asked.

"Austin is a growed man. He can either join us or he can go to hell."

"Let's ride. There's always another day. We'll hide up in the mountains, see which way Jensen runs out, then bushwhack him. Let's go."

The two men rushed for the horses hidden in the bend of the creek, behind the bank. They kept the cabin between themselves and Smoke until they were deep in the meadow and could belly down without him seeing them.

In the creek, the water red from the wounds in his butt, Kid Austin crawled upstream, crying in pain and humiliation. His pistols were forgotten, but they were useless anyway. The powder was wet. All he wanted to do was get away.

Left in the house, the two wounded men looked at each other.

"Help me," Evans said, his voice weak. "Help me get out of here."

Clarke frowned. "What for? You're hit a lot worse than me. You'll more'n likely be dead soon. Besides, I ain't goin' nowhere. I plan to kill Jensen and take the rest of the reward money for my ownself."

Outside and some distance from the cabin, Kid Austin finally managed to reach his horse hidden in the woods. Looking around, he realized that Smoke had not seen him.

He was getting away!

He stepped into the stirrups, hoisted himself in the saddle, and cried out in pain as his wound hit the saddle.

CHAPTER 21

"Looks like me and you's the only ones left now," Clark said, looking over at Evans.

The man was dead, having bled to death from the wound inflicted by the buffalo gun.

"I guess it's just me," Clark corrected with a pained chuckle of grim humor. "Hey, Jensen! What if I was to come outta here with my hands up in the air? Could maybe me and you just call this fight off, and go our own ways? I ain't after you no more. It ain't worth it."

Smoke didn't answer.

"Jensen, what do you say? How 'bout I give myself up? We could just shake hands, and have us a truce between us."

When there was still no answer, Clark realized he wasn't going to get far with that tactic. Angry, and knowing that he had lost the battle, he changed tactics, and began venting his hate and anger. "Hey, Jensen. Your wife don't look so good now. Not after one of our boys got through workin' her over with his knife!"

Clark's taunts had replaced the gunfire. Smoke had seen the others ride off but he remained still, his eyes burning with rage as he stared at the still form of his son.

"Yes, sir," Clark goaded him. "Me and the others had our way with that woman of yours. She was real good at it, too. Where at did you find her, anyhow? Did she used to work in one of them special kinda houses somewhere? 'Cause let me tell you, she sure knowed how to please a man."

Without replying, Smoke backed slowly away, keeping the woodpile in front of him. Carefully working his way around to the front, he looked in through the open door and grinned.

Clark was crouched in the back doorway, looking out. He held a pistol in his hand. The outlaw was still talking to the woodpile, to the muzzle of the Sharps that Smoke had left sticking out between the logs.

Smoke could have killed him easily, but that wasn't his intention. He took aim and shot the pistol out of Clark's hand.

The outlaw howled in pain and grabbed his numbed and bloodied hand as he fell to his knees. Smoke stepped over Grissom's body, then glanced at Evans.

Still on his knees, Clark looked up at the tall young man staring down at him with burning eyes. "You've near 'bout kilt us all. We was give a thousand dollars apiece to kill you, and it warn't worth it."

"Who paid you to kill me?"

"What makes you think I'm goin' to tell you that?"

"Actually, you don't have to tell me. I know who it was. It was Potter, Stratton, and Richards."

"Then what for did you ask? And if you know that,

then you also got to know that if we didn't get the job done, they'll just hire more people. You're a dead man, Jensen." Clark cackled a demonic laugh. "You're a dead man."

"So are you." Smoke kicked Clark in the side of the head, dropping him unconscious to the floor.

When Clark came to his senses several minutes later, it took him a moment to figure out where he was and what had happened to him. He was no longer in the cabin. He was outside lying on the ground a couple hundred yards away, spread-eagled and staked to the ground. He was also naked and could feel the irritation of something crawling on him. "What the hell? Where am I? What's going on here?"

"You'll figure it out, soon enough." Smoke began pouring something on Clark's naked body.

"What is that? What are you doing?"

"This is honey. And as you can see, I'm pouring it on you."

"What? Are you crazy? Why would you do that?"

"Turn your head and look beside you," Smoke said.

"What?" Clark turned his head and saw a huge mound of ants.

"No! My God, no! Jensen, you can't do that! I'm a white man," Clark screamed. "You can't do this to me." Slobber sprayed from his mouth. "What are you, half Apache? How can you do something like this to a white man? Shoot me, Jensen. God have pity on me. Just shoot me!"

Smoke glared. "Do you really think God could possibly have any pity on you after what you and the others did to my wife and my son? Not even God could, and I'm sure not Him."

"It warn't only me! Please, Jensen, I beg of you! Shoot me! Shoot me now!"

"No. You need time to think about what you did. This will give you an opportunity to make your peace." Smoke mounted his horse and rode away with Clark's terror-filled screams behind him.

"Shoot me, For God's sake, shoot me!" Clark pleaded. "It'll take me days to die like this. You're a devil, Jensen! You are a devil!"

Smoke blocked the screaming from his mind as he rode back to the cabin across the plain, so lovely with its profusion of wildflowers. Nicole had loved the wildflowers and often picked a bouquet of them to brighten the table for their meals.

Once he returned to the cabin, he went through the pockets of the four dead outlaws and Clark, the effort garnering him almost twenty-five hundred dollars. He dragged the bodies of Stoner, Grissom, and Poker into the cabin and left them lying in the middle of the floor beside Evans.

Smoke found a shovel and began a slow digging of two graves, one smaller than the other. He wasn't worried about whoever had gotten away. His horse would warn him if anyone was approaching. He paused often to wipe the tears from his eyes.

When Nicole and the baby were buried, Smoke took off his hat and stood alongside the graves, remembering having stood beside the graves of his ma and his pa. He thought of them.

"Ma, Pa. This is your daughter-in-law and your grandson. I didn't do any better keepin' them alive than I did with you two. I want you to look after 'em when they get there, though most likely you've already met them."

His words spoken, Smoke began dousing the cabin with kerosene. The entire structure was enveloped in flames as he rode away.

But no blaze could ever burn out the hatred in his heart.

"Felter, we got to go back for 'im," Canning said as he and his companions watched from a distance. They could hear Clark's faint, weakening screams. "We can't just leave 'im staked out like that."

"You really want to go back there and face Jensen? It would be bad enough facin' 'im any which way, but after what you done to his woman . . ."

"Here now, don't you be puttin' all that off on me. You had your turn with her just like ever'one else did," Canning said.

"Yeah, but I didn't cut her up like you did," Felter said.

"She was already dead when I done that, and you know it."

"You want to go down there and explain that to Jensen?"

"No." Canning shook his head. "No, I don't."

"Then leave Clark ascreamin'. We all took the same chance in comin'."

"I'm hurtin'," Kid Austin whined. "I'm hurtin' bad. You got to get me to a doctor."

"Tighten the cinch on your horse, Kid," Felter

said. "If your saddle don't move so much, it won't hurt you as much."

Austin turned his back to Felter and started to adjust the cinch.

Felter stepped up behind him, put his hand around Kid Austin's head, and drew his knife blade across the Kid's neck.

Austin collapsed, bleeding profusely and making a gurgling sound.

"What did you do that for?" Canning cried, shocked by what he had just seen.

"We have to ride, Canning. He woulda just slowed us down. Get his money. He won't be needin' it no more. I wish we had got the money from Stoner and the others."

After a ride of some twenty miles, Felter and Canning wound up in a miners' camp—one long street with tents and roofed shacks on both sides. Seeing that one of the tents served as a saloon, they went inside and stepped up to the bar. Blood splattered their clothes—Kid Austin's blood on Felter, Nicole's on Canning.

The bartender approached them, then stopped and stepped back. "Lord almighty, where have you two been? What happened to you?"

It wasn't until Felter saw the shocked look on the man's face that he realized just how much blood was on them. Ignoring the questions, he said, "Whiskey. The strongest you got. If you'd been where we been, and seen what we seen, you'd be wantin' a whiskey, too."

"Yeah." Canning didn't know what Felter had in

mind, but he was prepared to follow him, whatever it was.

Felter tossed the drink down in one gulp as if he were on the verge of shock. "I'm tellin' you the truth. It was about the most awfulest thing I ever seen. Them murderin' Utes raped a white woman, then they kilt her and her baby. They scalped her too, and done other things to her that I don't even want to talk about."

"Yeah," Canning agreed, picking up on it. "We was just lookin' around, seein' if we could track the In-juns that done it, when the next thing you know some crazy feller come up on us and commenced ashootin'. He kilt Stoner and Grissom and Poker and Evans right away. He shot Austin in the back, and we tried to bring 'im with us and done all we could for 'im, but he died on the way here."

"Then," Felter said, continuing the story, "this here feller took one of our wounded, a good man he was too, his name was Clark, and he staked him out over an anthill. Stripped him nekkid and poured honey over 'im. Well, you can imagine how poor ol' Clark suffered. We seen it from a distance, and we tried to go back to rescue him, but we knowed that this feller was usin' Clark as bait. He was hid out and he woulda kilt us both iffen we had tried. Why, there warn't nothin' we could do."

"Was this here feller you're atalkin' about a white man?" one of the miners asked.

"He were white, all right," Felter said.

"Why do you reckon he attacked you like that?"

"I don't know how to explain it," Canning said. "Could be that he just went crazy, is all."

"Mayhaps he thought it was us that done the killin' o' that poor white woman. I could see how a feller might get mad iffen he was to think that," Felter said. "But the thing is, he didn't even give us a chance to explain what happened."

"Not at all," Canning added. "He just showed up and commenced ashootin' without so much as a fare thee well. Why, Stoner and Poker and Evans and Grissom was all four kilt afore we even knew what was goin' on."

The miners listened to the story, but the glances they exchanged with each other indicated that they didn't quite believe what they were being told by the two blood-soaked men.

PSR Ranch, office

"Jensen is still alive!" Richards told his partners. "Story I've heard is that he killed all but two of them we hired."

"What kind of man is he?" Potter asked. "Who can be faced down by eight men and kill six of them?"

"We need to send more men," Stratton suggested. "Suppose we recruit about a dozen and tell 'em we'll give five hundred dollars apiece to everyone who comes back alive after Smoke Jensen is dead."

"We can't keep pouring out money to people just so Jensen can kill 'em," Potter objected.

Stratton smiled. "That's the beauty of it, don't you see? We don't pay anyone unless and until Jensen is dead. And if we're lucky, he'll kill all but one or two of 'em before they get him. That way, it won't cost us much money at all."

"Yeah," Richards said with a little chuckle. "Yeah, that's a good idea, Muley. A damn good idea."

The Pink House, Bury

"Something is going on," Janey told Flora. The two women were drinking coffee together in Flora's private quarters.

"What do you mean?"

"Josh, Wiley, and Muley have been closing themselves up in the PSR office and having a lot of really intense meetings. I'm not exactly sure what it is, but whatever it is has them scared to death."

"Scared of the law?" Flora asked. "How can they be afraid of the law? Hell, they own the law."

Janey shook her head. "No, not the law. From what I've been able to gather, it's one man. They have been spooked by one man."

"One man?"

"That's what it sounds like from the bits and pieces I've put together. They sent eight men out to kill him."

"They sent eight killers to take care of one man? They must have really wanted him dead."

"Yes, but it didn't work. As it turned out, he killed six of the eight men they sent after him, and he's still alive. Now, they're worried that he may be coming after them."

"What's the name of this man they're so afraid of?"

Janey shrugged. "I don't know. Josh hasn't spoken to me directly about this. What I do know, I've just picked up from overhearing parts of their conversations."

"Whoever it is that's after them must be one hell of a man," Flora said. "I wonder why he's coming after them. Do you think he might be a bounty hunter?"

"I think this is something personal."

CHAPTER 22

Preacher's cabin, July 1872

"You been hangin' around here for two weeks now," Preacher said, pushing open the front door. "Sittin' out on the porch and starin' off into the trees ain't gonna bring Nicole and the boy back to you."

Smoke looked toward Preacher with eyes that were more dead than alive. "I shoulda been there, Preacher. I shoulda been there when those men came."

"Smoke, you had things to do. You was seein' to your horses, you was takin' care of business. A man can't spend his whole life just sittin' around with his woman. Life is hard, boy. You should know that more'n almost anyone."

"I shoulda been there," Smoke said again.

"How many was there?" Preacher asked.

"I don't know. I killed four of them. I think Nicole must've killed one. And I found another one dead, not too far from the cabin. His throat was cut."

"So, six of 'em are dead?"

"Yes."

"How come two of 'em are still living?"

A grim smile appeared on Smoke's face. "That's a good question. I'll tell you this. They won't be living very long after I find them."

"Do you know where to start looking for 'em?"

"I thought I'd go back to the cabin and see if I could pick up the trail."

"No need," Preacher said. "I know where they are."

"You do?" For the first time in a while, animation replaced the dull lethargy that had Smoke in its grip. "How do you know where they are?"

"When I was at Schemerhorn's yesterday, I heard an old prospector tellin' about two men who came into a minin' camp where he was. The tale them two was tellin' was that they come upon some Injuns who had raped and killed a white woman and her baby. Said they fought the Injuns off, then a crazy man come and started shootin' at them. I figure they have to be the two men you're lookin' for."

"Yeah," Smoke said. "That has to be them. Do you know where this mining camp is?"

"Yeah, I know. It's 'bout forty miles southwest of here, on the Uncompahgre. You can't miss it. It's the only settlement within fifty miles in any direction."

Smoke nodded, then got up and went inside the cabin. Fifteen minutes later, he came back outside wearing his pistol.

Preacher had watched it all from his chair on the front porch. He didn't speak until Smoke was ready to mount. "Boy, take care of your business, but don't come back all shot up like I was."

Smoke's only response was a silent nod of his head as he rode out.

Uncompahgre mining camp, Colorado Territory

A dozen men came riding in to the camp. It didn't take but one glance to see that they weren't hard-rock miners. They weren't prospectors, either. All twelve were wearing pistols. One had a cross-draw rig, another was wearing a shoulder holster, a couple were wearing two pistols, and one was carrying a rifle with bullet-studded bandoliers making an X across his chest.

None of the miners recognized any of them, at least, not by name, but they knew gunmen when they saw them. What they didn't know was why so many of them had showed up, all at the same time, and why they had come to the mining camp.

The gunmen stopped in front of the saloon, hitching their horses to every hitch rail for two tent buildings on either side. Stepping inside, they almost doubled the number of customers. All conversation stopped as everyone turned toward the men bunched together, just inside the door.

"Felter," one of the men said, recognizing him.

"Hello, Deke."

Smiling, Deke went over to take Felter's hand. "We heard you needed some help."

"Where did you hear that? And who are all these men?" The expression on Felter's face was one of challenge.

"Same as you. We're ridin' for Richards, Potter,

and Stratton. Richards said I should look you up and tell you that you're in charge."

"He did, did he?" The look of challenge was replaced by a smile.

"Yeah. This feller, Smoke Jensen is it? Word we got is that Richards sent eight after him, and he kilt six."

"He only kilt four," Felter said. "He didn't have nothin' to do with Stoner or Austin. What's Richards payin' you?"

"He ain't paid us nothin' yet, but he said he'll give five hunnert dollars to each of us when we come back, after Jensen is dead. What is he payin' you?"

"Same thing. Five hundred when we go back and tell 'im the job is done." Felter made no mention of the fact that he and the others he'd started with had already been paid five hundred in advance.

"So, you're in command, Sergeant. What do we do next? Where do we find him?" Deke had served in the army with Felter, and been dishonorably discharged, as well.

"We don't have to find him. I'm willing to bet a dollar to a horseshoe nail that he'll find us." Felter grinned. "Onliest thing is, he thinks he's only lookin' for two of us. He don't have no idea how many of us there is now."

A solitary camp on the Uncompahgre, August 1872

Jake Johnson had been in Colorado almost as long as Preacher, and back in the day had made a few rendezvous with him. He knew his way around the mountains and the forests and had crossed every river in Colorado. At the moment, he was drinking coffee as he watched a spitted rabbit sizzle and brown over a campfire. Perhaps he was paying too much attention to his lunch, and that was why he didn't hear Smoke come up on him.

"You got friends in that mining camp downriver?" Smoke asked.

The sudden appearance of another man when Jake Johnson thought he was all alone startled him so that he spilled hot coffee on his hand. "Damn!" he shouted, dropping the cup and shaking his hand. "Where the hell did you come from?"

"You got friends in that mining camp?" Smoke asked again.

"Yeah, I got friends there. Why do you ask?"

"My name is Smoke Jensen. I want you to go down and tell any friend you have there to ease on out of camp, because in one hour I'm coming down."

"Smoke Jensen? You the one that's Preacher's friend?"

"Yes."

The man smiled and extended his hand. "Well, I'm mighty glad to meet you, Smoke Jensen. I'm Jake Johnson. Me and Preacher go back a long way."

Smoke returned the smile. "Yes, I've heard him tell a few stories about you."

"Yeah, well, don't be abelievin' none of 'em," Jake said, his smile broadening. "By the way, Smoke, most of the folks in that camp have heard of you, and near 'bout all of 'em is on your side. Felter and Canning come in there claimin' it was Indians that kilt your family, but there didn't none of us believe 'em."

"That's their names? Felter and Canning?"

"Yes, but, it ain't just them."

Smoke frowned. "What do you mean, it isn't just them?"

"There's twelve more that's come down to help 'em. Word we got is that someone is payin' 'em to kill you."

"Yeah. That's the word I got, too."

The old-timer looked straight at Smoke. "You're still goin' down there, though, ain't you?"

"Yeah, I'm still going. I've got to go."

"I understand. I would probably do the same thing."

"Jake, get your friends out of town. It's not going to be safe for them."

"All right. I'll go down there and warn the miners. I've got time to eat my lunch, don't I?"

"Sure, I never like to interrupt a man at his meal."

"Join me," Jake invited. "Half a rabbit makes a pretty good meal."

"Don't mind if I do," Smoke said.

"By the way, I almost hate to ask you this, 'cause I'm not sure I want to hear the answer. But I was told that Preacher was bad shot up, and that he went off somewhere to die."

Smoke pulled off some rabbit meat, stuck it in his mouth, then licked his finger before he replied, but the smile on his face eased Jake's concern, even before he said the words. "Jake, you know Preacher well enough to know that it's goin' to take more than a couple bullet wounds to kill that old man. He's still around, and still as ornery an old coot as he ever was."

"That's good to hear," Jake said with a relieved smile. "That's very good to hear."

*   *   *

An hour later, Jake gathered several miners around him at one of the mining shacks. "I met a fella this mornin', and he sent me down here to warn you. To tell you to leave town for a little while."

"Why?" asked one.

"Because he's comin' into town after Felter and Canning, and when he does, all hell is going to break loose. I don't think you want to be in the middle of it, Dugan, and neither do I."

"What's put the burr under this fella's saddle?" another asked.

Jake explained. "You know the story that Felter and Canning are telling, about how Injuns killed a woman and her baby? Well that woman was the wife of the man I met this mornin', and the baby was his, too. The story that Felter and Canning is telling is all lies. They was eight men who done the killin' and the rapin', and they wasn't Injuns. They was all white. It was Felter, Canning, and six others. The other six is already dead, and now he's comin' to town to kill Felter and Canning, too."

"Well, I can't say as I blame him for wantin' to kill Felter and Canning," the miner called Dugan said, "but maybe he don't know that they was twelve more men come here a couple days ago to join up with Felter and Canning."

Jake nodded. "Oh, yeah, he knows. I told him."

"Wait a minute," a tall, lanky miner named Henderson said. "Are you tellin' us that this feller knows they's fourteen men waitin' here for 'im, and he's acomin' anyway?"

Jake nodded again. "That's what I'm atellin' you, all right."

"What kind of damn fool would take on fourteen men all by his ownself? What's this feller's name, anyhow?"

Jake smiled. "His name is Jensen. Smoke Jensen."

"Smoke Jensen? Damn, I've heard of him," Dugan said in awe.

"Yeah, me too. If there's any one man who could take on fourteen all by hisself, it would have to be someone like Smoke Jensen."

"I'm takin' him at his word," said a miner named Clyde who wore a patch over his left eye. "I believe all hell is goin' to break loose, and I'm plannin' on watchin' it with this one good eye I got left."

"Not me. I'm getting' out of town. You should too, Clyde. Why, you'd be a fool to stay here and watch it. There's bound to be lead flyin' ever'where!"

"I didn't say I was goin' to stay here. All I said was I was goin' to watch it."

"How you gonna do that?"

Clyde smiled, then pointed to the rise on the northwest side of the canyon. "From up there. I'll be able to see ever'thing that happens, and it ain't likely I'll get shot neither."

"Yeah," another said. "Yeah, that's a damn good idea. I'm goin' to watch it from up there as well."

That idea was met with equal enthusiasm from all, and soon there was a mass exodus from the encampment.

It was going to be a show the likes of which that part of the country had never seen—and might not ever see again.

CHAPTER 23

Felter figured out what was happening as soon as the miners began leaving, and he asked Deke to get everyone together in the saloon.

"He's comin', ain't he?" Deke asked with a broad grin. "You was right. We didn't have to go lookin' for 'im. He's comin' to us."

"Yeah," Felter replied with a grin of his own. "The rabbit has fell into our trap."

"How many men does he have with him?" one of the new men asked.

"He don't have nobody but his ownself," Felter said. "You've heard the talk. Everybody else around here is too scared to throw in with him."

"Ha! This is gonna be a piece o' cake," one of the others suggested.

Felter frowned. "You think so?"

The man nodded. "Well, yeah. There are fourteen of us, and only one of him."

"We'll see," Felter said.

"Felter, you ain't afraid of this feller, are you?" Deke asked.

"Let's just say that I'm cautious," Felter replied.

Deke had another question. "When do you reckon he'll get here?"

Felter shrugged. "I don't know, but I think we had better—"

"Felter!" The powerful shout rolled down the hillside.

It was clearly audible inside the tent building, and several men jumped a little when they heard it.

"Felter!"

"Damn. How'd Jensen find out my name?" Felter asked.

"Clark musta told him," Canning said.

"Canning! Felter and Canning. I'm coming for you! . . . for you, for you, for you!" The last two words echoed and echoed from the canyon walls.

Felter and the other gunmen were the only ones in the saloon. The place had been abandoned by everyone who wanted to stay out of the line of fire, which was practically everyone in camp.

Felter stepped outside. Cupping his hands around his mouth, he called back, "I'm here! What do you want? . . . you want? . . . you want?"

"You and Canning want to settle this between us? . . . tween us . . . tween us?"

"Just the three of us, meeting standup out on the street, you two, and me. Two to one. What do you say? . . . you say? . . . you say?"

Deke looked over at Felter. "From what I've heard

of this feller, he ain't someone you want to go up against, not even two of you to his one."

"Don't worry. It ain't gonna happen that way," Felter replied.

"What do you say, Felter? . . . Felter? . . . Felter?" Smoke called down.

Felter cupped his hands around his mouth again. "Now, why would we want to do a thing like that, when we have twelve new friends down here, just waitin' for you? . . . for you? . . . for you?"

"You new men," Smoke shouted. "It's Felter and Canning I want. I don't have anything against any of you. Ride on out of here now, and you can live. Stay here, and you'll die! . . . you'll die! . . . you'll die!"

"Mister, that's mighty bold talk for a man that's outnumbered as bad as you are," one of the new men shouted back.

"I'm not outnumbered," Smoke replied.

"What do you mean, you ain't outnumbered? They's only one of you. They's fourteen of us."

"I've got fourteen bullets," Smoke shouted back. "Like I said, I'm not outnumbered."

"Who the hell is this man?" one of the men asked, awed by the response.

"He ain't nobody," Felter replied. "You men get into position. Let's end this thing now."

Shortly after the shouted dialogue with Felter and the others, Smoke shifted positions, slipping about twenty-five yards to his right. He saw a man dart from the camp, then start working his way up the side of the hill.

Smoke watched the man pause and get set to take a shot. Smoke raised the Henry rifle and put a slug in the man's belly, slamming him backward. The man screamed, dropped his rifle, and tumbled back down the hill. He landed in the single street, then struggled back to his feet. Smoke had worked the rifle's lever by then, throwing another cartridge in the chamber, so he shot him again.

The man fell forward. There was no further movement.

The miners across the way cheered.

Smoke watched as more men fanned out in the town, moving too quickly for him to get a clear shot. He fired anyway and hit one of the men in the lower leg. The wounded man shouted a curse, then darted into one of the many mining shacks that lined the street.

"Are you boys that close with Felter and Canning?" Smoke yelled. "You sure you want to stay around for this? It's gonna get pretty hot down there."

"You go to hell, Jensen!" The voice came from a shack.

A dozen other voices shouted curses at Smoke.

Two men sprang from behind the saloon tent, rifles in their hands. They raced into one of the small shacks. Smoke put half a dozen rounds into the shack, working the lever and firing as he swung the Henry from left to right. One man screamed and stumbled through the door, out into the street, dropping his rifle and dying in the dirt. The second man came out and Smoke aimed, but he held his fire. That man's chest and belly were already crimson. He sat down in the street, remained that way for a moment, then toppled over to die.

Smoke shifted positions once more, reloaded, and

called out, "Any more of you boys want to give it a try?"

Canning looked at Felter. They had left the saloon and were in the largest of the mining shacks, both crouched behind crates of machinery.

"Come on, Felter. Let's just kill Jensen and be done with it."

"Yeah, well, ain't that just what we're tryin' to do?"

"We ain't tryin' hard enough. There's fourteen of us, for cryin' out loud."

Felter shook his head . "Only eleven now. They's three men lying out there, dead in the street. Or ain't you noticed?"

"All the more reason for us to kill him and get this over with."

Felter was thoughtful for a moment. The whole plan had been a disaster from the very beginning. Jensen was a pure devil, right out of hell. They had torn the cabin apart searching for gold, but it had been fruitless. Maybe there wasn't any gold. For all Felter knew, Jensen's pa might've spent it all on whiskey and women.

One thing Felter was sure of, though. If he failed at the job, he could never set foot in the Idaho territory again. Richards, Stratton, and Potter would see to that.

"All right. Maybe there's only eleven of us now, but there's still only one of him," Canning said. "I say we rush him. We've got to kill Jensen, or he's goin' to kill us, sure as a gun is iron."

Felter was sorry he had ever gotten mixed up in it. For the first time in his evil life, he was really afraid of another man. He took a deep breath to screw up his courage. "You're right, we've got him outnumbered. It would be foolish to let him just pick us off, one at a time. Let's take the damn man."

He passed orders down the street, from shack to shack. The plan was for three men to advance on the right, three men on the left, and three men to circle around behind Jensen, coming in from the rear. Felter and Canning would remain behind to "offer help, where help was needed."

In truth, Felter hoped no help would be needed. It was his hope that Jensen would be killed before either he or Canning would have to encounter him.

Smoke walked into the empty saloon. From the lack of alarmed shouts in the camp, none of his enemies had seen him slip down the hillside and into the settlement. They were all too busy being scared and trying to figure out what to do next.

He went behind the bar, drew himself a beer from the keg the saloonkeeper had left behind, then drank it casually as he looked through the window and saw men moving carefully along the street. He strolled over to the open-flap doorway, picked out the man he had wounded, aimed, and fired. Another of the hired killers went down, screaming, spasmed a couple of times, then lay still as death claimed him.

"There are only ten of you left," Smoke shouted. "Still time for the rest of you men to leave. I've got nothing against any of you. It's Felter and Canning I want. You men don't owe anything to them."

"Damn it, Felter!" one of the new outlaws shouted, running across the dusty street. "Jensen is in the saloon!"

Smoke's Henry thundered again, and the outlaw who had given the warning spun in the street, crying out as a bleeding bullet hole soaked the front of his shirt red with blood. Dropping his gun, he tumbled forward into the dirt and didn't move again.

One of the other outlaws, thinking he could get lucky, ran down the side of the street, darting in and out of doorways shooting at anything he thought he saw.

Smoke went back to the bar, laid his rifle on the hardwood, and reached under it to pick up a double-barreled shotgun from the shelf. He checked to see that it was loaded and stuffed a handful of shells from a box sitting next to it into his pocket. He walked back to the entrance just as the panic-stricken outlaw approached.

"Over here," Smoke called as he stepped out of the saloon. The man lurched to a terrified halt only a few yards away. He looked like he wanted to be somewhere—anywhere—else, but there was no time to get there.

Smoke pulled both shotgun triggers. The blast lifted the man off his feet, almost cutting him in half.

Smoke reloaded the shotgun as he ducked behind one of the shacks and then started up the alley. He came face-to-face with one of Richards's hired bounty hunters. The bounty hunter fired, the lead creasing Smoke's left arm, drawing blood. Smoke triggered both barrels of the shotgun again and blew the man's head right off his shoulders.

Smoke stepped into an open door just as a man ran toward him, firing at him with a pistol in each hand. The thunderous volley echoed back from the slopes around the camp. Splinters from the doorframe gouged painfully into Smoke's cheek as he dropped the shotgun and pulled his pistol. He shot the man in the chest and the belly.

The street erupted in black powder, whining lead, and wild cursing. Gray powder smoke billowed. Spooked horses broke from their hitch rails and charged down the street, clouding the air with dust, rearing and screaming in fear. A bullet from Canning's gun punched into Smoke's right leg, and he flung himself out of the doorway and behind the protection of a water trough.

Canning hobbled painfully into the street, shouting, "I've got you now, Jensen. You are dead meat!" His pistols belched smoke and flame, and his eyes were wild with hate.

One of Canning's slugs hit Smoke in the left side, passing through a fleshy part and exiting out the back. The shock spun him around and knocked him down.

"Ha!" Canning shouted. "That hurts, don't it?"

Smoke raised up on one elbow and leveled his pistol. He shot Canning in the right eye, taking off part of his face. Canning's legs jerked out from under him and he fell on his back, dead.

"Probably not as much as that," Smoke mumbled as slowly, painfully, he stood up.

Two men ran into the smoky, dusty street, and Smoke shot both of them just as one fired at him. The outlaw's bullet ricocheted off a rock in the street, part of the lead hitting Smoke in the chest, bringing blood and a grunt of pain. He dragged himself into a doorway and quickly reloaded.

Bleeding from wounds in his side, leg, face, and chest, he returned the fire of another outlaw shooting at him. The man doubled over, dying in the center of the street.

Lead began whining down the alley, and Smoke, moving slowly and painfully, managed to find shelter behind a building, where he paused to reload.

Deke left the shack and called out to Smoke, firing as he yelled. His round struck the handle of a spare pistol Smoke had stuck behind his belt. Pain doubled him over for a second, but he lifted his pistol and dropped the outlaw in his tracks. It was almost over. Smoke took a deep breath, feeling a twinge of pain from at least one broken rib, maybe two.

Felter had not left the comparative safety of the machine crate in the mining shack. He'd watched the entire battle without taking part, counting the men Jensen had shot. He realized, with a real degree of shock and fear, that everyone—Canning, Deke, and all the others—had been killed. "No. No, that isn't possible."

He had started the day with an advantage of fourteen to one, and he was the only one left. He knew that he couldn't get away. Smoke Jensen was a man with a mission—to kill everyone who'd had anything to do with killing his wife and kid. Except for Felter, Jensen had done just that.

Felter lifted up the bottle of whiskey he'd brought with him when he left the saloon earlier and took several Adam's-apple-bobbing swallows. Then, lowering the bottle, he wiped his mouth with the back of his hand and shook his head. "You ain't goin' away, are you, Jensen? You know what? I believe I can take you now. You have to be running out of steam." He said it to bolster his courage and his confidence.

"Felter!" Smoke called. "Step out here and face me."

Felter stepped out into the street and was shocked at Smoke's appearance. "Well, now, boy, you look like you're hurtin' real bad." He smiled at the apparition in front of him. "Just about shot to pieces, ain't you?"

Smoke was bleeding from several wounds, which gave Felter a renewed courage. The two men advanced toward each other until they were separated by no more than twenty-five feet. Smoke's advance was slow and halting, each movement bringing him pain.

Felter lifted the whiskey bottle toward him. "Here's to you, Jensen," he said with a chuckle. "Damn if you didn't kill thirteen men here, today. You got shot up pretty bad doin' it, though, didn't you? I've got to give you credit. You almost pulled it off."

"Not almost. Goin' to." Smoke's voice was strained with pain. "I've only got one left."

"Ah, yes, only one left. But you see, kid, that one you got left is me. And you ain't goin' to get through me."

"I think I will. And after I take care of you, I'm going after your bosses."

Felter grinned. "That would be Potter, Stratton, and Richards, would it?"

"That's right."

"You've kilt how many men, now . . . eighteen? Just to get to Potter, Stratton, and Richards?"

"Nineteen," Smoke pointed out.

Felter disagreed. "No, only eighteen. Your wife kilt Stoner."

"Nineteen, and I'm not counting Stoner. I'm counting you."

Up on the hillside, the miners had watched the entire battle, listening not only to the pop of gunshots, but also the curses, the shouts of anger and fear and pain as, one by one, Smoke had killed those who were trying to kill him.

"Damn," one of the miners said. "Jensen looks half dead. There's no way he can take Felter now."

"Don't sell him short," Jake said. "There ain't very many men like Smoke Jensen . . . maybe nobody like 'im. But if you're wantin' to bet, my money's on him, even now, hurt as bad as he is."

Down below in the street, Felter chuckled again. "You know what, Jensen? I don't think you could beat me even if you wasn't all slowed down by them wounds. But I know damn well you can't do it now." He transferred the drink from his left hand to his right, then held it out toward Smoke. "Here, kid, take a drink. You look like you need it."

Suddenly, and without calling it, he dropped the whiskey and his hand streaked down to his pistol quick as a striking snake.

Felter was fast, but Smoke was faster. By the time the last echo of the single shot reverberated back down from the hillside, Smoke was still standing, a

ribbon of smoke drifting from the end of the barrel
of the pistol he was holding in his hand.

Felter lay dead in the street before him.

Smoke pouched the iron, then walked over to the
hitch rail and put his hand on it to keep himself erect.

The miners, who had watched the whole battle in
awe, came down from the hillside, pausing here and
there to look at a body. A couple of the more coura-
geous, moved hesitantly, cautiously, up to Smoke.

"You hard hit, son," one of the miners said.

"Yeah," Smoke said.

"You goin' to need some doctorin'."

"Yeah," Smoke said again. "I'll be gettin' some
doctorin' done. Help me on my horse."

A couple miners helped him get mounted, then
watched in awe as he rode away.

"Folks will be readin' about this day a hunnert
years from now," one of them said.

"I hope whoever does the writin', gets it right," another replied.

CHAPTER 24

Preacher's cabin

Smoke had been thinking of Preacher when he'd said he would find a doctor to treat his wounds. Preacher, he knew, could do more for him than any doctor he had ever met or known, but he was nearly dead by the time he reached the cabin more than a week later. He had holed up for a while and done what he could to stop the bleeding, which was the only reason he had lived this long. But the damage was tremendous and needed more care than he could give himself.

The smile on Preacher's face faded quickly when he saw how badly hurt Smoke was. "Boy, what the hell happened to you?"

"I got them, Preacher. The ones who killed Nicole and my boy. I got them, and I killed every last damn one of them."

"Yeah, well, I'm glad you did. But you look half dead yourself. How come you ain't gone to see no doctor?"

A small, pained smile spread across Smoke's face. "I thought I just did." He winced once. "And I don't mind telling you, Preacher, I'm hurting pretty bad."

Smoke sagged in the saddle, and would have fallen, if Preacher had not stepped up quickly to grab him.

"Come on in the house, boy. I'll do what I can for you, but I don't know as I've ever doctored anybody shot up as bad as you."

PSR ranch house, parlor

"All of them?" Richards asked, gasping the words out in disbelief. "Surely you aren't telling me he killed all of them, the twelve new men we sent, as well as Felter and Canning."

"That's what folks are saying," Potter said. "They're saying that when the shooting was over, that miners' camp looked like the battlefield at Shiloh."

"What the hell kind of man is this?" Stratton exclaimed. "There ain't no one man who can take on fourteen men, all by hisself, and kill 'em all! Is there?"

"Yeah? Well, if what Wiley is sayin' is true, this one can," Richards argued.

"Well, there is one more thing," Potter pointed out.

"What's that?"

Potter grinned. "The word is, he was so shot up his ownself that it's more than likely he's dead now."

"Good," Stratton said emphatically.

"What do you mean, *good*?" Richards asked. "Bein' bad shot up ain't the same thing as bein' *dead*. Nobody has found his body yet, have they?"

"No," Potter said, shaking his head. "There ain't nobody found his body."

"Then, far as I'm concerned, Jensen isn't dead. And that's the way we're goin' to treat it."

"What are we goin' to do now?" Stratton asked.

"We can hire some more people." Potter smiled. "After all, that last bunch we hired didn't cost us nothin'."

"And the first bunch only cost us half of what we said we was goin' to give 'em," Stratton added.

Richards shook his head. "That hasn't gotten us very far, has it?"

"Well, we have to do something about him. I mean, he's goin' to find us sooner or later. I don't know about you two, but I don't want to face Jensen, not even with the odds three to one," Potter said.

Richards wasn't giving up. "Let me think about it for a while. I'll come up with something, and when I do, I'll run it by the two of you to see what you think about it."

"Yeah, well, come up with it pretty quick," Stratton said. "I don't cotton to the idea of Jensen being out there, hangin' around, waitin' to strike."

The three men had just finished their conversation when Janey came into the parlor. "Good evening, gentlemen. Why, Josh, are your friends are sitting here without a drink in their hands? What kind of host are you? Mr. Potter, Mr. Stratton, would you like a drink?"

"Well, now that you mention it, yes, I believe I would," Potter replied with a smile.

She smiled at him. "Bourbon and branch."

"You remember. I'm flattered."

She laughed. "That's not hard to remember. All three of you have the same preference."

Janey came back into the parlor a few minutes later,

carrying four drinks on a tray. "I hope you gentlemen don't mind if I drink with you."

"Ha! Why should we mind? If we go to any saloon in town, we have to pay to have a drink with a pretty woman."

"Yeah, well, as long as you understand that this pretty woman belongs to me," Richards griped.

"That's right, Josh, honey. I'm your woman." Janey walked over to him and planted a kiss on his cheek.

The four of them engaged in light talk for a few more minutes, then, as they finished their drinks, Potter and Stratton stood.

"You will let us know when you come up with an idea, won't you?" Potter asked.

"You can count on it," Richards replied.

He waited until after his partners left before he turned to Janey. "All right," he snapped. "What is it?"

"What is it? Why, honey, what on earth do you mean?"

"Most of the time when I'm with Potter or Stratton, you can't leave fast enough. You've made it very clear to me that you don't like them. But here, today, you were all sweetness and smiles. I know you want something, so, why don't you come right out and tell me what it is?"

"I want to go to Kansas City."

Richards frowned. "What do you mean? For good? Are you pulling out of here?"

She returned his frown with a smile. "Now, honey, I've got a very good thing here with you. Why would I want to give that up? No, I don't want to go to Kansas City for good. I just want to go for a visit. Of course I'm coming back."

"Oh," Richards said.

"Besides, I would be going for you."

"What does that mean?"

"I keep your books, remember? I know we're getting a bit overstocked with cattle. I intend to visit the slaughterhouses while I'm in Kansas City to make arrangements to sell off some of the PSR cattle."

It was Richards's time to smile. "Well, I'll be damned. Yes, that would be a good idea."

"And since it would be a business trip, it would also pay for my visit," Janey pointed out.

"Meaning I would pay for the visit," Richards said.

"Well, of course you would, darling. They *are* your cattle, after all. Why should I be expected to pay for the trip to sell them?"

Richards chuckled and shook his head. "Janey, Janey, Janey. You are as crooked as I am. The only difference between us is, you're better looking."

Summit County

Two days after the conversation between Janey and Richards, three men were waiting alongside the Union Pacific tracks in a remote area of the county. A few minutes earlier, they had placed one stick of dynamite under the south rail. They waited far enough away from the track so that when the train derailed, they would be in no danger.

Janey was a passenger on that train bound for Kansas City. It was true that she was going to arrange with one of the packinghouses for shipment of some PSR cattle, but it wasn't the only reason she was going to Kansas City.

She was beginning to get more and more troubled about her relationship with Richards. As the train moved along the tracks, Janey was lost in thought.

It isn't just that Josh is crooked and that his entire operation could collapse someday if an honest lawman got word of everything he's doing. I could handle that. I have squirreled away enough money to survive such a thing.

Lately, I've been hearing disturbing rumors, stories about hiring a lot of men to kill one man . . . a man who, supposedly, was carrying on some personal vendetta against Josh and his cronies.

I've heard the man's name. Ironically, it's the same last name as mine.

Smoke Jensen, he's called.

Over the years since she had left home, she had run into more than one person named Jensen, none of whom she was related to or had ever heard of. As far as she knew, Smoke Jensen was just another man named Jensen.

Except, from what she had been able to learn, he was no ordinary man. It was being said that he had killed as many as twenty men that Richards had sent after him. The man Smoke Jensen could be dangerous, not only to Richards but indirectly to her, as well.

It was her intention to find out if it was safe for her to return to Kansas City. She thought of her time there.

*   *   *

I was on the line, but it was a good house, with women who became such good friends they were almost my sisters.

It's where I met Elmer Gleason, an older, rather strange man who was a frequent visitor of the house. He often bought the time of some of the girls, but rarely their services. He preferred just to talk with them.

He never shared my bed, either, though I probably would have had he asked. He wasn't handsome or polished and he was considerably older than me, but he was decent, through and through. I sometimes wonder if things had been different, perhaps we—

Janey didn't hear the explosion that derailed the train. One minute they were flying across the open land at better than twenty-five miles per hour, and the next minute the car had left the tracks, where it bumped along for several feet before it turned over, rending a crash of metal and the shattering of glass. Men shouted, women screamed, and children cried as they were thrown violently from their seats, crashing into each other.

Janey was on top of the pile, so she wasn't as badly hurt as some of the others. The screams, shouts, and cries stilled, replaced by low moans and whimpers.

She looked for a way out of the car lying on its left side and quickly climbed on a seat and poked her head and shoulders through one of the windows from the right, which had become the top.

She saw the reason for the crash. The train had been purposely derailed and was being robbed.

"Hey, what's going on here?" shouted a man who had just climbed out of the car in front of her and dropped to the ground.

One of the robbers turned his pistol toward the shouting man and fired. The bullet drove into the man's chest and threw him backward.

She quickly dropped back down into the car and saw some others trying to get out. "No, stay where you are! This train is being robbed, and they're killing passengers who get out of the cars." She began tending to some of the more injured passengers, periodically looking out to see if the robbers were still there.

Not until she saw them ride away did she give the word. "The robbers are gone! Those of you who can, help me get the injured out of the train."

Once again, this violent land had brought death and destruction to the innocent . . . and the not-so-innocent.

CHAPTER 25

Half an hour later, everyone was out of the train. There were only ten among all the passengers who, like Janey, had been uninjured, but of those, only five had enough wits about them to help. The dead—six men, two women, and two children—were laid out in one place and the injured in another. The injured were separated according to the severity of their injuries.

Except for one black porter, the entire train crew had been killed—engineer, fireman, express man, brakeman, and conductor. The porter was one of only two men who had not been injured. The other uninjured male passenger was in his mid-seventies and not able to do much. As a result, Janey took charge, though it wasn't something she asserted, it was just something that happened.

The porter, whose name was Toby, had crawled through the wreckage to find what first-aid material was available. He produced bottles of alcohol and precut bandages for use in treating the injured.

"Ma'am, we got to get a flagman out behind us to stop the next train," Toby said. "If we don't, it'll come plowin' into this one, 'n we'll have us a lot more hurt folks."

"That's right. I hadn't thought of that. Mr. Sealy, why don't you walk up the track and watch for the train, then flag it down when you see it?" Janey chose the older man primarily because he was the one she could most easily spare.

Toby shook his head. "No, ma'am, don't be sendin' him. The engineer see a white man flaggin' down the train, he mos' likely think it's somebody tryin' to stop 'im so as to rob 'im, and he'll go whizzin' on by. I should be the one. They see my black face, and me in my porter's uniform, they'll know somethin' has happened."

"Toby, you're the only one strong enough to do the lifting and the moving." Janey frowned in thought. "What if we send a woman back there to flag the train? They would stop for a woman, wouldn't they?"

"Yes'm, I expect they would. Unless they think maybe the robbers put out a woman to fool 'em."

"What if the woman has blood on her?"

Toby said solemnly. "Yes, ma'am. They see a woman standin' there with blood on her, they'll know for sure somethin' bad has happened."

"I'll do it." The volunteer had already identified herself as Maxine. "I'll get some of my husband's blood. Lord knows there's enough of it."

Maxine's husband was one of the injured, though most of his injuries seemed to be superficial cuts. She smeared her face with his blood, gave him a hug, and walked down the track behind the train.

During the next half hour Janey and the others cleaned, bandaged, and comforted the injured as best they could. Then they heard the whistle of the approaching train.

Janey looked toward the porter. "Do you think he will stop, Toby?"

"Lord, let's pray he stops, Miss Janey, 'cause if he don't, we goin' to be havin' us a lot more injured folks to be dealin' with than we got now."

The train's long whistle changed to a series of short blasts, and a big smile spread across Toby's face. "Yes, ma'am. You hear all them whistles? That means he's goin' to stop."

Janey nodded, heaved a sigh of relief, and went back to work.

Preacher's cabin

A little more than three weeks had passed since Smoke, bloodied and wounded, had arrived at Preacher's cabin. During that time, the weather turned cooler and leaves changed colors, but he didn't notice. Preacher had tended to his wounds, sewing shut the ones he could, treating with herbs and poultices those that couldn't be sewed shut.

Preacher fed him as much as he could. The first two days, Smoke could keep down only broth, but by the third day he was eating venison, fish, eggs, bacon, and biscuits. Preacher had even sacrificed a few of his chickens for him. He also made him stews of squirrel and rabbit, potatoes, and noodles that he made from flour and broth.

Smoke slept twelve to fifteen hours a day, feeling

his strength slowly returning to him. His dreams of Nicole, her soft arms soothing him, helped to melt away the hurt and the fever, calmed his sleep, and gradually brought him back to health.

As he healed, he began to grow anxious and soon knew that he was ready to ride, ready to move.

One day, he carefully checked his gun, loaded it, then rubbed oil into his holster until the deadly pistol slipped in and out of it smoothly. That done, he saddled Seven and waited for Preacher to return from his fishing trip.

Preacher noticed the saddled horse right away. "You fixin' to leave?"

"Yes."

"I figured the time was near 'bout here when you would be leavin'. Where are you agoin'?"

"Thought I'd go back to Denver and check in with Marshal Holloway."

"Hell, boy. It's been nigh two years since you done any deputyin' for him. What makes you think he'd take you back now?"

Smoke shrugged. "I don't know. Maybe he won't. But I thought I'd give it a try."

Preacher held up one fish on his line. "Well, you may as well go see 'im. I ain't got enough fish for the both of us anyhow. Not the way you eat."

Smoke chuckled. "I didn't figure you'd come back with much, no better a fisherman than you are."

"Ha! I'm a hell of a lot better fisherman than anyone you ever seen, 'n don't you be aforgettin' that."

"There's a lot about you I won't be forgetting, Preacher," Smoke said, the smile gone, replaced by an expression of deep and abiding friendship. "One thing I won't forget is how you saved my life. If it hadn't been for you, I would have crawled off into the woods somewhere and died."

"Yeah? Well, don't you go gettin' all mushy on me now. I mean, you ain't gonna try and hug me or any-thin' foolish like that, are you?"

With a mischievous smile, Smoke snatched Preacher's hat off, leaned over, and kissed him on the bald spot on top of his head.

"What?" Preacher shouted. Grabbing his hat from Smoke, he started hitting him with it. "You get the hell out of here now, you hear me? Git! Git, I tell you!"

Laughing out loud, Smoke mounted Seven. With-out looking back, he threw a wave over his shoulder as he rode off.

More than his physical wounds had been healed in the high country.

His broken soul was starting to knit back together, too.

Denver

"Why, if it isn't Deputy Jensen!" Annie Wilson said enthusiastically. "I was beginning to think we'd never see you again."

"You know what they say, Miss Wilson. A bad penny always comes back."

"Why, no such thing, Deputy Jensen. You're not a bad penny. You aren't a bad penny at all. Do you want to see Marshal Holloway?"

"Yes, if he isn't too busy."

"He isn't too busy at all, and I know he would love to see you. Why, he speaks about you all the time."

"All I want to know, Smoke, is if it is true," Marshal Holloway said once Miss Wilson had ushered the younger man into his office and the two men had shaken hands.

"You're talking about the little fracas at the mining camp on the Uncompahgre?"

"Little fracas? I heard you'd killed thirty men, before you got killed."

"As you can see, I'm not dead," Smoke said. "And the other part isn't right, either. Nineteen were killed there, and Nicole killed one of them herself, before they killed her."

Marshal Holloway's rugged face grew solemn. "Yes. I heard what happened to your wife and child. At first, I didn't put any credence in it because I didn't even know you were married."

"It all happened pretty quick after I left here."

"I can't tell you how sorry I am to hear that."

"Is there a warrant out for me?" Smoke asked.

"For those killings?" Marshal Holloway shook his head. "No. After I heard the story from two or three different sources, including from some of the miners who witnessed what happened, I was convinced you were in the right. When the county sheriff came to me with a suggestion that maybe you should be charged . . . if you were still alive . . . I told him you were acting on official business. As it turned out, you were. At least six of the men you killed did have federal warrants out for them, and therefore, by association, the others were equally as guilty."

"I'm glad to hear that. That means I can still work for you. That is, if you're willing to take me on again."

"I'm more than willing," Marshal Holloway said. "If you'll hang around Denver, I'll give you the very next assignment."

"I'll be here," Smoke promised.

Kansas City, Missouri

Because she had "acted heroically and with great compassion" after the train wreck, the Union Pacific provided Janey with free, round-trip passage to Kansas City. When she arrived, she went straight to the Pretty Girl and Happy Cowboy House, once run by Maggie Mouchette.

"Honey, if you're lookin' for your husband, he ain't here," one of the girls said when Janey stepped into the parlor.

Janey decided to play along. "How do you know he isn't here?"

"Because any man who is married to you would be a fool to come here," the girl replied.

Janey laughed, then looked around at the girls who were lounging in the parlor. She didn't recognize any of them. "Well, I'm not looking for my husband. Believe it or not, I used to work here. I was just dropping in to see if any of my old friends were still around."

"Blimey," an attractive young blonde said with a definite Cockney accent. "You used to work here, luv?"

"You?" another girl asked. "The way you're dressed? What did you do, find yourself a rich husband?"

"No," a familiar voice said. "What she did was save my life."

Looking toward the speaker, Janey smiled broadly when she recognized Louise. The smile froze, however, when she saw how badly scarred the girl was. A large, puffy mass, like a purple flash of lightning, ran through and disfigured her left eye, then slashed across the corner of her lips, leaving some of her teeth and gum exposed.

Louise saw Janey's reaction to her appearance and smiled, or at least, tried to smile. The effort served only to emphasize the disfigurement. "Hello, Abigail"—she addressed Janey by the name she had used when she'd worked at The Pretty Girl and Happy Cowboy House—"or whatever you're calling yourself these days."

"It's Janey. Janey Garner." She gave only half her real name. "I didn't know if I would find any of the old girls still here."

"Well, I'm the only one still here. But as you can see, I wouldn't make much these days." She passed her hand across her face then smiled. "But I'm one hell of a madam."

"Yes, she is," said the girl who had greeted Janey. "She really is."

"His name is Josh Richards," Janey told Louise when the two of them went out for dinner. "He and two others own a huge ranch, and I'm the business manager for the spread."

"Oh, my. That's very impressive." Louise raised a glass of tea to her lips. "How did you get that job?"

"By sleeping with him," Janey replied.

Louise laughed just as she was taking a drink, and she sprayed tea on the table. Janey laughed with her, and both giggled as they picked up their napkins and began wiping the table.

"Oh, Abigail . . . I mean, Janey . . . it's so good to see you again. I've been worried about you ever since you left. You just dropped off the face of the earth after that night."

"I didn't have any other choice."

"I know. I do credit you with saving my life."

"Maggie had more to do with it than I did," Janey said. "And it cost her her life."

"Yes," Louise said, her mood more somber. "She was such a dear woman."

"She was, indeed. How did you . . . ?" Janey finished her question with a wave of her hand, but Louise understood the implication.

"How did I wind up with the Pretty Girl and Happy Cowboy?"

"Yes."

"Because you were gone."

"What?"

"Maggie had a will drawn up. It said that if anything happened to her, she wanted everything left to you. And if you were no longer with the house, then she wanted everything left to me. Oh!" Louise realized something. "I suppose the house belongs to you, now."

Smiling, Janey reached across the table to put her hand on Louise's hand. "No it doesn't. Didn't the will say that if I was no longer with the house, that it would belong to you?"

"Yes, but . . ."

"But nothing. It belongs to you. The only reason I came by was to look up any old friends who might happen to be around, and I found the one who was dearest to me."

Louise gave Janey a rundown on all the girls who had been there when she was there. Two had gotten married, one had gone back to St. Louis, and she had lost track of three of them.

"What about Abigail Fontaine?" Janey asked. "Is the law still looking for her? For me?"

Louise shook her head. "They came around a few times for the first month or two after you left, then they just gave up."

"Nobody came looking for Janey Garner, did they?"

"Honey, as far as I know, nobody here has ever heard that name. You don't have a thing to worry about."

Janey smiled. "That's good to know."

What Janey didn't say out loud was that if everything fell apart in Bury, and she had a feeling that might happen sooner, rather than later, she could always come back.

CHAPTER 26

PSR Ranch, office

"**B**oys, I have found the answer to our problem," Richards told the other two members of his alliance as they sat in chairs, smoking cigars and drinking whiskey.

"What is it?" Stratton asked.

"In order to stop someone who is good and fast with a gun, we need to find someone who is better and faster."

"And you've found someone who is better than Smoke Jensen?" Potter's tone indicated his skepticism.

Richards smiled. "Yeah."

"Who?" Stratton wanted to know.

"Clell Dawson."

"Clell Dawson?" Stratton repeated. He and Potter looked at each other, then Stratton went on. "Yes, if there's anyone who could beat Jensen, it would be Dawson. But from what I've heard, he's pretty particular about how he hires out his gun."

"That's the beauty of it. We won't be hiring him. He'll be taking care of business for us without even knowing that's what he's doing."

"Josh, I don't know what you have in mind, but I sure hope it works," Potter said.

"Oh, it will work all right. Believe me, it will work. And we won't be bothered by the likes of Smoke Jensen, ever again."

Richards put his cigar in his mouth, clamped his teeth down on it, and smiled.

Denver

For the first two weeks after Smoke returned, nothing of any significance happened. Then he was called into Marshal Holloway's office for a new assignment.

"I've got a request here from the sheriff up in Summit County. There have been a series of incidents up there over the last eighteen months, and the sheriff says he needs help. By any chance, do you know Sheriff Jesse Hector?"

"No. Why do you ask? Should I know him?"

"I can't say as you should. But he knows you. At least, he asked for you by name."

Smoke smiled. "Well, if someone asks for me by name, I can't very well turn them down now, can I? Summit County, you say?"

"Yes, in Breckenridge. Miss Wilson will show you on the map where it is."

Smoke went back into the outer office and found Miss Wilson waiting for him with a map spread out on her desk. As Smoke stood beside her, she used a slender finger to indicate a spot on the map.

"That looks like a good long ride," Smoke said as she pointed out the location to him.

"No need for you to ride." She briskly rolled up the map and put it back in a case. "There is train service to Breckenridge. I'll arrange for your rail fare."

"I don't mind riding. I've got a good horse and a soft saddle."

"A soft saddle? Why, I've never heard of such a thing."

Smoke laughed.

"You shouldn't make fun of a helpless lady like that," Miss Wilson teased.

"A lady you are, Miss Wilson. But helpless you are not."

The building stood alone on a country road. It had started out as a general store, but because it was the only establishment of trade in that part of the county, its business grew.

As business improved, the building began to expand. One section was added to accommodate a blacksmith shop, the saloon occupied another extension, while a second-story addition provided a hotel. The finished project reflected its hodgepodge origins, the construction spreading out in erratic styles of architecture, mismatched types of wood, and varying shades of paint.

Smoke stood for a moment just inside the door, studying the layout. To his left was a bar. In front of him were four tables; to the right, a potbellied stove, sitting in a box of sand. The stove was cold, but the stale, acrid smell of last winter's smoke still hung in the air.

One man was behind the bar; a customer was in front. Several men sat at a table. A woman was at the back of the room, standing by an upright harpsichord. Her heavily painted face advertised her trade, and she smiled provocatively at Smoke, trying to interest him in the pleasures she had to offer.

Smoke stepped up to the bar.

"You're new in Pin Hook, ain't you?" the bartender asked, wiping the bar in front of him with a soiled rag.

"Pin Hook?"

"This here town is called Pin Hook," the bartender said. "Or it will be when a few more buildin's get built. As you can see, we got us a start."

Smoke chuckled. "Looks like a pretty good start, too. Tell me, do you serve food here?"

"We sure do. Mabel's cooked up a stew today that's not half bad, if I do say so myself. But bein' as Mabel is my wife, I prob'ly ought not to brag so."

"Well, I'll have a bowl and see for myself," Smoke said with a smile.

A short while later, Smoke was enjoying his stew, which actually was quite good, as he listened to the conversation being carried on by the four men at a nearby table.

"They say he rode into town with the reins of his horse clenched betwixt his teeth, and blazin' pistols in each hand, and he kilt thirty-five men without gettin' a scratch on 'im."

"Fifty, I heard, but you're wrong 'bout him not gettin' a scratch on 'im. He kilt the last one, just as that feller kilt him."

"I don't believe Smoke Jensen is dead. No, sir, not for a minute of it," the third said. "And I don't believe he kilt all that many people like you said he done, neither. Maybe ten or twelve. We prob'ly ain't never gonna know. I mean the way stories like that get told and then they get told again, and somethin' gets added with ever' tellin'."

"Legends, they call them," one said.

"What's that?" asked another.

"Legends. Like Robin Hood is a legend. He never actually existed."

"Look here. Are you atryin' to tell us that there ain't no Smoke Jensen?"

"No, I'm not trying to tell you that. I am merely pointing out that once so many different stories get told about the same thing, then they move into the field of legends. Maybe a better way of explaining it is to compare them to tall tales."

"Yeah, well, I heard he kilt fifty of 'em, and that ain't no tall tale."

Smoke smiled at the overheard conversation, then, finishing his meal, he stepped up to the bar to pay for it. "You tell your wife that her stew was quite tasty."

"Yes, sir, I'll do that. And who shall I tell her was the gentleman who expressed his appreciation?"

"Jensen. Smoke Jensen." Turning toward the four men at the table who only a few moments earlier had been talking about him, he threw them a little wave.

All four looked back, their mouths open in wordless shock.

Breckenridge, Summit County

It was just after dark several days later when Smoke approached the town. From the small houses on the outskirts, dim lights flickered through shuttered windows. The kitchens of the houses emitted enticing smells of suppers being cooked.

A dog barked, a ribbony yap that was silenced by a kick or a thrown rock. A baby cried, and a housewife raised her voice in one of the houses, loudly enough to share her anger with anyone who might be within earshot.

The middle of town was a contrast of dark and light. Commercial buildings such as stores and offices were closed and dark, but the saloons were brightly lit, splashing pools of light out into the dirt street. As Smoke rode down the road, he passed in and out of those pools of light so that to anyone watching, he would be seen, then unseen, then seen again. The footfalls of his horse made a hollow clumping sound, echoing back from the false-fronted buildings as he passed them.

By the time he reached the center of town, the night was alive with a cacophony of sound—music from a tinny piano, a strumming guitar, and an off-key vocalist. He gave a passing thought to stopping in one of the saloons, but he was tired from the long ride, so he reined up in front of the hotel and went inside.

"You are Deputy Jensen?" the desk clerk asked as Smoke signed the register.

"Yes."

"Sheriff Hector left this message for you, sir."

"Thanks." Smoke unfolded the paper. The message was printed in capital letters.

DEPUTY, PLEASE MEET ME FOR BREAKFAST TOMORROW MORNING AT SUZIE'S CAFÉ.

"Can you board my horse?" Smoke asked, looking up from the note.

The clerk nodded. "Yes, sir, I can do that for you."

"Thanks. And do you have bathing facilities in this hotel?"

"Yes, sir, we do. They're located at the end of the hallway."

Forty-five minutes later, with Seven comfortably boarded and the trail dust washed away, Smoke, refreshed by his bath, went to bed.

From the saloon next door, he could hear through the open window the deep guffaws of men interspersed with the occasional high-pitched laughter of women. Hollow hoofbeats echoed from a horse that was being ridden up the street, and he heard the mournful wail of a coyote just outside of town.

Gradually the sounds subsided and one by one the lights across the town were extinguished until at last it lay as a cluster of dark buildings, visible only because of the silver wash of the three-quarter moon.

In the hotel room, Smoke gasped and sat up, reaching for his gun in the gun belt he had coiled and placed on a chair beside the bed where it would be handy. As he closed his hand around the Colt, he stared at the figure standing beside the bed.

"Pa?" he whispered, surprised to see his father.

But how could that be true? His pa was dead.

"Son," Emmett *said in his well-remembered voice. "I seen what you done to them men that kilt your wife and boy, and I don't mind tellin' you, I think you done the right thing.*

"I know that you're alookin' for Richards, Potter, and Stratton, them bein' the men what shot Luke and kilt me. But what you need to know is, they're lookin' just as hard to find you, so they can kill you. So, what I got to say to you is, be careful. And don't trust nobody but Preacher.

"I'm gettin' tired now, so I'll be agoin'." Emmett *began fading away right before Smoke's eyes, as if he were being enveloped in a swirling mist.*

"Pa? Pa, no, don't go! Don't go!" Smoke called.

"Bye, son. Bye . . . "

A different voice said, "Bye, son. Bye. Write to your ma and me."

"Giddyup!" The shout to the team was augmented by the loud pop of a whip, then the creak and rumble of a stagecoach pulling away.

"Bye!" others called.

The sounds associated with the departing stagecoach were floating up from the street as Smoke woke up with a jolt and opened his eyes. A bright splash of sunlight spilled through the open window, showing a wall covered with paper so faded that the original pattern and color was indistinguishable. A soft breeze filled the muslin curtains and lifted them out over the wide, unpainted plank floor.

"A dream," Smoke said. The calls of good-bye had been incorporated into his dream. It had seemed so real, he was sure he had been talking to his pa.

As a general rule, Smoke awakened with first light,

but the long hard ride of the day before had left him tired, and he had slept harder than usual.

He stepped into Suzie's Café a short while later and was met by Sheriff Hector and two other men.

"Deputy Jensen?" the sheriff asked.

"That's right," Smoke said with a nod.

"I'm Sheriff Hector, this is Dan Adams, the prosecuting attorney, and this is His Honor, Judge Drew Martin. I've invited them to have breakfast with us because this concerns the entire community. Gentlemen, this is Smoke Jensen. He's a deputy for Marshal Holloway down in Denver."

"I've heard about you, young man," Judge Martin said as they were seated. "You have been making quite a name for yourself. Especially that business on the Uncompahgre."

"How many men did you kill? Twenty? Thirty?" the prosecutor asked. "You must be some kind of one-man army to go after so many men all by yourself."

"Actually, I had no idea there were so many," Smoke replied. "I only wanted to bring two men in to face murder charges. The rest of it just sort of happened."

"Still, it was quite a prodigious effort on your part," Judge Martin said. "And, as it turned out, many of them were wanted men, so you not only avenged the despicable murder of your wife, you also served the cause of justice. That has made you famous throughout the West."

"It was never my intention to be famous, Your Honor. I just wanted justice for Nicole and my boy."

Sheriff Hector nodded. "Understandable. Indeed, that is exactly why we have asked you here."

Before he could continue, they were approached by a woman carrying a small tablet and a pencil. "What can I get for you gentlemen this morning?"

"Suzie, give the deputy anything he wants for breakfast," Sheriff Hector said, pointing to Smoke. "The county will be paying for it." He looked to the judge and the prosecutor. When they nodded, he added, "We'll just have our usual."

Suzie was a heavyset woman, and she stuck out her bottom lip, then blew a stream of air up toward a displaced strand of blond hair. "What will it be, Deputy?"

"Do you have any pancakes?"

"Yes, sir, I have pancakes."

"I'll take half a dozen pancakes, a couple fried eggs, about eight pieces of bacon, a couple biscuits, and a side of gravy. And maybe some fried potatoes."

She smiled. "Oh, my. I love a man with a good appetite."

"My goodness, Sheriff, are you sure the county can afford breakfast for this man?" Prosecutor Adams asked.

"Well, I don't know," Sheriff Hector replied with a laugh. "I suppose it depends on whether or not he orders seconds."

Smoke grinned. "I think I can get by on this."

"I hope so," Suzie said. "Otherwise I'll have to put on three or four more cooks." Laughing, she started toward the kitchen.

"I hope Deputy Jensen is up to the task we're

going to give him. He is already costing us a ton of money," Judge Martin teased.

"I'll do my best for you," Smoke promised with a good-natured chuckle.

"First, I want to thank you for coming," Sheriff Hector said. "Did Marshal Holloway fill you in on what's going on here?"

"Not really. He just said you were having some problems. Some *incidents*, he called them."

"I'll say we are. Bloody incidents over the last eighteen months. We've had a stagecoach dynamited, with five people killed—the driver and shotgun guard, a man, his wife and their little boy. The criminals did that all for eighty-seven dollars. Eighty-seven dollars, mind you, and five people were killed."

Judge Martin added, "Some men broke into a banker's house where they held his wife and little girl hostage while they forced him to bring them thirty thousand dollars from the bank."

"And more recently a train was robbed, again using dynamite that caused it to derail. Ten people were killed and twenty-three were injured," Prosecutor Adams concluded.

"It was horrible," the sheriff said. "We're convinced the same bunch is responsible for both the stagecoach holdup and the train robbery."

"Because of the dynamite angle," Smoke said, nodding slowly.

"That's right. And since witnesses told us it was three men who caused the train wreck, we suspect they're the same ones who terrorized the banker and his family."

"More than likely," Smoke agreed. "You've had some busy people up here."

Suzie and two others brought their breakfasts then.

Suzie served Smoke. "Here you go, hon. If you need anything else, you just let me know."

"Thanks, I will," Smoke replied with a friendly smile.

What he really needed, Suzie couldn't provide. That was a lead to the whereabouts of the ruthless outlaws responsible for the carnage in Summit County.

CHAPTER 27

The four men started on their meals before Sheriff Hector resumed their conversation.

"You said we have had some busy people up here, and that is true," he told Smoke, "but like any operation, someone is always at the head, and if you cut the head off, the snake will die."

"You have any idea who that might be?" Smoke asked as he slathered molasses over his pancakes.

"Yes, we have a very good idea," Hector said. "We believe Clell Dawson is behind it."

Smoke paused just before forking a bite of pancakes into his mouth and looked at the sheriff. "Clell Dawson? That's who you think is behind all this?"

"Like I said, we have a very good idea that he is."

"I'd say that it's more than just a very good idea," Adams said. "We are sure he is behind it."

"Well, you're free to say that, Dan," Judge Martin said. "After all, when the deputy brings Dawson in, it will be your job to prosecute him. But I will have to sit in judgment over him, so it is incumbent upon me to maintain some sense of detachment. Therefore, I can't allow myself to say anything more."

"I'm interested, Deputy Jensen, why you question this?" Hector asked. "Do you know Dawson?"

Smoke shook his head. "No, I've never met him. But I do know who he is. I've never heard of him doing anything like this before."

"It's him, all right," Hector insisted. "But the thing is, Dawson is too good with a gun for me to take him, and I don't mind admitting it. He's killed I don't know how many in gunfights. I've complained to the capital about him but haven't gotten any help. Since you've heard of him, you know it's going to take someone who's really good with a gun—someone like you—to be able to bring him in."

"Do you have any idea where I might find him?"

"Oh, yes, we know exactly where he is," Sheriff Hector said confidently. "That's another reason I asked for you. He isn't in Summit County anymore. He's moved to Boggsville. That's down in Bent County. But you have the same jurisdiction there that you do here."

"Boggsville?" Smoke nodded and filed the information away in his brain. "All right, I'll go look him up."

The three men at the table smiled and nodded, obviously well pleased with the results of the meeting.

"Thank you, Deputy," the judge said. "The people of Breckenridge appreciate your help."

"Better save your thanks until I've caught up with Clell Dawson and seen what's what," Smoke responded dryly.

Boggsville, Bent County, Colorado Territory

During the great Western migration, the town had become a stopover place for the wagons. Army troops at Bent's Fort made the route safe, and the improved road over Raton Pass made wagon travel relatively easy. When Richens L. Wootten established his toll road in 1866, even more wagon trains used the Mountain Branch because, although longer, it was safer and had more water than the Cimarron Cutoff.

Boggsville grew from a convenient resting place for the wagons to a settlement providing a stagecoach station, as well as lodging; grocery, dry goods, leather, hardware, and gun stores; saloons; and gambling halls so that it was no longer just a convenient settlement but had become a thriving town, servicing several ranches in the area. By the time the Atchison, Topeka, and Santa Fe Railroad reached the community, it was on its way to being a small city.

When Clell Dawson had come to Boggsville one year earlier, he'd bought a part interest in the Trail Blazer Saloon. It had been his intention to settle down in Boggsville and lead a quiet life, supported by his share of the revenue earned by the Trail Blazer.

But that wasn't to be. Twice in the last year, he had encountered obstacles in his quest for a quiet life when he had been confronted by gunslingers looking for a reputation.

Both had found a grave, instead.

Down the street from the Trail Blazer, in the Circle Thirty-four Saloon, the groundwork for a third such confrontation was being laid by a discussion between John Norton and Darren Draper.

"Well, my point is, you're good with a gun," Norton said. "You're good and you're fast. Very fast. But the question is, are you as good as Clell Dawson?"

Draper shrugged. "I figure I am."

"You may be, but—and here is why I'm asking the question—nearly everyone has heard of Clell Dawson. But there ain't nobody who has ever heard of you . . . not more than a dozen or so people, at any rate."

Draper smiled. "When somebody is as good as I am and there ain't that many people who know it, that gives me a big edge, don't you see? And the fact that I've managed to keep myself off the reward dodgers and out of newspapers . . . that just shows how smart I am."

Norton chuckled. "You seem awful sure of yourself."

"Yeah, I suppose I am. But you got to consider this. When a fella is in my profession, he has to walk a real narrow line between bein' real sure of hisself and bein' downright conceited."

"I suppose so. But it's too bad," Norton said.

"What's too bad?"

"It's too bad that we ain't never goin' to know which one of you is the best."

Draper pulled the makings out of his pocket and began rolling a cigarette. "What makes you think we ain't never goin' to know?" He struck a match with his thumbnail and began puffing until the cigarette was lit, then he blew out a long cloud of aromatic smoke.

Norton frowned. "Well, how we goin' to know which of the two of you is best?"

"I'll tell you which one."

"All right. Which one of you is best?"

"Which ever one of us is still standin' when this is over." With that pronouncement, Draper eased his pistol out of the holster, opened the guard, and spun the cylinder to check his loads. That done, he walked out of the Circle Thirty-Four and down to the Trail Blazer Saloon.

Those who had been listening in to the conversation between Draper and Norton followed. They entered the saloon at the same time.

Clell could tell by the way Draper was walking why he was there and knew that the others had come to watch the show. "I've been about halfway expecting you, Draper."

"Only halfway expecting me?"

"Yeah. I thought maybe you would have sense enough to go on your way and leave this behind you."

"I was about ready to move on," Draper said. "But I can't leave without finding out."

"Finding out what?"

"You know what I'm talking about."

Clell nodded. "Yeah, I suppose I do."

"You understand that, don't you, Dawson? If I let this pass, how would that make me look? Why, I'd be the laughingstock of the territory."

"That might be true, but on the other hand, you would still be alive," Clell pointed out.

"What makes you so sure that I won't still be alive after we play out this hand we've been dealt?" Draper asked.

"You'll be dead." Clell spoke the words calmly and

with little emotion as if he had been asked whether he wanted a cup of coffee.

"On the other hand, you might be the one who winds up dead." Draper tried to preserve some bravado.

"You can walk away now, and we'll both still be alive."

Draper smiled, thinking perhaps Dawson was human after all. Perhaps he was a little frightened. *That could be my edge.* "I can't do that. We're going to have to deal with it, both of us, right here, right now. Too many people have come to see us shoot it out." He smiled and took in the crowd with a wave of his left hand. His right never strayed far from the butt of his gun. "Look how many people are here. Don't you think we owe them a show?"

"Why should I have to kill you, just to satisfy them?" Clell asked.

Again his words had a disquieting effect on Draper, but a rapid blink was the only demonstrable evidence of his reaction.

"Is that really what you want, Draper?" Clell went on.

"Yeah, that's really what I want. I think the talkin' is over. It's come time for me and you to settle this thing, once and for all. That is, unless you want to back out and admit that I'm better'n you. What will it be, Dawson?"

Clell didn't give in. "You dealt the cards. It's up to you to hold 'em or fold 'em."

"I'm goin' to hold 'em," Draper said. "I've been wonderin' which of us was the fastest. Hell, ever'body has been wonderin'."

"I haven't been wonderin.' " Clell shook his head. "And I doubt that many others have been wonderin'. I know that they know. And deep down, Draper, even you know."

For the first time since he had confronted Clell Dawson, Draper was beginning to have second thoughts. *What the hell was I thinking, to push things this far?* Those second thoughts turned to apprehension, that apprehension turned to outright fear, and that fear was mirrored in his eyes and in the nervous tic on the side of his face. His tongue came out to lick his lips.

Clell waited for Draper to make his move, an easy grin spreading across his face.

Even that, the grin in the face of an impending shoot-out where he could be killed, had the effect of unnerving Draper. With all that was in him, Draper wanted to turn and walk . . . no . . . *run* away.

But he couldn't do that, of course. If he did, he could never show his face anywhere again.

Suddenly, and without calling it, Draper's hand started for his gun, but Clell's gun was out just a heartbeat faster. That heartbeat of time was all the advantage Clell needed, for he fired first. Draper caught the slug high in his chest.

Draper dropped his unfired gun and slapped his hand over his wound. He looked down in surprise as blood began streaming between his fingers. He took two staggering steps toward his shooter, then fell to his knees. He looked up, his eyes registering shock, fear, and then the dreadful realization that he was dying. "You . . . you killed me."

"Yes, I have," Clell replied, returning his pistol to his holster.

"I never would have believed it." Draper smiled, then coughed, and flecks of blood came from his mouth. "I was sure I was faster than you."

"It's a little late for you to be learning this, but nothing in life is sure," Clell said easily.

Draper fell facedown on the saloon floor.

"I'll be damned," someone said. "That beats anything I've ever seen."

Smoke arrived in Boggsville on the next morning's train, having left Seven behind. Before he left the station, he bought two return tickets on the afternoon train to Breckenridge.

"Will someone be going back with you?" the ticket agent asked.

"I expect so."

"Well, it's too bad you can't stay in town a little longer and enjoy some of our hospitality." The agent stamped the tickets, then passed them across the counter in exchange for the fourteen-dollar fare.

"It looks like an interesting enough town," Smoke said. "Maybe I'll come back someday."

"We had us a real famous person who lived here for a while, you know."

"You did, did you? And who was that?"

"Why, it was none other than Kit Carson, that's who."

"That's very interesting." Smoke restrained a

chuckle, thinking Preacher and Carson had been close friends at one time. He remembered the story.

"Until he got to makin' eyes at the same Injun girl I was interested in," Preacher explained.

"Which one of you got the girl?" Smoke wanted to know.

"Why, I did, of course. Me and her was married for one whole winter."

Smoke was still grinning as he stepped out into the street. A rather sizeable cluster of people were gathered around the front of the hardware store. For a moment, he wondered what had their attention.

He didn't have to wonder for too long. Someone in the crowd moved, and Smoke saw what they were all looking at. Standing upright in the window was an open coffin, and inside the coffin was a body. A sign was pinned onto the shirt of the cadaver.

Too far away to read it, he decided to walk down to see what it said.

"Fastest damn thing I ever seen," someone was saying as he approached the crowd.

"Yeah, and what makes it so amazin' is that Draper was real fast his ownself. They say that he already kilt six men."

"Number seven wasn't very lucky for him then, was it?" another said.

A ripple of nervous laughter came at that pronouncement.

Close enough, Smoke read the sign.

DREW DRAPER
THOUGHT HE WAS FASTER
THAN CLELL DAWSON
HE WASN'T

"Has anybody seen Dawson this mornin'?" one of the men in the crowd asked.

That was a lucky break for Smoke. It meant he didn't have to ask the question himself.

"He's where he's always at. He's astandin' at the end of the bar down at the Trail Blazer like nothin' at all happened."

"I thought maybe after the shoot-out yesterday he might not come in to the saloon today."

"Hell, with somebody like Clell Dawson, yesterday was just another day."

"How many men you think Dawson has kilt now?"

"Ten, twenty. Who knows?"

"Yeah, well, most of 'em was prob'ly like Draper. Some young punk who come up to 'im, tryin' to get a reputation for hisself. You'd think they'd know better by now."

Despite his youth, Smoke knew some men were so full of the need to make a name for themselves that they never learned.

He had killed too many of them not to know it.

CHAPTER 28

Smoke waited until less than ten minutes before departure time for the train, then went after Dawson. He figured that by doing it that way, he would have less time to worry about keeping Dawson under guard in a town where he might have friends who would try to rescue him.

Stepping into the Trail Blazer, Smoke saw a tall, slender man standing at the far end of the bar. Dressed in blue serge trousers, a white shirt, and a tan cashmere jacket, the man stood out from the others. The hem of his jacket was pushed back to expose a pistol nestled in a black leather holster.

Smoke was reasonably certain that was Clell Dawson, but he wanted to be sure before he made his move. He didn't have to wait very long.

The bartender moseyed to the end of the bar. "Mr. Dawson, we're gonna have to order some new bottles of bourbon pretty soon. We're runnin' low."

"You talk to Tommie Kay about it?"

"Yes, sir, and she said go ahead and do it, if it's all right with you."

Dawson nodded. "Sure, go ahead."

Upon hearing the conversation, Smoke walked down to the well-dressed man and stepped right up in front of him. "Mr. Dawson?"

"Yes?"

"I am a deputy United States marshal, and you are under arrest."

Without so much as one word of response to Smoke's comment, Clell reached for his gun.

It wasn't there! His hand groped at an empty holster.

"Are you looking for this?" Smoke held out Clell's gun, pointed directly at him.

Clell's reaction was a surprise. It was a broad smile. "I'll be damned! How did you do that?"

"Never mind how I did it," Smoke said. "The point is, you are under arrest. I hope you agree to come peaceably. From what I've heard about you, you're the kind of man I wouldn't want to take any chances with, and that means I'd have to kill you."

"Look here, Deputy," the bartender said. "If this is about the killin' yesterday, if you ask around, ever'one in this town will tell you that Mr. Dawson didn't do nothin' wrong. When he kilt Draper it was self-defense, pure and simple. Draper drawed his gun first."

"This has nothing to do with what happened yesterday. I didn't even know about it until I saw Draper's body standing up in front of the hardware store." Smoke turned his attention back to Clell. "You didn't answer my question. Are you going to come peaceably?"

"I'm not going to give you any trouble, Deputy, but can I have a minute to explain the situation to my business partner? It wouldn't be right to just walk out of here without a few words of explanation."

Smoke nodded. "No more than a minute. We're taking the next train out of here."

"Rex, would you go get Tommie Kay?" Clell asked.

"Yes, sir." The bartender disappeared through a door at the end of the bar, then came back a moment later with a very voluptuous woman whose pretty face was framed by fire-red hair.

"What's going on here, Clell?"

"Tommie Kay, it would appear that I'm going to have to go somewhere with this gentleman."

"When will you be back?"

"I'll be honest with you, my dear. I'm not sure I will be coming back." Clell looked at Smoke. "Deputy, you would have no objections if I kissed my business partner good-bye, would you?"

Smoke was a little surprised by Clell's reaction. He wasn't sure what he expected, but he hadn't anticipated such a cool demeanor. "I suppose so, as long as you don't do anything foolish."

Tommie Kay approached Smoke and, holding her arms out, thrust her chest forward, emphasizing her breasts. A considerable expanse of enticing flesh spilled out over the top of her low-necked dress. "Do you want to check to see if I have a gun, Deputy?" she asked with a coy smile.

The others in the saloon, including Clell, laughed.

"That's all right, miss," Smoke said with a grin. "I can see that you aren't hiding . . . anything." He stared pointedly at the creamy tops of her breasts, and again the others laughed.

"My dear, he is quite right," Clell said, holding his arms open in invitation.

Clell and Tommie Kay shared a long kiss in front of everyone, eliciting more than a few comments.

As they separated, Smoke heard the whistle of the approaching train. "I hate to break this up, Mr. Dawson, but we need to get going."

"All right. And it's Dr. Dawson, actually."

"Doctor?" Tommie Kay asked, surprised by the remark. "What do you mean, *doctor*?"

"You mean I've never told you that I'm a physician? No, I don't suppose I have. I guess it's just never come up before."

Smoke put Clell's hands in cuffs, then led him back down to the depot. His decision to wait until just before the train was due to depart was a good one. Several people gathered along the way between the saloon and the train station.

"What are you arrestin' him for? He ain't done nothin'!"

"If you're goin' to try him, try him here, where we know he'll get a fair trial!" another shouted.

Fortunately, the complaints never got beyond a few shouts, and five minutes later they were on the train, heading back to Breckenridge.

"Breckenridge?" Dawson mused. "Well, that will be an interesting experience for me. I don't believe I've ever been to Breckenridge."

"It's in Summit County," Smoke told him.

"Good. I've never been there, either. I'm looking forward to the visit."

Smoke laughed. "I'll say this for you, Dawson. You are one of the coolest characters I've ever encountered. You're being taken back to stand trial for the murder of fifteen people, and you act like you're going to a church social."

Dawson raised an eyebrow in surprise. "I haven't killed fifteen people. I've only killed eleven, and witnesses will tell you that every one of those eleven gentlemen was trying to kill me."

"The ten people on the train were all trying to kill you?"

Dawson got a confused look on his face. "What train? Deputy, I have to confess that I don't know what this is all about. I've never killed anyone on a train."

Smoke leaned back against the bench seat and tried not to frown. He considered himself a pretty good judge of people.

And it sure sounded to him like Clell Dawson was telling the truth.

Breckenridge

"Why didn't you kill 'im?" Sheriff Hector asked.

"I beg your pardon?" Clell replied.

"When Jensen came to arrest you, why didn't you kill 'im?"

"You'll excuse me for saying this, Sheriff, but isn't that a rather strange question for you to ask?" Clell was in the jail and, at the moment, he and the sheriff were the only two men in the building.

Hector glared at him through the bars on the door of the cell. "You do know what you're facing, don't you? You are going to be tried, found guilty, and hung. I would think that with all that hanging over your head, you wouldn't have just let Jensen bring you in so easy."

"Yes, that's something I wanted to talk to you about. Deputy Jensen said something about me killing people on a train."

"That's right. You are being charged with dynamiting a stagecoach and killing five people, including a woman and child; holding a woman and child hostage, while you forced her husband, a banker, to take thirty thousand dollars from the bank to pay ransom; and finally dynamiting a train where ten people were killed, making the total fifteen people you murdered."

"I didn't do any of that!" Clell insisted.

Sheriff Hector chuckled and shook his head. "It doesn't matter."

"What do you mean, it doesn't matter?"

"That's what you're going to be charged with, the prosecutor is going to make the case, and the judge is going to sentence you to hang."

Clell didn't like the sound of that. "How can you be so sure of that?"

"Can I let you in on a little secret?" Hector knew he shouldn't boast, but lording it over a famous gunman like Clell Dawson was just too tempting to resist, even if things hadn't gone according to plan.

"Please do, because none of this is making any sense to me."

"I know you didn't do any of those things. Those jobs were pulled by Pete Kotter, Eddie Spence, and Merlin Mathis. I know exactly who did it because"—Hector paused, looked around, then smiled a broad, conspiratorial smile—"I set the jobs up for them."

Clell frowned. "You did?"

"Yes." Hector laughed. "Now, you tell me what can be a sweeter deal than that? I control the law, so I can control the people who are actually doing the killing, by protecting them from the law. They're more than willing to share their take with me, and I don't mind telling you, this has been a very good deal."

"Why *are* you telling me this, Sheriff?"

"I'm telling you so that you know where you fit into things. Three other men, Potter, Stratton, and Richards, have come to me and asked me to do a job for them. A very big job."

Clell gave the sheriff his full attention. "And, somehow, I am supposed to fit into this job that they want done?"

"That's right."

"How?"

"These three men want Jensen dead. I expected you to kill him, damn it, not let him arrest you."

Things were starting to make a little sense. "Ah. How do you know I'm good enough to kill him?"

"I just assumed that you were, but you're right. I should have taken that into consideration. That's why I've come up with an alternate plan."

"And what would that plan be?"

Sheriff Hector held up a finger as if telling Clell to

wait for a moment, then he walked over to his desk, opened a drawer, and pulled out a pistol. "Here is the plan. I'll find some reason to get Jensen in here so that there are only the two of you. You can use this gun to force him to open the cell for you. Then, once he does that, you kill him and be on your way. Oh, and to sweeten the pot, I'm leaving five hundred dollars for you in the center drawer of my desk. Meet me in Boreas in one week, and I'll let you in on a deal that can mean even more money for you. A lot more money."

Clell frowned. "What if I don't want any part of this?"

"Think about it, Dawson. On the one hand you will be tried, found guilty, and sentenced to death by hanging. On the other hand, you'll have your freedom, five hundred dollars, and the opportunity to make a lot more money."

"What if I choose to go to trial and testify about this offer you just made?"

Sheriff Hector laughed. "So, you're going to tell the judge that I'm behind all the robberies, and that I tried to pay you to kill a deputy United States marshal. How far do you think you're going to get with that story?"

Clell ran his hand through his hair and grimaced. "Not very far, I don't imagine."

"You have only one way of coming out of this alive, Dawson. Now what will it be?"

"I guess I'm going to have to take you up on your offer."

"Now you're showing some intelligence." Sheriff Hector opened up the desk drawer and held up a packet of money with a string tied around it. "There are fifty ten-dollar bills in this packet . . . and as I said, a lot more where that came from if you join me in Boreas next week." He put the bills back in the drawer, then walked back over to the cell and passed a pistol through the bars. "And here is the gun you can use to make your escape."

Clell took the pistol. "Suppose I want to make my escape now?" He pointed the gun at the sheriff. "Open the door to this cell now, or I will shoot you."

"Go ahead, shoot," Hector said with a smile.

"The gun's empty, isn't it?"

"Yep, it sure is."

"Let's just see." Clell pulled the trigger, and there was a metallic *click* as the hammer fell upon an empty chamber. "How am I supposed to kill Jensen with an empty pistol?"

"You won't kill him with an empty pistol. Once you bluff him into opening the cell, you'll disarm him and kill him with his own gun. Won't that be something?"

"Yes, I see the irony in such an act."

Hector frowned. "The what?"

"I agree. That will be something," Clell said without trying to explain. "But let me ask you this. What makes you think I can bluff him into opening the cell? I wasn't able to bluff you."

"Ah, but I knew the gun was empty, don't you see? Jensen won't know that. You'll have the drop on him."

"I'll have the drop on him," Clell repeated.

"Yes." Hector nodded, happy Dawson was finally getting his plan.

"That doesn't matter. Even if the gun I was holding was loaded, it wouldn't matter."

"What do you mean, *it wouldn't matter*?"

"Reaction time," Clell explained.

"Reaction time? What is that?"

"Someone who is good with a gun—I mean very good—someone very good like Smoke Jensen can draw and shoot before someone like me . . . or you . . . holding a pistol on him could even pull the trigger. That's because once you see him start his draw, you have to react to that and pull the trigger. And in the time you are thinking about—reacting to—his move, a fast gun like Jensen will have already drawn and fired."

"Well, if that's the case, it wouldn't matter whether the gun you're holding is loaded or not, would it?"

Clell chuckled and shook his head. "I guess you've got me on that one, Sheriff. No, it really doesn't matter. All right, get Jensen in here. If I'm going to do this, I want to do it, and get it over with."

After Hector had hurried out of the jail, Clell stood in the cell looking down at the empty weapon in his hand. After a moment, he laughed.

It was a grim sound.

Smoke was having a cup of coffee in Suzie's Café when Sheriff Hector came in.

"Hello, Sheriff. Join me in a cup of coffee?" Smoke asked.

"Well, I will when you come back."

"When I come back from where?"

"Dawson wants to talk to you. It's something about

three men who have hired some people to kill you. I don't know what he's talking about. I think he may be trying to come up with something that he can use in his trial. I mean, do you have any idea what he's talking about?"

"Three men, he said?"

"Yeah. Does that mean anything to you?"

"Yes, it does mean something," Smoke said. "Would you excuse me, Sheriff? I reckon maybe I'd like to hear what he has to say."

"I'll be right here when you get back," Hector said. "Suzie? What kind of pie do you have left?"

CHAPTER 29

"Dawson, I understand you have something to tell me about the three men who are trying to kill me," Smoke said when he stepped into the cell block a few minutes later.

"Is that the ruse he used to get you over here?" Clell asked. "He told you I have something to tell you?"

"Yes. What do you mean, *ruse*? Are you saying you don't have anything to tell me?"

"Oh, yeah, I've got something to tell you, all right. I've got the damnedest story you ever heard."

Smoke shook his head. "I don't have any idea what you're talking about."

"No, I don't imagine you do. But I'll start out with this. I confess that I held up a stagecoach in Pueblo County several months ago. I didn't get that much money out of it, and nobody was hurt." Clell smiled. "The newspapers called me the Gentleman Bandit. I admit that was wrong, but I didn't have anything to do with those robberies where the stagecoach and the train were dynamited. Sheriff Hector was behind those robberies. He told me as much. He set us up, Deputy. You and me. And now he is doing it again. The reason he wanted you to come see me is because he wanted me to kill you."

"How did he plan for you to do that?"

"He gave me this gun to use," Clell said, producing the gun but holding it by the barrel, butt first. "It's not loaded."

Smoke frowned. "It would be kind of hard to kill me with an unloaded gun, wouldn't it?"

"Oh, well, I'm supposed to bluff you with it, make you open the cell door, then take your gun and use it to kill you."

"Did he really think you could do that?"

"I don't think it matters. Supposedly, if I could pull it off and kill you, that would be good. On the other hand, if you killed me, they would try you for murder, for shooting me in the cell. Either way, it would accomplish the same thing. You would be dead."

So far, what Dawson was saying made no sense to Smoke. "Do you have any idea why the sheriff wants me dead?"

"Do the names Peters, Stratford, and Richards mean anything to you? They are the ones who want you dead."

"Do you mean Potter, Stratton and Richards?" Smoke asked quickly.

"Yes, sorry, I just heard the names once, but that's them. Apparently, those names mean something to you."

"Yeah, they mean a lot to me," Smoke said. "I've

been looking for them for a number of years. And I want them dead as much as they want me dead."

"Uh-huh. Well, they're the ones who hired Hector to get it done."

Smoke smiled and shook his head slowly. "I have to hand it to you, Dawson, you said you were going to tell me the damnedest story, and I'd say that you just did."

"You don't believe me?"

"Not one word of it. Except the part about Potter, Stratton, and Richards. I know they're trying to kill me."

"Look over there in the sheriff's desk," Clell said. "If you pull out the middle drawer, you'll find five hundred dollars there. That is the money I'm to be given for killing you. I'm supposed to meet him in Boreas next week, to join him in some sort of deal that he claims will make me a lot more money."

Smoke walked over to the desk and opened the drawer. "I'll be damned." He reached in and picked up the packet of money.

"Here's the thing, Deputy. Suppose the bluff did work. Suppose I killed you, and took that money. There would be wanted posters out on me quicker than a wink. I'd be wanted for killing a deputy U.S. marshal. And if you don't believe me now, who would believe me then?"

"You have a point," Smoke said. "But what convinces me is this money. What sheriff, making forty dollars a month, is going to have five hundred dollars of honest money lying around?"

"So, where do we go from here?" Clell asked.

"Your word alone isn't going to be enough to convict a sheriff. We're going to have to have something more, and the best way to come up with that, I think, would be to go to Boreas."

"You'll let me have a loaded gun, won't you?"

"Sure, I don't see why not," Smoke replied with a chuckle.

Sheriff Hector returned to the jail a short time later to find that both his prisoner and Jensen were gone. The first thing he did was check the middle desk drawer. He was surprised to see that the money was still there.

Leaving the jail, he rode out to a place called Hidden Canyon, which got its name from the fact that a pinnacle rock guarded the entrance to the canyon. Someone who just happened to be riding by wouldn't even know it was there.

Reaching the entrance to the canyon, he pulled his pistol, fired two shots, waited a couple seconds, then fired one more shot. A moment later, he heard the answer—one shot, a pause for a couple seconds, then two shots.

Hector rode on down into the canyon toward a small cabin that was built against the back wall. Glancing over to the right, he saw someone behind a boulder covering him with a rifle. The man smiled at Hector as he stepped out from behind the boulder.

"I thought that might be you," Eddie Spence said.

"Are Kotter and Mathis in the cabin?"

"Yeah. You got a new job for the three of us?"

"For the four of us," Hector replied grimly.

"Four of us?"

"I'll explain it all inside."

The one room cabin was furnished with three cots, a table, three chairs, and a wood-burning stove. The place smelled of bacon recently fried and the musky odor of men who bathed infrequently. A pot of coffee was on the stove, and Sheriff Hector accepted the offer of a cup.

"What's up?" Pete asked. "Do you have a new job for us?"

Eddie jumped right in. "He said he's going to pull the job with us."

Pete frowned. "You are? Do you think that's a good idea? I mean, you bein' the sheriff and all."

"Something has come up," Hector said. "I'm not sure it's going to be safe for me to stay around much longer. So after this job I plan to leave. I would advise you boys to do the same thing."

"Go where?" Merlin asked.

Hector smiled. "Texas, California, Oregon. Hell, when this job is done, we'll have enough money to go anywhere we want."

Merlin's eyebrows shot up in wonder. "Really? How much money?"

"Oh, I'd say about twenty-five thousand dollars apiece."

"Damn! Where are we gonna get that kind of money?" Eddie asked.

"We're going to hold up a gold shipment."

CHAPTER 30

Boreas, Summit County

Shortly after they arrived in town, Smoke and Clell learned that the Boreas mine would soon transfer some gold bullion to Denver. The amount being shipped was said to be worth one hundred thousand dollars.

"That's why you were to meet the sheriff here," Smoke said. "If he really is behind those robberies, he isn't going to let this shipment get away."

"Yeah, I think you're right," Clell said.

"How much did you get?" Smoke asked.

"What?"

"You said you held up a stagecoach. How much did you get?"

"Fifteen hundred dollars."

"Good, there'll be enough to cover that."

"Deputy, I don't have an idea in the world what you're talking about. Enough to cover what?"

"Just this," Smoke replied. "I plan to set up a little surprise for Sheriff Hector and his cronies, and I'm asking you to join me. You don't have to, of course, but there are some pretty big rewards out for the men who dynamited the coach and the train, and because I'm a lawman, I can't collect any of it. That means all of it would go to you."

"Yeah!" Clell said. "Yeah, that's right!"

"You would probably get enough reward money to pay back that fifteen hundred dollars you stole."

"Jensen, you and I both know that paying that money back isn't going to get me off the hook for that robbery."

"No, but if you help me bring in these people, and if you pay back the money you stole, Governor Elbert will grant you a pardon."

"How do you know that?"

Smoke had a ready answer. "Marshal Holloway and the governor are good friends, and the marshal and I are good friends. I'll talk to Holloway. I know we can get it done."

"All right," Clell said, nodding his head. "All right. It's about time I settled down anyway. I've got a good thing going with the saloon and Tommie Kay. I've been afraid to take it any further, but if I get this all put behind me, I could. You've got yourself a deputy, Deputy."

Smoke shook his head. "I can't deputize you. If I do, you won't be eligible for the reward. You're just going to have to volunteer as a good citizen."

Clell smiled. "All right. As a good citizen, I hereby volunteer to help you bring to justice Sheriff Hector and his cohorts in crime. Where do we start?"

"We start with the Boreas Gold Mining Company."

* * *

"Deputy, I appreciate your offer to guard the gold." Scott Matthews was the president of the BGMC. "But the amount of gold being shipped is valued at more than one hundred thousand dollars. I simply cannot allow you to use that money as bait."

"Mr. Matthews, you don't understand," Smoke said. "There will no risk for your gold because it won't actually be the bait. My friend and I will be."

Matthews frowned. "What do you mean?"

"When do you plan to ship the gold?" Smoke asked instead of answering the question.

"Thursday morning."

"What arrangements do you normally make when you have a shipment of gold? Who knows how much gold is being shipped? And when and how it is to be shipped?"

"Well, we notify the board of directors for the mine, so they know. We notify the teamsters and guards who will actually be taking the gold, so they would know. And we send a telegram ahead to the bank in Denver, so someone there would know."

"Does the newspaper carry an announcement of the shipment?"

"Oh. Yes, the announcements in the papers let the stockholders know how well the mine is doing. When it is a particularly large shipment, as this one is, those announcements sometimes bring in additional investments."

Smoke quickly formulated a plan. "All right. I want you to do everything just as you normally do it, but with one little change. I want you to tell all the same people you normally tell that you actually plan to send it out a day earlier, with only two private detectives guarding it. However, you should tell them that you don't want anyone else to know that."

"Deputy, didn't you just assure me that the gold wouldn't be used as bait?" Matthews asked.

"I did, and it won't be used as bait. The gold won't actually be in that wagon. It will still be here, safe, ready for you to ship the next day, just as planned."

Matthews smiled. "Oh. I think I see where you're going with this. You think that someone is going to let the secret out, don't you?"

"I don't just think it, I'm counting on it. When there is this much money involved, someone can be bribed."

"But what if that doesn't happen? What if there is no attempt to rob the gold?" Matthews asked.

"We'll carry a letter from you to the president of the bank where the gold is being shipped. He will announce that the secret shipment of gold has arrived safely, then you can ship the gold later without anyone knowing about it."

Matthews contemplated the proposal for a moment or two, then nodded. "All right. I'll go along with the plan. But what about you and your partner? Won't you be putting yourselves in a great deal of danger?"

"You let us worry about that."

Breckenridge

Amon Thomas scurried into the sheriff's office. The fussy little man was the railroad telegrapher.

Sheriff Hector looked up. "Yes, Mr. Thomas, what can I do for you?"

"I'm not sure."

"What do you mean, you aren't sure?"

"I intercepted a telegram this morning which gave all the details about the gold shipment from Boreas to Denver, and I brought that to you."

"Yes, you did. And I paid you for it, as you recall."

Thomas nodded. "Yes, sir, but I just now intercepted another telegram between Boreas and Denver, and it has me confused."

Hector frowned. "Confused, how?"

"You take a look at it and see what you think." Thomas handed the telegram to the sheriff.

TO FIRST BANK OF DENVER STOP
PURSUANT FIRST TELEGRAM STOP
OPERATION MOVED UP TWENTYFOUR
HOURS STOP

"Well, now," Sheriff Hector said with a smile. "I do believe they're trying to pull a fast one."

"Is this telegram worth something to you?" Thomas asked.

"Yes, Mr. Thomas, it is." Hector gave the telegrapher a twenty-dollar bill.

"Thank you," Thomas said, smiling broadly at his unexpected fortune.

Boreas

As the steel-rimmed wheels rolled away from the mine and across the hard-packed earth, they picked up dirt, causing a rooster tail of dust to stream out behind them. The wood of the wagon was bleached white. In the wagon bed were several boxes, covered by a tarpaulin. The boxes were empty, but covered they presented the illusion of actual cargo.

Clell was driving. "You really think Hector is going to make a try at this?"

Sitting to his right and wearing a sheepskin jacket against the cold, Smoke kept his eyes peeled. "Yeah, I do. After he returned to the jail and found you gone and me not dead, he had to know that he couldn't stay there any longer. And with this much money at stake, he has to make a try for it. He has no choice but to leave."

They drove on for another half hour, then Smoke saw that two men on horseback were trailing them. They were riding just fast enough to overtake the wagon, but not so fast so as to arouse suspicion.

"Clell, there are two men coming up behind us."

"Yeah, and there are two more ahead."

"This can't be a coincidence. Be ready. You take the front two, I'll take the ones in back," Smoke said.

As if validating Smoke's declaration, the four riders broke into a gallop, closing in with guns drawn.

"Now!" Smoke shouted. The time had come to put their plan into action.

Clell stopped the wagon, then leaped down from it, darting to his left and taking cover in the ditch that paralleled the road. Smoke did the same thing on the right side.

Gunfire started. The valley rang with the sound of shots, and gunsmoke roiled up from the ditches and over the road. None of the robbers dismounted. They were counting on superior numbers to carry the fight, and that was their fatal mistake.

The shooting was all over in less than thirty seconds when four horses, their saddles empty, came galloping by. Two bodies lay in the road ahead of the wagon, and two more were in the road behind.

"Ha!" Smoke shouted. He stood up. "Good shooting, Clell! We got 'em all!" With his Colt still in hand, he stepped into the middle of the road. "First, we'd better make sure they're all dead. I'll check the ones in the back, you check the ones in front."

"Maybe you'd better check them all, partner," Clell said from the other side of the road. His voice sounded strained.

"Clell?" Smoke holstered his gun and hurried over to him.

The physician turned gunman was sitting up in the ditch but leaning back against the opposite bank. He was holding his hand over a wound in his right side.

"You're hit! I'm sorry, I didn't realize that."

"Damn," Clell said. "Looks like I'm not going to get to spend that reward money, after all."

"Come on. Let me help you. I'll put you in the wagon and take you to a doctor."

"No. If you do that, I'll be dead before you get me to the wagon. Just let me lie here for a moment or two, then it'll be over."

"You don't know that, for sure."

Clell forced a chuckle. "Yes, I'm afraid I do. I'm a doctor, remember? From the location of this wound, my guess would be that both the spleen and the liver are involved. That means the wound is fatal."

Although he had heard of Clell Dawson, Smoke had only recently met him, and he believed that a friendship might have developed between them. Now, that wasn't to be.

"I wonder," Clell said.

"You wonder what?"

"If you hadn't taken my gun from my holster back in the saloon that day, do you think you could have beaten me?"

"I don't know," Smoke confessed. "That's why I took your gun."

Clell smiled. "I thought . . . that might be . . . the case," he said as he drew his last breath.

CHAPTER 31

From the *Bury Bulletin:*

SHERIFF KILLED IN THE LINE OF DUTY

Didn't Die Alone

(*Special from the Summit County Journal*)

Sheriff Jesse Hector of Summit County, Colorado, was killed on the 7th instant, while attempting to arrest the perpetrators of a string of deeds so foul as to defy description.

Though the gallant sheriff was shot down, he didn't fall until he had brought the most severe justice on his assassins. The four men who fell before his deadly shooting were Peter Kotter, Edward Spence, Merlin Morris, and Clell Dawson.

Dawson, discerning readers will notice, had become known throughout the West as a "fast gun." Said by witnesses to a few

of his fights, to be "quick as thought."
Dawson, Kotter, Spence, and Morris are
known to be the deadly gang which, over
the last two years, have not hesitated to use
dynamite in their deadly assaults against
their innocent victims.

PSR Ranch, office

"Damn," Richards said as he read the article.

"What is it?" Potter asked.

"That worthless sheriff got himself killed, and
Jensen is still alive."

"How do you know he's still alive?"

"Hector had some kind of plan in mind that involved Clell Dawson, but Dawson and the sheriff are
both dead, and there is no mention of Jensen."

"We've got to get rid of him, Josh," Potter said.
"He is going to be trouble, big trouble. We've got
plans, I've got plans. I intend to be governor of this
territory. I can't have him causing trouble."

"We have twelve full-time hands working here at the
ranch. The Bury city marshal and both his deputies
are on our payroll. I think it's time they begin to earn
their pay. We'll put the word out that Jensen is to be
shot on sight."

Stratton had listened to the conversation between
his partners without comment. Finally, he had something to say. "Yeah, well, there might be a problem
with that."

"There's no problem," Richards said. "If they don't
want to kill him, then they're fired."

"You said they are to kill him on sight. What does
he look like?"

Richards frowned. "What?"

"Smoke Jensen. What does he look like? There ain't a one of us that's ever actual seen 'im. We've heard what he looks like, big man, broad shoulders, muscular, light hair, but there can't none of us say that's for sure."

"Muley is right," Potter said. "There ain't none of us that really knows what he looks like."

"I ain't worried about that," Richards bragged. "There's enough folks that has seen 'im that we'll get word when he comes around. And he will come around, you can damn well count on that. I intend to be ready for 'im when he comes."

Denver, early spring 1874

Marshal Holloway knew Smoke had spent the winter months with Preacher and obviously hadn't shaved or cut his hair in that time. His hair fell almost to his shoulders, and he wore a full beard. That changed his appearance quite a bit, but Holloway knew him right away despite that.

The marshal was glad to see Smoke. After a heartfelt greeting, he looked at the wanted poster Smoke had given him.

WANTED
DEAD OR ALIVE
The Outlaw and Murderer

SMOKE JENSEN

$10,000 REWARD
Contact the Sheriff at Bury, Idaho Territory.

"Don't worry about it, Smoke. I'll get these pulled," Holloway said.

"No, don't pull them, Marshal. Leave them out there."

"What?" Marshal Holloway replied. "Why in heaven's name would you want to do that?"

"As you can see, the reward is being posted by the sheriff of Bury, Idaho. I've never been there, but that tells me where Potter, Stratton, and Richards are. I know they're behind this, and they've either lied to the sheriff or they have him in their pocket. Either way, I want to play this out, so don't do anything to stop it."

"Ten thousand dollars is a lot of money, Smoke. You'll have every bounty hunter in the West looking for you. This much money will bring out people who've never thought about bounty hunting before."

"Including Buck West," Smoke said.

"Who?"

Smoke smiled. "Buck West. That's who I'm going to be calling myself for a while. I'm going to Bury to join the hunt for Smoke Jensen."

"Smoke, you're crazy as a loon. Did anyone ever tell you that?" Marshal Holloway asked with a little laugh.

Smoke chucked. "Some have told me a few times. Preacher has told me that more times than I can count."

"You should listen to that old coot more often. All right. If that's the way you want it, I won't do anything to call them in."

Holloway took a sheet of paper from his desk, wrote something on it, then gave it to Smoke. "But if you get picked up by a legitimate officer of the law, show him this."

> *To whom it may concern. Kirby "Smoke" Jensen is a deputy U.S. marshal working undercover on a case for me. If you have questions, contact by telegraph Uriah Holloway, United States Marshal, Denver, Colorado Territory.*

Somewhere between the Big Lost River and the Craters of the Moon, Idaho Territory

The bearded, long-haired man who called himself Buck West had left the train with his horse at Idaho Falls and had been riding for a few days since then, acting like a drifting bounty hunter would. When he came upon a trading post, he dismounted, tied his horse, and went inside.

He almost wished that he hadn't stopped. The place was dark, filthy, and filled with the stench of sour beer and rotgut whiskey. Smoke bought bacon, beans, and coffee from an ugly clerk who smelled as bad as his store.

He saw some wanted posters on the wall, including one for him. "Thirty thousand dollars for Smoke Jensen? Last one I saw was for ten thousand."

"I reckon they want him pretty bad," the clerk said.

"They who?" Smoke asked.

"The sheriff up in Bury."

"Still, thirty thousand dollars. That's a lot of money for a county sheriff to be puttin' up, don't you think?"

"Word I've heard is that there's some wealthy businessmen up in Bury that's actually the ones that's puttin' up the money."

"Why would they do that, do you think?"

"Damned if I know. I reckon they're just good citizens, is all."

"A man could sure do a lot with thirty thousand dollars," Smoke mused.

He thanked the clerk, moved to the bar, and ordered a glass of whiskey—not because he particularly wanted it, but because he wanted information and bartenders seldom talked to anyone who wasn't drinking.

"The good stuff," he told the bartender.

The man replaced one bottle and reached under the counter for another. "This here is the best we got." When Smoke nodded, he poured.

Smoke paid for the drink, then lifted the glass. It smelled like bear piss. Keeping a bland expression on his face, he took a sip, and decided that it tasted even worse.

"Come from the East, did you?" the bartender asked.

"What makes you think I came from the East?"

"That's the way you rode in."

Another voice asked, "Did you see four men riding together?" The question came from one of the cardplayers behind Smoke.

Smoke turned around, taking in the measure of the man. "As a matter of fact I did. And so did the Blackfeet."

"Blackfeet? Damn. You reckon the Injuns got them four?"

"I expect they did. I didn't hang around to see."

The man was astonished. "You mean you just rode off without so much as lending a hand?"

"I was just one more man. Nothin' I could've done to help."

"Then I reckon that makes you a coward, don't it?" the cardplayer said accusingly. The man stood up.

Smoke put the shot glass of bear piss on the rough bar slowly and deliberately. Obviously, his antagonist knew his way around guns. He was wearing two. One was low and tied down.

"I suppose you could say that," Smoke replied. "You could also say I was just being careful."

"Nah, you weren't careful. You was scared. You know what I think, slick? I think it makes you yellow." The man's dirty hands hovered over his guns. "I think I'll just kill you for that."

Smoke shook his head. "No, you won't. You might try to kill me, but you won't get the job done. Fact is, if you do try, you're goin' to wind up dead, yourself. Is that really what you want?"

Without another word, Smoke's challenger made a lightning-fast dip toward his gun, but Smoke's draw was faster than lightning. His pistol roared. The bullet plunged into the gunman's heart, and he was dead even before he collapsed over the table in front of him, scattering cards along with the greenbacks and coins in the pot.

The other men in the game didn't move as Smoke holstered his gun.

After a long moment, they began gathering up the money. One of them took hold of the dead man's coat and hauled him off the table and onto the floor.

The game went on.

CHAPTER 32

"Any of you other boys have an argument with me?" Smoke asked as the men at the table resumed playing.

No one responded to his offer.

"This man have a name?"

"Luke," one of the men said without looking up from the cards in his hand.

Smoke frowned. "Just Luke?"

"That's the only name any of us ever heard."

"Damn. It'll be hard collectin' a bounty on him if nobody knows his last name."

Finally, the speaker looked up at Smoke. "What makes you think he's got a price on his head?"

"His kind always do."

Curious, the cardplayer asked, "What's your name?"

"West. Buck West."

"You a bounty hunter, West?"

Smoke grinned a crooked grin. "Now just what gave me away," he asked sarcastically.

"What are you doin' this far away?"

"This far away from what?" Smoke asked.

"Everything. Hell, it's so far away we don't hardly get nobody to come around, not even outlaws."

"There's one up here, I reckon. I've been tracking that damn Smoke Jensen for a while now, and near as I can figure, he's most likely around here somewhere."

"That's funny. We been trackin' 'im, too. I would ask if you want some company, but you look like you ride alone."

"That's right."

Smoke looked at the dead gunman's body. His eyes were still open but had turned opaque. His mouth was open, as well.

Smoke made a motion toward him. "None of you feel like you need to avenge your friend here, do you? 'Cause you seem like a nice bunch of fellas, and I'd hate to kill any more of you."

"He warn't our friend. He was just someone we met up with out on the trail a week or so ago."

"Good. I reckon I'll be goin' now." Smoke turned and left the saloon.

The men watched as he rode away, ramrod straight in the saddle.

"That young feller is faster than greased lightning," one of them said.

"I think Potter needs to know about this man," another said. "I think I'll take me a ride later on. But I want to let that West feller get good and gone."

Later that same afternoon, a stranger rode up to the trading post and walked inside. He cradled a

Henry repeating rifle in the crook of his left arm. "I seen they was a fresh grave out back," he said to the barkeep. "Friend of yours?"

"No friend o' mine . . . or anybody else, near as I can figure."

"A man ought to have some kind of a marker though, don't you think?"

"I'll get around to it one of these days. Maybe. Luke was what they called him."

"Better than nothing," Preacher replied, grateful that it wasn't Smoke's grave. He didn't really expect it to be, but validation was always good. "I don't reckon he died of natural causes?"

"Not likely. You want to talk all day or buy a drink of whiskey?"

The old man tossed some change on the wide rough board bar. "Will that buy me a jug?"

"I reckon it will." The bartender put a jug of rotgut on the counter. "No, sir, this fella Luke fancied hisself a gunhand, but I guess he run up against somebody a lot faster than he was. A feller by the name of Buck West. Funny that I never heard of him, bein' that fast. But I expect people will be a knowin' him afore too long. Says he's a bounty hunter. I know this. He's one bad hombre to mess with."

"Fast, is he?"

"He was so fast you couldn't even see him draw. Ol' Luke didn't much more than touch the butt of his pistol when lead hit him in the center of his chest. He was dead before he hit the ground."

The old man smiled. He knew only one man that fast.

"Say, ain't I seen you before?" the bartender asked. "You're a mountain man, ain't you? Ain't so many of you ol' boys left."

"Not me, partner. I'm retired from the East. I came out here to pass my golden years amid the peace and quiet of these here beautiful mountains."

The bartender laughed. "And you're just as full of bull now as you was forty years ago, you old goat!"

The old man laughed. "Well, you just keep that information inside that head of yours and off your tongue. You do that and I won't tell nobody I know where old Jay Kelly retired to. You still got money on your head?"

"Yeah, but don't nobody aroun' here know that. I heard you got kilt. Heard you was shot all to hell and back, and crossed over the Great Divide."

"Part of it's true," Preacher said. "I did get shot up pretty bad and figured I was about to die, but a couple friends of mine managed to pull me through."

"Yeah, well, I'm glad to see you're still around, Preacher."

The old man nodded, picked up his jug of whiskey, and rode off.

Smoke followed the Big Lost River north, pushing hard to put as many miles as possible between himself and the trading post. He had a hunch that the cardplayers would be heading for Bury. They were bounty hunters, had even offered to let him join up with them in their quest for the thirty thousand dollars being offered for Smoke Jensen. He wondered how they would react if they knew just how close they had been to the very man they were looking for.

Smoke found himself a hidden vantage point where he could watch the trail and settled in for the evening. He built a hand-sized fire and fixed bacon and beans and coffee. Using tinder dry wood, the fire was virtually smokeless. He kept his coffee warmed over the coals.

Just at dusk, he heard the sounds of approaching riders. Three of them passed his hiding place at a slow pace, heading north toward the trading post at McKay. He watched, listening to the sounds of the steel-shod hooves fading into the settling dusk. Then, using his saddle for a pillow, he settled down for the night.

He wanted to take his time getting to Bury for two reasons. For one, he wanted the story of the shoot-out at the trading post to reach the right ears, namely those of Potter, Stratton, and Richards. Men like that could always use another gun, and he intended to be that gun. Two, he still had that nagging sensation of being followed. And it annoyed him. He knew—*felt*—someone was back there. He just didn't know who.

Bayhorse, Idaho Territory

It was the first community Smoke came to after leaving the trading post—just one short business street with more saloons than anything else. Tents and shacks and a few permanent-looking homes huddled to the north. Most of the shacks were so flimsily constructed it looked as if they would blow away in a stiff breeze.

He stabled his horse and taking his Henry repeating rifle, a change of clothing, and his saddlebags, walked toward the town's only hotel. After checking in, he went to a bathhouse, where a young Chinese man kept the water hot with additional buckets of water. After soaking off the dirt, he dressed in dark trousers, white shirt, and vest, and leaving his boots to be shined, stepped into the attached barbershop for a haircut.

"Cut it short," he told the barber. "And trim my beard."

"Passing through?" the barber asked.

"Could be, or I might stay. Mostly, I'm just drifting."

Being an observant man, and one raised on the frontier, the barber noticed Smoke's tied-down gun. He knew a fast gun when he saw one. And he knew the man sitting in his chair was a fast gun. He also knew the man was no tinhorn trying to make a name for himself. The butt of his pistol had no marks carved in the wood to signify kills, the way foolish young wannabe gunmen did.

There was something else about the young man. Confidence. And a cold air about him. Not unfriendly, just cold.

The barber started a friendly conversation. "If you're up here lookin' for silver, there's a big strike north and east of here. Close to the Lemhi River."

"Not for me," Smoke told him. "Too much work involved in that."

"Ha. You handy with them pistols?"

"Some folks say that."

"You head north from here, follow the Salmon

River to where it cuts to the Lemhi Range, then head east. You'll come up on the town of Bury."

Smoke mumbled, "Why would I want to go to Bury?"

"Maybe you don't. Then again, you might find work up there. From what I hear, three men up there seem partial to hirin' folks that's good with a gun. You might find Bury real interestin'."

"I might at that. By the way, how's the law in this town?" Smoke set the stage with that question.

"Tough when they have to be, but as long as it's a fair fight, they won't bother you."

"I never shot no one in the back," Smoke said, purposely making the response rather harsh.

"Wouldn't think you had. You don't have that look about you, that's for sure." The barber's voice was very bland.

"Where's the best place to eat?"

"Marie's, just up the street. Beef and beans and apple pie. Good-sized portions, too, and she don't charge an arm and a leg for 'em."

They weren't just good-sized portions; they were huge, and the food, though simple, was well prepared. The apple pie was delicious. Smoke pushed the empty plate away and leaned back in his chair, chosen because it was against the wall. He lingered over a third cup of coffee and watched the activity through the window.

He was waiting for the law to make an appearance, and he didn't have to wait long. The town marshal entered the café, and his deputy, carrying a sawed-off, double-barrel shotgun, was right behind him.

Smoke felt a momentary start. He recognized the

marshal. He had run across him back in Colorado, when working a case for Marshal Holloway. He had seen him only once, and that for a short period of time, but he remembered him. Smoke had been one of three deputy U.S. marshals working the case, though, and it was possible the marshal wouldn't recognize him.

The man sat across the same table as Smoke. "Coffee, Marie."

"Comin' right up, Marshal," the heavyset woman said. "What about you, sir? Your coffee need freshenin'?"

"I'm good, thanks," Smoke said, lifting his cup.

"You just passin' through?" the marshal asked.

"Yeah, though I might stay around a couple days, just to get some rest from the trail."

"What's your name?"

"There aren't any dodgers out on me."

"That's not what I asked. What's your name?"

"Buck West."

"You look like you know how to use that hogleg. Ever killed anyone?"

"Nobody that wasn't tryin' to kill me." Smoke placed the marshal's name. It was Dooley. From what he remembered, Dooley was a fair man.

Dooley pointed toward the north. "Up at that end of town, you'll find the better houses, the ones that's been painted, and kept up. Do you know anyone who lives there? Any friends or relatives?"

"Nope. Don't know a soul in this entire town."

"Then I'll thank you to stay away from 'em. Decent folks livin' there, and I got a feelin' you're the kind of man that draws trouble."

Smoke started to reply, but Dooley held up his hand. "I ain't sayin' you'll be the one to start it. But I don't reckon you would run from it, neither."

"Not likely."

The marshal finished his cup of coffee, then set the cup down and stared at Smoke for a long moment. "Son, I got the feelin' me and you have met somewhere. The name Buck West don't ring a bell, but your face is awful familiar."

Smoke chuckled. "That's 'cause I've got what folks call a warm, friendly face."

The marshal nodded. "Sure you do," he said sarcastically.

CHAPTER 33

PSR Ranch, office

"You say this fella's name is Buck West?" Richards asked.

"That's what Cornett told me," Potter said. "He's blinding fast with a gun, too."

"As fast as Smoke Jensen, do you suppose?"

"Well, he drew on Luke Simmons, and they say Luke started his draw first, but this man West shot him before he could even get his hand wrapped around his pistol."

"Damn. Simmons was fast. That's why we hired him. Luke swore he was faster than Smoke Jensen."

Potter smiled. "Yeah, maybe he was. And that means this man, Buck West, is probably faster too."

"I wonder how we can get in touch with West."

"There's no need to. It's more than likely he'll get in touch with us. After he kills Smoke Jensen for us."

"Yeah." Richards nodded. "Yeah, that's right, isn't it? Potter, our problem may soon be over."

"I've already got my campaign pitch that I'll make to the people of Idaho. I helped rid the West of the murderer and outlaw, Smoke Jensen."

"You don't need to campaign to the people. Just to President Grant."

Potter grinned. "I don't even need to do that. As long as I can buy off his brother-in-law."

Bayhorse

Smoke finished his supper and headed down to the saloon to have a beer.

He was standing there, slowly nursing his beer, when a man standing at the other end of the bar turned toward him and spoke. "Hey, saddle bum, are you plannin' on drinkin' that beer or are you just gonna stand there and look at it with your face hanging out?"

Smoke ignored him.

"Boy, don't you hear me talkin' to you?" the cowboy asked, his voice even more belligerent.

Smoke turned. "I'm sorry. Were you talking? I thought I just heard you fart, and I'm too much of a gentleman to have commented on it."

The cowboy took a step backward, a puzzled look on his face.

Smoke knew the type. The cowboy was big and muscular, and probably used to getting his way. Smoke was sure he had been a bully all his life.

The cowboy's frown deepened. "What did you say, mister?"

"Don't you speak English?"

The barkeep leaned forward and whispered urgently, "That's Harry Carson, stranger."

"Is that supposed to mean something to me?" Smoke asked, not bothering to keep his voice to a whisper.

"And his buddy is Wade Phillips," the barkeep offered.

The deputy who had been with Marshal Dooley earlier that day slipped away from the bar and out of the line of possible gunfire, taking his beer with him.

"Carson, back off. Drink your drink and leave me be," Smoke said.

Not wanting to be left out of the fun, Phillips stuck his ugly nose into it. "You've got a smart mouth, you know that, buddy?"

Smoke turned to face the two men, forcing a grin. "It would appear to me that, somehow, we've gotten off on the wrong foot. Why don't the two of you let me buy you a beer, and we just drop this now?"

"Oh yeah, you'd like that, wouldn't you? But there ain't no way we're gonna drop this," Carson said confidently. "You done smart mouthed me, and I don't intend to let that go."

"I'm sorry to hear that. Like I told you, I'm willing to drop this. I'm not looking for trouble, but if I'm pushed into it, so be it."

"Oh, yeah. You're wearin' that fancy gun rig, but I bet you ain't got the sand to duke it out."

Smoke's smile was faint. He knew that both men realized neither of them could beat him if it came to gunplay, so they would push him into a fight. And if he didn't fight them in their own game, he would be branded a coward.

Smoke took off his gun belt. Spotting the deputy, he handed the belt and the holstered gun to him. "Look after this, would you?"

"Be glad to, West. But watch these two boys. They fight dirty."

Smoke finished his beer. "Yeah, well so do I."

With a wide, confident smile spread across his face, Carson had watched and listened to the exchange between Smoke and the deputy. "All right, so—"

Smoke smashed the empty beer mug into Carson's face. The heavy mug shattered, breaking the man's nose on impact. He jabbed the broken edges into the man's cheek, sending the bully screaming and bleeding to the sawdust-covered floor.

Phillips came toward Smoke, shouting, "You son of a—"

Smoke hit him with a short, brutal punch, preventing him from finishing his profanity. Powerful in his own right, Smoke didn't like to fight with his fists, but sometimes it was the only option.

Phillips dropped to his knees and Smoke brought his knee up. The crunch of broken bones was loud and Phillips went down and out.

The fight was over in a handful of seconds. Carson lay squalling and bleeding on the floor beside the unconscious Phillips. Smoke turned around. Marshal Dooley was standing by his deputy.

"Any law against a fair fight, Marshal?" Smoke asked as he retrieved his gunbelt. "It was two against one."

"And they were outnumbered at those odds," Dooley said with a smile. "No, West, there is no law against it, but there is something about you that I can't quite put my finger on."

"Pueblo," Smoke said.

"What?"

"Marshal, can we go somewhere to have a little private conversation?"

"All right. I don't know what this is all about, but I have to confess that I'm damn curious. Let's go to my office."

They left the saloon together and walked the few steps to the marshal's office.

"Coffee?" Marshal Dooley asked a few minutes later.

"Don't mind if I do," Smoke replied.

Dooley stepped over to the stove and, using a pad, removed the blue steel coffee pot. He poured two cups and handed one of them to Smoke. "Now, what is this about Pueblo?"

"Two years ago a man named Keefer led a bunch of his men into town and announced they were taking over. You were one man against eight, so you asked Marshal Holloway to send you some help. He sent Cephus Prouty, Lee Tanner, and—"

"Smoke Jensen!" Dooley said, pointing at Buck. "You're Smoke Jensen."

"Yes."

"Damn! I thought I recognized you. And now you're a wanted man. What happened? Where did you go wrong?"

"The only people who want me are some men up in Bury. Evidently they have enough money, power, and influence to get the sheriff there to put paper out on me. As it turns out, I'm looking for them, too. I have something here I want you to see."

Smoke pulled out the note that Marshal Holloway had written and showed it to Dooley.

The lawman read it, then looked up and said, "So, you're working undercover?"

"Yes. If you need to validate that, you can contact Marshal Holloway."

"There's no need for that. You didn't have to tell me who you were." Dooley handed the note back. "I'll keep your secret."

"I appreciate that, Marshal."

"But I have to warn you, the two men you ran into in the saloon? They aren't going to let this pass. Look out for them, Jensen."

"Thanks for the warning."

CHAPTER 34

The marshal's warning was correct. Smoke had just stepped out into the street when he saw two men walking toward him, their hands near their pistols, ready to draw. Doors and windows facing the street banged shut as the townspeople scurried to get out of the line of fire from the bullets they believed were about to fly.

"You know, we can stop this now if you want to," Smoke called out to them. "There's no reason either of you have to die today."

"What makes you think we're the ones who'll die?" Phillips asked defiantly.

Smoke's smile had an unnerving effect on the two men. No more than fifty feet separated them from him. He was close enough to see the sweat on their faces. Phillips was licking his lips nervously, and there was a visible tic in Carson's jaw.

Smoke studied his two adversaries. He knew he could not afford to draw first. He had to let them make the initial move in order for it to be called self-defense.

"Have you thought you might be the one to die?" Carson asked, trying, by bravado, to ease his own fear.

"Well, we all have to die sometime," Smoke acknowledged. "Whether or not it happens for you two today is up to you. There's no need for you to turn your backs on reason and good sense. Why don't you come into the saloon and have a beer with me? I made that offer before our little scuffle, but you turned it down."

"You want to show some reason?" Carson said. "Beg, and we'll let you turn tail and run away."

"No, I don't think I'd like to do that." Smoke's face creased with an easy smile.

"Then die!" Phillips shouted as he clawed at his gun.

Smoke let him clear leather before he drew his own Colt. He fired twice, the first bullet hitting Phillips in the belly, the second one sending out a little spurt of blood as it plunged into the center of his chest.

Phillips fell backward, mortally wounded.

Carson, obviously surprised by Phillips's draw, had not reached for his gun at the same time. He watched it all in shock.

His mouth and eyes open in fear, he looked toward Smoke still holding the smoking pistol in his hand.

"Back off, Carson," Smoke said easily. He pouched the iron. "Just because your friend died today doesn't mean you have to."

"I ain't agoin' to draw. I'm agoin', I'm agoin'!"

Carson held his arms forward, palms facing Smoke as if pushing him away.

"You're smarter than I gave you credit for," Smoke said.

Carson turned and started to walk away, and seeing that, Smoke also turned and started toward Marshal Dooley, who had watched everything from the porch in front of the jail.

With a look of triumph on his face, Carson pulled his gun.

"Look out!" Dooley suddenly shouted.

Smoke spun quickly, drawing his pistol and firing before Carson could pull the trigger.

The shock he felt was etched clearly on his face before he collapsed, twitched once, and then lay still.

"Damn. How did he do that?" someone asked. "Carson already had his gun out and was fixin' to shoot!"

Shortly after the echo of the last shot reverberated through the street, the townspeople came streaming back out to the street from where they'd taken cover. Like carrion to a recent kill, they gathered around the two men who lay dead in the street.

Smoke walked back toward Marshal Dooley. "Thanks for the warning."

"You know that beer you were going to buy them?" Dooley mentioned.

"Yeah?"

"How 'bout you buy one for me and my deputy, instead?"

Smoke chuckled. "I'd be glad to."

Fifteen minutes later, Smoke, Dooley, and the marshal's deputy were sitting at a table in the back of the saloon.

"I want you to run me out of town," Smoke said quietly.

Dooley frowned. "Why?"

"It wouldn't look all that good for you to be friendly with a wanted man, now would it? I wouldn't want it getting back to Richards and the others that we were pals."

Dooley's frown changed to a small nod. "Yeah, I see what you mean."

"Besides, it might look good for us in the next election if we ran out a fast gun like Buck West," the deputy added.

Dooley smiled. "It might at that."

"You have to do it in public, though," Smoke said.

Dooley looked around the saloon. Twelve to fifteen other customers were in the saloon, in addition to the bartender and the working girls. Close to twenty in total.

"What about here?" Dooley asked. "Is this place public enough?"

Smoke looked around. "I'd say so."

"You 'bout finished with your beer?" Dooley asked.

Smoke drained the last of it, set the mug down, then ran the back of his hand across his lips. "I am now."

Marshal Dooley stood up, then looked down at Smoke, speaking loudly enough for everyone in the saloon to hear him. "All right, West, you asked me to let you stay long enough to have a beer, and you've had it. I'll not have my town filled up with would-be gunfighters lookin' for you so's they can make themselves a reputation. I want you to get your gear together and get out of town."

"You're throwin' me out of town, Marshal?" Smoke replied.

Dooley crossed his arms. "I am doing just that."

"What if I don't want to leave?" Smoke asked belligerently.

"You don't have that option, West."

"This is a right friendly place you have here," Smoke said with a sneer on his face.

"As a matter of fact, it is. But there is somethin' about you that just invites trouble, boy." At Smoke's sputter, Dooley held up a hand. "I know, I know. You didn't start the fight that got Carson and Phillips killed. But you didn't avoid it, either, and if you hadn't ever come into this town, it wouldn't have happened in the first place."

"All right, all right. I'm goin'," Smoke muttered. He stood up and strolled to the door.

"Damn, did you see that?" he heard someone in the saloon say. "Marshal Dooley just stood Buck West down."

"I've always said the marshal has sand," another replied.

Smoke kept a passive expression on his face until he stepped outside, then he smiled. His next stop would be Bury, but he wasn't in a hurry. He wanted the word about him to spread first.

One of the witnesses to the gunfight between Smoke and the two challengers was an old mountain man named Lobo. Nobody knew Lobo's real name, and some insisted he didn't know it himself. He came by the name because it was rumored that he'd once lived with a band of wolves, a story that he neither confirmed nor denied.

Leaving Bayhorse, he met up with a band of mountain men camping at the base of Gray Rock Mountain, about halfway between the Sawtooth Wilderness area and the town of Bayhorse. He told them about the gunfight he had witnessed. "Fastest thing I ever seed. Those two poor sumbitches din't have no idee what they was lettin' theyselves in for. Why, that boy snatched his gun out of the holster so fast it was a blur. I don't believe hummin'birds can beat their wings no faster than he got his gun out."

"What was the boy's name?" Beartooth had not had a tooth in his head in over forty years.

"West, his name was. Buck West."

"No, it warn't," Preacher said. "His name is Smoke. Smoke Jensen."

"Smoke Jensen. Ain't that your boy?" Greybull asked.

"Yeah."

"Why is he callin' hisself Buck West?" Lobo asked.

"'Cause them three that kilt his pa has paid the sheriff up in Bury to put paper out on 'im. So he's took to callin' hisself Buck West. But he ain't runnin' from 'em, I can tell you that. He's headin' straight to Bury, and he plans to settle scores with Potter, Stratton, and Richards."

"It don't bother him none that they's three of them to his one?" Beartooth asked.

"Four of 'em . . . no, five if you count the sheriff and his deputy. 'Cause I'm tellin' you right now them two is in the pocket of Potter, Stratton, and Richards, sure as a gun is iron," Greybull pointed out.

"Hell, there's a lot more of 'em than that," Lobo said. "They's all the cowboys that works out at the ranch for Richards, and then, I wouldn't be surprised if half the town wasn't on Stratton's payroll."

Preacher nodded. "That's how come I been trackin' Smoke."

"Does the boy know you been followin' him?" Pugh asked.

"Damn, Pugh, you want to stand downwind a mite? When the hell's the last time you took a bath?" Lobo had little room to talk, since he hadn't taken a bath in three months.

"Why are you so damn persnickety? Hell, I took me a bath back in seventy, it was. Or maybe it was seventy-one. I don't rightly recollect exactly when it was."

"Four years? How come you ain't molded?" Beartooth asked.

"Prob'ly 'cause even the mold can't stand to be close to him," Greybull said.

"Yeah, well, that still don't answer the question I asked Preacher," Pugh said. "Does the boy know you been followin' him?"

"No, he don't know. He'd run me off if he knowed that I was followin' him. More'n likely he'd be worried maybe I might get hurt or somethin'. I was shot up pretty bad some time back, and Smoke, bein' the good boy he is, was some troubled by it."

"Yeah, well, if it was just you, I could see how, maybe, he might be a mite worried. But they's five of us now," Greybull declared.

Preacher was surprised. "You men don't have to take a hand in this. I mean, it ain't your fight."

"That's a hell of a thing for you to say to friends. We been together in these mountains for damn near fifty years," Beartooth said.

"Yeah," Greybull said. "Well, not actual together, seein' as we'd go most a year without seein' one another 'ceptin' at the rendezvous and such. But Beartooth is right. Iffen it's your fight, then by damn, it's our fight, too."

"All right," Preacher agreed. "If you boys feel that way, I'd be downright proud to have you come along."

"Good." Greybull voiced it as the others nodded in agreement.

"Now that that's settled, why don't we just amble on over to Bury? If I know Smoke, and I reckon I know 'im better'n about anyone in the world, seein' as I raised 'im, why he'll take his time gettin' there. More'n likely, he'll lay back in the timber for a day or so and give the situation a good lookin' over."

"What do you figure we should do, Preacher?" Lobo asked.

"I figure we'll cross the Lost River Range, head for the flats and turn north, then make camp in the narrows just south of Bury."

"I got me an idee," Pugh said.

"What is it?"

"Once we get there, whyn't I get Deadlead and Powder Pete to join up with us?" Pugh suggested. "I know where at they're camped right now."

"Sounds like a pretty good idee to me," Lobo said. "What do you think, Beartooth?"

"I like the idea, but it's up to Preacher. This here is his range."

Preacher nodded his agreement. "Yeah, Pugh, go ahead and do it."

"We need to get started," Greybull said. "As old as we are, hell, if we wait around here much longer some of us is liable to die of old age afore we get there."

The group of mountain men made their camp in the timber of the Lemhi Range about ten miles south of Bury.

"So, Pugh, are you goin' to go find Deadlead and Powder Pete?" Beartooth asked as soon as they set up.

"Yeah, but I thought maybe I'd take me a bath first, seein' as you folks is so put off by my smell and all."

"You ain't takin' a bath here, are you? 'Cause I'm afraid if you done that, you'd more than likely kill the fish for five miles downstream." Beartooth grinned a toothless grin.

"You just a barrel of laughs, ain't you?" Pugh said as he took off his clothes, then waddled down to the stream.

"I reckon I'll ride on into Bury to buy some bacon, beans, coffee, flour, and salt," Lobo said. "And while I'm there, I'll also have me a look around the place, keep my ears open for talk of anything that might be of some use to us."

"They's a tribe of Flathead Indians some east of here," Preacher said. "I think I'll ride over there for a bit."

"What you going there for?" Beartooth asked.

"Just to visit some. I might have me a daughter there, or else mayhaps a granddaughter, or even a great grandkid. Injuns gets started whelping pretty early, so it can build up real quick."

Lobo put his hands on his hips and frowned at Preacher. "Well, do you or don't you?"

"Do I or don't I what?"

"Have any Injun kids or grandkids there?"

Preacher gave a very small smile. "Don't know for sure, but it's more 'n likely that I do."

Pugh came back from the water, dripping wet, but considerably cleaner.

"Damn, there really was a man under all that dirt," Lobo said.

"Yeah? Well, has it crossed anyone's mind that I'm the cleanest one here?" Pugh asked. "Don't none of you get too close to me. I wouldn't want to get none of your dirt or stink on me."

"So, you're good for another four years now, right, Pugh?" Lobo asked with a laugh.

"If I live that long," Pugh said, giving a serious answer to a joking question.

CHAPTER 35

Bury

Muley Stratton was in the office of the town's only newspaper as the week's edition was being printed. He watched as the editor, Harold Denham, pulled one sheet off the Washington Hand Press, put it on the stack of papers already printed, then put a blank page on the bed and pulled down the typeset platen to print the next copy of what would be a two-hundred-copy press run.

Stratton wasn't a newspaperman, but he was a businessman, and as such, he owned the *Bury Bulletin*. He picked up one of the completed papers and perused the stories, finding one that caught his interest. "Where did this story come from?"

"The copy came from the Associated Press, Mr. Stratton," Denham said. "It's where all the stories come from, unless they are local."

"Do you think it's true?"

"Well, I see no reason why it wouldn't be true. The stories are pretty well vetted, otherwise the paper originating the story would be dropped by the AP. Nobody wants that."

Stratton nodded, then left the office.

PSR Ranch Office

"Look at this." Stratton handed the paper to Richards. "Seems to me, this is the man we need to get." Richards read the article Stratton pointed out.

SHOOT-OUT IN THE STREETS OF BAYHORSE

Two Men Killed

Gunshots rang out in the street of Bayhorse Thursday last, when two local men, Harry Carson and Wade Phillips, confronted Buck West. Though West was a stranger to the citizens of the town, he has inscribed his name indelibly in the memory of all who witnessed the gunfight.

Challenged by Carson and Phillips, it is reported that West made every effort to avoid gunplay, even offering, as an act of friendship, to buy a beer for each of the two men who accosted him. Carson and Phillips refused the offer and carried their challenge to fruition. Doing so was a fatal mistake on the part of the two men, for even though they drew first, West was able to dispatch them through the skillful and deadly employment of his pistol. Marshal

Dooley, himself a witness to the events herein described, declared that as it was justifiable homicide. The gunfight clearly being an act of self-defense, no charges will be brought against West.

It is said that Buck West is a bounty hunter in search of the outlaw and murderer, Smoke Jensen. Jensen's expert employment of the pistol is well known throughout the West, and though the name of Buck West is not yet known, those who observed his performance in the gunfight in the street of the town of Bayhorse are in agreement that his efficacy with the handgun must surely be commensurate with the proficiency so often demonstrated by Smoke Jensen.

Richards looked up after reading the article. "What do we know about this man, West?"

Stratton frowned. "What do we need to know about him? Cornett told us he was faster'n Luke. And you read it yourself, he is looking for Smoke Jensen. Those who saw him say that he is as good as Jensen."

"That's what they said about Kid Austin and Clell Dawson . . . and you know what happened to them. How do you propose to get in touch with this"— Richards checked the newspaper article again to get the name—"Buck West?"

"Why is it necessary for us to get in touch with him? According to the news articles that have appeared in papers all over the West, he is already looking for Smoke Jensen. If he finds him and kills him, then he'll be coming here to see Sheriff Reece. When that happens, our troubles are over."

"Yeah." Richards stroked his chin as he examined the paper for a moment longer. "I wish I was as confident as you are."

"What have we got to lose? If this man West doesn't do the job, we aren't out any money."

"No, but we will still have Smoke Jensen to deal with."

Bury

In his office, Sheriff Dolan Reese was reading the same article that Josh Richards had just read. Reese tried unsuccessfully to place Buck West, but he couldn't come up with a face to put with the name, and that was unusual. He knew most of the outlaws and gunhands throughout the West. He had been a sheriff in three other communities before coming to Bury.

But it wasn't just because he was a sheriff and it was his job to know the outlaws, for he hadn't always been a sheriff. In the past, he had ridden on the other side of the line as an outlaw. As a matter of fact, he had ridden the outlaw trail more times than he had worn the star of a lawman.

Reece knew about gunfighters because he was one of the best. He had been in gunfights as an outlaw and as a lawman, and he wasn't against selling his guns to the highest bidder. In the past, he had taken a lawman's job primarily as a way of *hiding* from the law, but most recently the highest bidder *was* the law, or at least the law as established by Potter, Stratton, and Richards. They had hired him and were paying him almost ten times more money than any other law position paid, no matter where it was located. In addition, there had been times when the "Big Three", as they were often called, had paid him bonuses for special jobs.

They had given him a thousand dollars to put paper out on Smoke Jensen, and they had raised the reward quite often. It was currently at thirty thousand dollars.

Sometimes Reese daydreamed about facing down Smoke Jensen. His daydreams about such an event predated the reward that the PSR had put out for Jensen. In the past, he'd contemplated going against the man strictly for the notoriety killing Jensen would bring him.

Whoever did kill Smoke Jensen would be famous all right. Jensen was one of, if not *the best* known gunfighters ever. If Reese made money from his gun, just think how much he could sell it for if word got around that *he* was the one who had killed Smoke Jensen.

That would be after he collected the thirty-thousand-dollar reward. But Buck West might be in his way.

Reese's thoughts were interrupted when his deputy Adam Rogers came into the office, calling out, "Hey, Sheriff, you ever heard of this fella Buck West?"

"No, I haven't."

"I haven't, either, but that's near 'bout all anyone

in town is talkin' about, especially since Denham run that story about 'im in his paper."

"It isn't Denham's paper."

Rogers sat in the chair in front of Reese's desk. "Well, yeah, I know that Stratton owns the paper just like he purt' nigh owns ever'thing else in town. But you know what I'm talkin' 'bout. I mean Denham does all the work. Anyhow, what do you think about West?"

"I don't think anything at all about him."

"Don't it kinda make you wonder though? I mean, him bein' as good as the paper says and all. How come neither me or you ever heard of 'im?"

Reese shrugged. "You got me, pardner."

"You know what I think?"

"No, but I reckon you're goin' to tell me."

Rogers ignored the sheriff's attempt at humor. "I think it's more'n likely this here West feller ain't really all that good."

"Why do you think that?"

"Well, first of all, like I said, we ain't neither one of us ever heard of 'im. You, bein' as good as you are, and bein' as you've been almost ever'where, if he was really as good as the paper makes out in this story, why, you woulda heard of him. I mean, don't you think?"

"It would seem so," Reese agreed.

"Besides which, them two he kilt down in Bayhorse? Well, I knowed Harry Carson, and he was a big man what liked to fight, only mostly what he liked to fight with was his fists, is all. He warn't no gun hand. If you ask me, this here Buck West is gettin' hisself a reputation based on doin' nothin' more'n killin' people that don't know one end of the gun from the other."

"Yeah." Reese agreed with his deputy, primarily because he wanted to agree with him. He didn't want to think about anyone killing Smoke Jensen before he got the chance.

CHAPTER 36

Smoke rode down the three long blocks of the business district of Bury at midmorning. Stores and saloons lined both sides of the wide street.

He had spent the last several days and nights camped some miles away, watching the one road that led into the little town. During that time, he'd watched the stagecoaches that came and went twice a day, primarily serving the outlying towns as a connector to the railroad in Bury. Freight wagons, peddlers, and tinkers had rolled in and out, too.

The first place he went was the livery stable, where he arranged a stall for his horse. Stashing most of his gear in Seven's stall, he took his rifle and saddlebags and started toward the hotel. On the way, he passed a very pretty, dark-haired, hazel-eyed young woman. He smiled at her and she blushed.

Smoke paused just long enough for her to walk on toward the edge of town, then he crossed the street to get a better look at her without her knowing that she was being observed. He saw her push open the gate on a white picket fence and walk up onto the porch of a small house. Going inside, she disappeared from view.

"Nice," he muttered.

"Yeah, she is," a voice said from behind him.

Turning, Smoke saw two men. Identified by the stars they wore on their shirts, he knew they were the sheriff and his deputy.

"I'm Sheriff Reese. This is Rogers, one of my deputies. I don't know you."

"There's no reason you should know me, Sheriff. My name is Buck West."

"So you're Buck West. Yeah, I've heard of you. You're the gunhand who shot down Carson and Phillips back in Bayhorse."

"I don't deny that, Sheriff, but if you check with Marshal Dooley, he'll tell you that the shooting was justifiable."

"Whether it was or wasn't is none of my business, since it didn't happen in my jurisdiction," Reese said. "But what happens here is. So tell me, West, how long are you planning on staying in my town?"

Smoke frowned. "Your town?"

"Yeah, my town."

"I've heard that there are three men here who might have a better claim to this town than you do. But, be that as it may, I'm not sure I can answer you as to how long I'm going to be here, seeing as it all depends."

"Depends on what?"

Smoke shrugged. "On how long it takes me to get rested up and resupplied. Also, I'll need to find out more about this Smoke Jensen character, and how I go about collecting the reward money."

Reese smiled. "Yeah, I heard you were a bounty hunter. Well, if you are planning on collecting money on Smoke Jensen, the first thing you're gonna have to do is find him."

"Oh, I'll find him, all right," Smoke said.

"Will you now?" Sheriff Reese asked.

Smoke smiled. "I think I can just about guarantee that, Sheriff."

Rogers had heard enough and couldn't keep silent any longer. "You know what I think? I think you're all talk."

Smoke looked at him. "Is that right?"

"Yeah, that's right. And here's another thing. You stay away from Sally Reynolds. I got my eyes on her. Besides, she likes me."

"So that pretty lady I was just looking at is Sally Reynolds, is she? Well, that's good to know. Thanks for telling me."

"Miss Reynolds is our schoolteacher," Reese said. "And I'm pretty sure that someone like her wouldn't want nothing to do with no damn bounty hunter like you, West."

"Yeah. You're probably right, Sheriff. Anything else I need to know about Bury and its citizens?"

"Just stay out of trouble."

"I'll try and do that, Sheriff." Smoke smiled, though the smile seemed more challenging than friendly. "The problem, or at least I've been told this, is that I'm the kind of man trouble seems to seek out."

"Yeah, I wouldn't be surprised."

Without losing the smile, Smoke touched the brim

of his hat in what was almost a mocking salute, then turned his back on the two men and walked on up the boardwalk toward the hotel.

"I don't like him," Rogers said after Smoke was out of earshot. "I think I'll kill him."

"I don't like him, either," Reese said. "But you don't do nothing until you're told to do it. You understand that, Rogers?"

"Yes, sir."

"I just saw Stratton ride in. I'm going to go see him and find out what he thinks about this man West."

"What's your impression of him?" Stratton asked after Sheriff Reese told him that Buck West was in town.

Reese hesitated. He didn't care much for Buck West, but he knew better than to play the game any way other than straight. He leveled with Stratton. "I think he's who he says he is. And I think the rumors are right. He's one hell of a gunfighter."

"How do you know?"

"Mr. Stratton, you know me, and you know my background. I've been around enough gunfighters to know one when I see him."

"Do you think he could take Smoke Jensen in a gunfight?"

"He might just be able to do that."

"Good. But keep an eye on him."

"Yes, sir."

*   *   *

In the hotel, Smoke bathed and shaved. After getting dressed, he buckled his gunbelt around his waist and tied down the low-riding holster. That done, he stepped out onto the boardwalk and carefully looked all around him, as was his habit, before heading for the café, choosing that over the hotel dining room.

He took a seat inside, and saw that he was but one table over from Miss Sally Reynolds. Because the normal lunch hour was over, they were the only customers in the café. He smiled at her. "Pleasant day."

"Very," Sally replied. "Now that school is out for the summer, it's especially so."

"I regret that I don't have more formal education. The War Between the States put a halt to that."

"It's never too late to learn, sir."

"You're a schoolteacher?"

"Yes, I am. And you . . . ?"

Smoke gave a slight smile. "I'm what they call a drifter, I'm afraid."

"Oh, I think *adventurer* would be a more accurate term than *drifter*," the young woman said, meeting his gaze.

Smoke chuckled. "Adventurer? Yes, I'll take that."

"Why do you wear a gun?"

"Force of habit, I suppose."

"I sometimes think many of the men who wear guns do so for show, without adequate skill to handle them. But I don't get that impression about you."

Smoke leaned back in the chair. "What makes you think that?"

"I don't know. It's just a feeling I have. Are you skilled with a pistol, sir?"

"Some say that I am."

Conversation waned as the waitress brought their lunches.

Before conversation could resume, Deputy Rogers entered the café, sat down at the counter, and ordered coffee. Seeing Sally and Smoke close together, albeit at different tables, vexed him, and he showed his irritation by glaring at them.

"Will you be in Bury long?" Sally asked Smoke.

"All depends, ma'am."

"Lady of your quality shouldn't be talking to no bounty hunter, Miss Reynolds," Rogers said. "It ain't fittin'."

"Mr. Rogers," Sally said coldly. "The gentleman and I are merely exchanging pleasantries over lunch, and I'll not be told by anyone who I can and who I can't speak to, whether you wear a lawman's badge or not."

Rogers flushed, placed his coffee mug on the counter, and abruptly left the café.

"I'm afraid, Miss Reynolds, that Deputy Rogers doesn't like me very much," Smoke said.

"Why?" Sally asked bluntly.

"I imagine it's because I make him feel somewhat insecure."

"Very interesting statement from a man who professes to have little formal education, Mister . . ." She paused and chuckled. "I seem to be at a disadvantage here. You know my name, but I don't know yours."

"It's West, ma'am. Buck West."

"Buck West? I believe I read an article about you in the paper, and I was right. You do know how to handle a pistol. That is, if the article is factual."

THIS VIOLENT LAND
333

"Did it have anything to do with a little fracas over in Bayhorse?"

"It did."

"Then, yes, ma'am, the article is factual."

"Are you a bounty hunter, Mr. West?"

"Bounty hunter, cowhand, gunhand, sometimes trapper. Whatever it takes to make a living."

"Oh, then I was right about the other thing, too. You really are an adventurer. A soldier of fortune, one might say."

Smoke grinned. "I think your appellations may be more romantic than realistic."

"*Appellations*? Oh my. And you say you aren't educated?"

"I read a great deal."

"Never underestimate the value of self-education, Mr. West."

"You're from east of the Mississippi River, ma'am?"

"New Hampshire. I came out here a few years ago after replying to an advertisement in a local paper. The pay is much better out here than back home."

"I sort of know where New Hampshire is. I would imagine living is much more civilized back there."

"To say the least, Mr. West. And also much duller."

"Would you mind taking a walk with me, Miss Reynolds?" Smoke blurted. "And please don't think I'm being too forward."

"I would love to walk with you, Mr. West."

The sun was high in the afternoon sky and Sally opened her parasol as they strolled along the street a few minutes later.

"Do you ride, Miss Reynolds?" Smoke asked.

"Oh, yes. But I have yet to see a sidesaddle here."

Smoke nodded. "They aren't too common a sight out here."

As they walked, his spurs jangled.

"Which employment are you currently pursuing, Mr. West? Bounty hunter, cowhand, gunhand, or trapper?"

"Not many beaver here in Bury," Smoke replied with a little chuckle.

A group of hard-driving cowboys picked that moment to burst into town, whooping and hollering and kicking up clouds of dust as they spurred their horses, sliding to a stop in front of one of the saloons.

Smoke pulled Sally into a doorway and shielded her from the dust that had been kicked up. When the dust was settled, he stepped aside and Sally resumed her walk beside him.

"Those are men from the PSR Ranch," she said. "Rowdies and ruffians, for the most part."

"PSR?" Smoke asked, knowing full well what the letters stood for.

"Potter, Stratton, and Richards. It's the biggest ranch in the state, so I'm told."

The door opened behind them, and a very pretty lady emerged from the dress shop. "Hello, Sally," she said with a smile.

"Hello, Janey." Sally smiled.

"That is the business manager for PSR," Sally said as Janey walked on down the boardwalk.

Smoke had just seen his sister for the first time in more than ten years. Or was it the first time? He could swear she was the woman he had seen in the Denver depot.

Sally frowned at him. "You have a rather odd look in your eyes, Mr. West."

"I guess I'm surprised that such a pretty woman would be a business manager."

"Not surprising when you get to know her. She is a very intelligent lady. She speaks three languages. And she is my friend."

Smoke kept his face neutral. *How in the devil did Janey learn three languages? I thought she quit school in eighth grade.*

CHAPTER 37

"Oh, here she comes again," Sally said, pointing to a carriage that was being pulled down the street by two magnificent-looking black Andalusian horses. "Isn't that a beautiful carriage?"

It was a grand carriage, all right. The coachman was a black man, all gussied up in a military sort of outfit. As the carriage passed, Smoke removed his hat and bowed gallantly.

Even from the boardwalk, Sally could see that the woman in the carriage flushed with anger and jerked her head to the front. Sally suppressed a giggle. "Oh, my, I think you made her mad, Mr. West."

"She'll get over it, I reckon."

Smoke remembered the time, back before the war, when he had pushed over the family outhouse with his sister in it. She'd chased him all over the farm, throwing rocks at him.

"That is a funny look in your eyes, Mr. West. What are you thinking?"

"I'm thinking about my sister," he answered honestly.

"Does Janey remind you of her?"

"Not the sister I remember. I'll probably never see that girl again."

"Oh, why do you say that?"

"She's not there anymore. Everything and everyone is gone." He took Sally's elbow as they continued their walk toward the edge of town.

They had not gone half a block before the sound of hooves drumming on the hard-packed dirt came to them. Two men reined up in the street, turning the horses to face Smoke and Sally.

Smoke had never seen either of those men before, but he had seen their kind and he recognized, at once, that they were trouble. Gently but firmly, he moved Sally to one side. "You had better stand clear," he said in a low voice. "This looks like trouble."

"What kind of—"

"You run along now, schoolmarm," one of the men cut her off. "This here might get messy."

Sally stuck her chin up. "I will stand right here on this boardwalk until the soles of my shoes grow roots before I'll take orders from you, you misbegotten cretin."

Smoke chuckled at Sally's remark.

"What the hell did she call me?" the cowboy asked his friend.

"Damned if I know."

The cowboy swung his eyes back to Smoke and demanded, "Are you the one they call Buck West?"

"I am."

"I hear tell you're lookin' for Smoke Jensen. Is that right?"

"That's right."

"Well, here's the problem with that, West. Me and my pard here are lookin' for him, too, and we don't plan to share that reward money with nobody. Most especial not some greenhorn like you who I ain't never heard of afore you got your name put in the paper for shootin' down a couple men that most prob'ly didn't know one end of a gun from another. So you got fifteen minutes to get your gear and get gone."

Smoke's hands hung down by his sides. "If it's all the same to you, I think I'll just stay."

"Boy, do you know who I am?"

Smoke shook his head. "I can't say that I do."

"The name is Dickerson. Mo Dickerson from over Colorado way." He smiled confidently. "I reckon you've heard of me."

Smoke had heard of him, but he decided not to let Dickerson know that. The man was a top gun, quick on the draw, and men like him were inordinately proud of their reputation. "Sorry, I can't say as I have." He saw the irritation in Dickerson's face.

"This here," Dickerson said with a jerk of his thumb, "is Frank Russell."

Smoke hadn't heard of Russell, but he figured if the man rode with Dickerson, he'd be good. "Pleased to meet you," Smoke said politely.

Dickerson gave Smoke an exasperated look. "What's the matter with you, boy? This here ain't no social meetin'. There ain't nobody pleased to meet nobody here."

"Oh. Well, in that case, there's no sense in continuing this conversation, is there? So, if you gentlemen will excuse me, I'd like to continue my walk with Miss Reynolds."

Dickerson and Russell dismounted.

"Only place you're goin' to is Boot Hill, boy," Dickerson said.

Several citizens, drawn by the increasingly threatening conversation, had gathered around to watch.

"I've bothered no one," Smoke said to the crowd, without taking his eyes from the two gunhands. "And I'm not looking for a fight. I just want to make that public."

"West, the only way you are going to avoid a fight is to get on your horse and ride away," Russell said. "And do it right now."

"I'm staying."

"You folks are getting a little too close," Dickerson said to the gathering crowd. "You don't want to take a chance o' gettin' hit when the bullets start flyin', do you?"

"They aren't in any danger," Smoke said.

"What do you mean they ain't in no danger? Boy, don't you understand that if you don't close your mouth and do what we tell you, that there's goin' to be shootin' here? And someone could be hit by a missed shot."

"There will only be two shots fired—and I won't miss. Neither of you will even get a shot off. Like I said, they can stand as close as they want."

"Then draw, damn you!" Dickerson shouted. He went for his gun, and out of the corner of his eye Smoke saw Russell slapping leather, as well.

Smoke's hand swept up with blinding speed, and

the Colt belched smoke and flame. He returned his pistol to his holster as quickly as he had drawn it.

Dickerson and Russell lay on the dusty street. Both were dead. Their guns were beside them in the dirt, and Smoke had been right. He had fired twice, both shots had found their mark, and neither Dickerson nor Russell had had time to cock and fire.

"Good Lord almighty!" cried a young cowboy in the crowd. "Where did those shots come from?"

"From West," one of the others said.

"But how? I never even seen the gun in his hand!"

Sheriff Reese and Deputy Rogers came running up the wide street.

"Drop that gun, West!" Reese yelled. "You're under arrest."

"I'd like to know why," Sally said, stepping up to stand beside Smoke, her face pale from what she had just witnessed. She pointed to Dickerson and Russell. "Those two started it. They ordered Mr. West to leave town, and when he refused, they drew first. I'll swear to that in a court of law."

"She's right, Sheriff," a cowboy said.

Reese gave the cowboy an ugly look. "Which side are you on, Cecil? These two men worked for the PSR same as you."

"I ain't workin' for 'em anymore."

"What? Since when?"

"Since right now. They don't want cowhands, Sheriff. What they want are gunhands. They are dead set on killin' someone named Smoke Jensen for some reason, and I don't want nothin' to do with it. This feller was in the right, and Dickerson and Russell was wrong."

"Cecil and the schoolteacher are right, Sheriff," put in another witness.

"Anyone here who has a different story?" Reese asked in exasperation.

Nobody responded to what was almost a plea.

"Any charges, Sheriff?" Smoke asked.

There was open dislike in Reese's eyes as he stepped closer and glared at Smoke. "No, not now. But you're nothin' but trouble, West, and you and me both know it. I hope you crowd me, gunfighter. 'Cause when you do, I'll kill you!"

"You might try," Smoke replied in the same low tone.

Reese flushed and stepped back. "Watch your step is all I got to say."

"Was this your first gunfight?" Smoke asked Sally a few minutes later as they continued their walk.

"It's the first one I was this close to," Sally answered, thinking about the incident the first day she'd arrived in town.

"Well, it's a big, wild country out here. The laws are simple and straight to the point. Justice comes down hard. Out here a man's word is his bond, and that's the way it should be everywhere. Tinhorns and shysters don't last long in the West."

They had reached Sally's front gate.

"Would you like to have supper with me this evening?" Smoke asked. "Maybe at the hotel dining room? Not having eaten there yet I can't testify as to how good the food is, but I know I will enjoy the company."

"I have a better idea. Why don't you come here and let me fix supper for you? I'm a pretty good cook, if I say so myself. That way we can enjoy the food and the company."

"You're on," Smoke agreed with a broad smile.

PSR Ranch

Janey looked out the window of her bedroom. Ever since she had seen that arrogant young man in town, she had struggled to recall where she had seen him before. She knew she had.

But where? She just could not remember. And startling news had come that the young man had killed Russell and Dickerson in a standup gunfight.

That was incredible.

She sighed and turned away from the window that overlooked the northern vastness of the PSR ranchlands. The face of the tall gunslick remained in her mind, and she knew that his name would come to her in time.

"I never see nothin' like it before, and I've seen some fast guns. Neither Dickerson nor Russell got a shot off, and they drew first," Sheriff Reese reported as he took the news of the gunfight to Richards, Potter, and Stratton.

"This man West is a bounty hunter?" Richards asked.

"That's what he claims."

"If he is as good as you say, he might be someone I'm going to want on the payroll. I think I'll look him up in the morning. Let's eat. I'm hungry."

The four men trooped out of the study and into the dining room. Janey was already there.

The expression on her face elicited a question from Richards. "Something the matter?"

"That Buck West. I've seen him before, somewhere."

"Can you remember where?"

She shook her head. "Not yet. But I will." She looked him directly in the eyes. "He's trouble, Josh."

"That's just your imagination, my dear. I believe he would be a good man to have on our side."

"Watch him," she cautioned. "I don't trust him."

"You don't even know him."

"Yeah, I do. I just can't remember where it's from, is all."

"It'll come to you."

"Bet on it."

Bury

"That was a fine supper, Miss Reynolds," Smoke said as the two them sat out on the front porch after the meal.

"Sally."

"I beg your pardon?"

"Don't you think we've spent enough time together to be on a first-name basis? My name is Sally, and I would like it if you would address me so, Buck."

"Uh . . ."

"Oh, I'm sorry," Sally said quickly. "Am I pushing this relationship too quickly?"

"No, it's not that. It's . . . well, I need to know what you think about the three men who seem to own this whole town. Potter, Stratton, and Richards."

Sally was quiet for a moment. "If those men are friends of yours, I'm sorry, but I have to be honest. I think they are despicable. No, it's more than that. I think they are evil."

Smoke smiled. "I had to ask you that, Sally. I mean, being as they own everything I supposed that, being a schoolteacher, you are actually working for them."

"I work for the children I teach. And they don't own everything. A very good friend of mine owns the Pink House."

"The Pink House?"

"It's a brothel. Does it shock you that I can be friends with such a person?"

"No, it doesn't. It tells me that you can trust your gut to look inside someone."

Sally laughed out loud. "What a quaint way of expressing intuition. My intuition tells me something about you."

Curious, Smoke asked, "What does it tell you?"

"It tells me that you are holding something back. What is it?"

He sighed, then stuck his hand down into his pocket and pulled out his badge. He showed the star to Sally. "I'm a deputy United States marshal, Sally, and my name isn't Buck West. It's Smoke Jensen. I've come here to arrest Potter, Stratton, and Jensen for murder."

He could tell she was shocked by the revelation, but she was also quick-witted and recovered from her surprise in a matter of moments. "Buck . . . I mean, Smoke . . . they're surrounded by bodyguards. They aren't going to let you just arrest them."

"I know. I'm going to have to kill them," he said

flatly. He looked at her. "Do you still want to be friends with me?"

"More than friends," Sally said, leaning closer to him.

Smoke hesitated, but he didn't pull back. For the first time since Nicole died, he kissed a woman.

CHAPTER 38

PSR Ranch

Janey tossed and turned in the comfortable bed, deep in the grip of a nightmare. The events in her dream weren't bizarre, frightening fantasies. They were memories of a day back home in Missouri.

She'd been leading on an older boy in school. He caught her in the barn and started tearing her clothes off. He would have raped her, no doubt about that, but her brother Kirby came along and interrupted it. He managed to put a stop to it and chased the boy away. Kirby, already tall and strong and fearless . . .

With a gasp, Janey awakened from her dream and sat up in bed with her heart pounding. That was why Buck West had looked so familiar to her. She knew who he really was.

Buck West was her brother Kirby.

Buck West was Smoke Jensen.

She knew that, for some reason, Richards and the other two were terrified of the mysterious Smoke Jensen, but despite the last name, she had never connected their nemesis with Kirby. She didn't know when he had taken the name *Smoke* but she was sure he was calling himself Buck West in order to keep his identity a secret from Richards and the others.

Should she tell them?

No. She had already told Richards that Buck West was trouble, and he had dismissed her warning. As far as she was concerned, Richards and the others were on their own.

She rolled over and went back to sleep.

Bury

Having tea with Flora in the parlor of the Pink House the next day, Janey asked, "Have you heard of a man named Buck West?"

"Are you kidding? Who in town hasn't heard of him? Why do you ask?"

"I must see him. Do you think you could get a message to him to meet me here?"

"I suppose I could. He's been hanging around Sally for the last few days."

Janey smiled. "Good. I think she would be very good for him."

"What?" Flora asked with a frown. "What do you mean?"

"Please, just get him to come here. But don't tell

him who he's coming to see. Oh, and maybe you had better bring Sally, too." Janey took a deep breath. "She needs to hear what I'm going to say."

"I hope you've got some coffee to drink," Smoke said as he stood in the foyer of the Pink House with his hat in his hand and Sally beside him. "All this lady has been giving me is tea, and tea has no taste at all."

"What? Why haven't you told me?" Sally asked.

"I didn't want to hurt your feelings."

"Then why did you say something like that to Flora?"

Smoke didn't hesitate with his answer. "Well, it won't be hurting her feelings if I ask for coffee."

Flora laughed and looked at Sally. "I'm sure that makes perfect sense to a man. Go on into the parlor, both of you. There's someone there who wants to talk to you."

In the parlor, Smoke and Sally saw a woman standing in front of the window, looking out. Even though her back was to them, both recognized her at once.

"Janey, how nice to see you," Sally said.

Janey turned around. "Hello, Kirby."

"Hello, sis."

Sally gasped in surprise and took a step back to allow Smoke and Janey a small bit of privacy.

"When did you figure out who I was?" Smoke asked.

"I knew the first time I saw you, that I had seen you before. It just took me a while to place it. Remember, you were only fourteen last time I saw you. I didn't know if you or Pa or Luke were alive or dead."

"Pa's dead," Smoke said. "Luke is, too, as far as I know."

Janey nodded. She didn't seem surprised by the news.

"Janey, I'm told you are hooked up with Richards."

She nodded. "I was. I'm not anymore. I'm leaving today." She had come to that decision in the middle of the night, and it was like a giant weight off her shoulders. The time had come to put the whole PSR part of her life behind her, just as she had other parts and times in the past . . . when things were too painful to bear or even think of.

Smoke nodded. "I'm glad."

"Why are you after them? I know all three of them are crooked as a dog's leg, but why are you, specifically, after them?"

"They're the ones who shot Luke, back in the war, and they're the ones who killed Pa."

"Oh!" Janey gasped. "They killed . . . both of them?"

"Yes."

"I didn't know that." Her face and voice showed the anguish she felt.

"Janey, what happened to you? How did you . . ."

"I make no apologies, Kirby. I was a young woman . . . no, I was a girl, really, and you may recall that I was left on my own. I made my way as best as I could. I don't ask for your understanding . . . or your forgiveness."

"Sis, both of us have been through some hard times. I make no judgments. Believe me, with all the things I've done, I have no right. I understand perfectly, and there is nothing to forgive."

Janey's eyes glistened with tears. "I'm leaving today, but I'm glad I had the opportunity to see you again."

She opened her arms, and Smoke drew her to him, hugging her tightly.

Her eyes weren't the only ones glistening with tears. Sally . . . and Flora, who had followed her and Smoke into the parlor . . . were crying, as well.

Janey walked out to her carriage, where her black driver, Mr. Jefferies, sat in the driver's seat, waiting patiently for her. She looked at him and asked, "Mr. Jefferies, if you had this carriage and team in a place like Denver, do you think you could find some way to make a living with it?"

"Yes, ma'am, I expect a body could make a good livin' hirin' out to folks who wanted to go somewhere in an elegant carriage like this."

She nodded and climbed into the carriage. "Take me to the depot, please."

"Yes, ma'am."

After leaving the Pink House, Sally and Smoke strolled through the town and out to Canyon Creek where they sat on the bank and watched and listened to the whisper of the quietly flowing stream.

"You recognized Janey the first day you saw her, didn't you?" Sally said.

"Yes."

"That was why you had the strange look in your eyes."

"I have to confess that I haven't had good thoughts about her all these years. I guess I wasn't being fair. Like she said, she was a girl of no more than sixteen last time I saw her. I have no right to pass judgment on her."

"Janey and Flora are my friends. There are people in town who pass judgment on me for that."

"I don't," Smoke said with a broad smile. "I can't think of anything you might do that would give me pause."

"Not even this?" Leaning toward him, Sally kissed him.

"Especially not that," Smoke replied after their lips parted.

"I must keep reminding myself that I'm a lady." The twinkle in her eyes told him that while a lady she might be, there were a lot of hot coals banked within. "Smoke?"

"Yes?"

"Tell me about Smoke Jensen."

Sally listened attentively for a full ten minutes, not interrupting, letting him tell his story his way. When he had finished, she sat quietly for a moment, mentally digesting all she had heard.

"And to think that I actually worked for those creatures." She hurled a small stone into the water. "Well, I shall tender my resignation immediately, of course."

Smoke's smile was hard. "Stick around, Sally. The show is just about to begin."

"You do know, don't you, Smoke, that I am quite fond of you?"

"I hope so. 'Cause Lord knows, I feel that way about you."

Just as their lips touched, a voice came from behind them. "Now if that ain't 'bout the most disgustin' thing? I mean, a great big, full-growed man a moonin' and a sparkin' like some kid. It's plumb disgustin', I tell you."

Smoke pulled away quickly. "Preacher!"

"We got to make some plans," Preacher said after Smoke had introduced him to Sally.

"What are you doing here?"

"You didn't figure I was gonna let you take on Richards and his men all by yourself, did you? I got Lobo, Beartooth, Greybull, Pugh, Deadlead, and Powder Pete camped just outta town. I figure the eight of us, countin' you, ought to be able to handle things all right."

Smoke laughed. "Yeah, I would think so. How did you find me, anyway?"

"Hell's fire, boy! I just followed the bodies! Can't you keep them guns of yours in leather?"

"Come on, Preacher! Tell the truth. I know you would rather lie, but try hard."

"I didn't have to find you, I been followin' you for a coon's age." Preacher looked over at Sally. "Do you see how unrespectful he is, missy? Can't a pretty thing like you do no better than the likes o' this fella?"

"I'm going to change him," Sally said primly.

Preacher grinned. "Ha. I'd love to see that. Smoke ain't easy to change."

Smoke frowned. "You had better get used to calling me Buck, Preacher. You might slip up in town and that would be the end of it."

"I ain't going into town. Not until you get ready to make your move, that is. When things is about to happen, we'll be there." Preacher looked at Sally. "You look after this boy now, you hear me?"

Sally smiled and looked at Smoke. "Oh, I intend to, Mr. Preacher. I'll be looking after him from now on."

Preacher mounted his horse, and with a nod to the two of them, rode off.

"I like your friend," Sally said. "He is the old man you were talking about when you told me your story, isn't he?"

"Yes, and when he dies it will be the end of the old mountain men, the end of an era."

"No it won't, Smoke," Sally said. "Not as long as you're around."

On the train to Denver

Janey Jensen rode comfortably in the Wagner Palace Car. Elam Jefferies was on the same train, but in a different car. He had a huge smile on his face. In one pocket was one hundred and fifty dollars in cash. In another pocket was the signed deed to an elegant Brewster Brougham and a team of matched, Andalusian horses.

CHAPTER 39

PSR Ranch, office

"Who did you say he was?" Richards shouted the question so loud that spittle sprayed from his mouth.

"The feller that's callin' hisself Buck West is actually Smoke Jensen." Morgan was a thin, baldheaded man who ran the leather goods store in Bury.

"How do you know this, Morgan?"

"On account of I seen 'im back in Red Cliff. This here is Smoke Jensen, all right."

"I'll be damned," Richards said under his breath. "She was right."

"Who was right?" Stratton asked.

"Janey. She told me this Buck West was trouble."

Stratton frowned. "Where is Janey, anyway? I ain't seen her in a day or two."

"I don't have any idea, and to be honest with you, I don't care. I've had about as much of her as I want to put up with. Get the word out. We'll divide the thirty-thousand-dollar reward among all the men who take part in killing Smoke Jensen."

Stratton nodded and left to do as Richards had ordered.

Bury

"You're Smoke Jensen, ain't ya?" The PSR cowboy who had stepped out from behind a building was already holding a pistol in his hand.

At that moment, Smoke realized his identity had been compromised. "I'm Buck West."

"No, you ain't. You're Smoke Jensen, and Richards and ever'one else knows that now. Only I'm the one who's goin' to kill you and collect that thirty thousand dollars."

"What's your name, cowboy?" Smoke asked.

The cowboy smiled. "I may as well tell you, seein' as I'm goin' to be rich and famous after today. Folks call me Sunset."

"Sunset? A fitting name, seeing as the sun is about to set on your life."

"What are you talking about?"

"Put the gun back in your holster, Sunset, and walk away. If you do that, I'll let you live."

Sunset laughed. "You're the one that's goin' to die." He raised the pistol to fire, but before he could cock it, Smoke drew and fired. Sunset died with a shocked expression on his face.

Smoke hurried back to Sally's house. "Sally, they know who I am. Come with me. I'm taking you down to the Pink House. You'll be safe there."

"All right," Sally said without question.

Smoke led her through the alleyways until they reached the big, pink building. They found Flora in her parlor.

"Yes, of course I'll keep her here," Flora said. "She'll be safe with me. We'll lock the doors, and I've got enough shotguns for everyone."

"Thanks." Smoke leaned toward Sally, then stopped and glanced toward Flora. "Look away, would you?"

"Oh, for heaven's sake. Kiss her, then go take care of your business."

Smoke kissed Sally, then with a wave toward both of them, left the house.

"Help me say a little prayer for him, Flora, would you?" Sally asked after the door closed behind Smoke.

"I've already started. You've grown quite fond of him pretty quickly, haven't you?"

"Fond of him? Flora, I love him."

"That all happened fast, didn't it?"

"When you know it's the right man, it doesn't take you long to make up your mind," Sally replied.

Flora smiled. "Make up your mind about what?"

"About marrying him. I intend to be Smoke Jensen's wife."

"If he lives through this."

"He will," Sally said confidently.

Smoke headed back downtown, encountering Sheriff Reese and three other men.

"Hold on there, Jensen!" Even as Reese shouted,

he pulled the trigger on the shotgun he was carrying. But he fired too quickly. Smoke, who was coming up from the alley, had not yet stepped into the street from behind the building. He leaped back just as the double load of buckshot tore into the corner of the building.

He stepped out then and started shooting, taking down a deputy and one of the other men. Reese, having expended both barrels of the shotgun, didn't represent any immediate danger. Two men turned and ran, while Reese dropped the shotgun and went for his pistol.

Reese was fast, faster than Smoke had expected, but he was able to shoot just before Reese brought his pistol to bear.

From outside of town, Preacher heard the gunfire of more than the occasional gunshot and knew that it was significant. "Grab your rifles, boys! The fun has started!"

Grabbing the assorted buffalo guns, Creedmores, Henrys, and Winchesters, the seven mountain men took up positions overlooking the pass that was the only way into town from the PSR Ranch. A veritable army of more than twenty heavily armed men were on their way into town.

"I'm gonna take the first shot," Lobo said, raising the Henry to his shoulder.

"All right. Go ahead," Preacher said, considering himself the leader.

Lobo pulled the trigger, and the riders kept coming.

"You missed!" Preacher jeered.

At that moment, one of the riders lurched, then fell out of his saddle.

Lobo grinned. "I didn't miss. It just takes this damn Henry a little longer to get the job done."

Beartooth was next, the boom of the buffalo gun sounding like an explosion.

After that, all seven mountain men opened fire, and the pass rang with the echo of gunfire.

Less than five minutes after the shooting started, the pass lay somber under the heat of the sun. Bodies were everywhere; men and animals sprawled, soon to be bloated by death. Among the dead were gunhands who had been gathered from all over the country; Telford, who was wanted in Wyoming, Olds, who had paper on him from Nevada, and Peyton, who had been one of Reese's deputies, and was wanted for murder back in Iowa. The pass was quiet now that the gunfire was over, and, except for the circling buzzards, still.

PSR Ranch, office

"There ain't nobody left, Mr. Richards." Bozeman was the only one who had survived the fight at the pass, and even he had not come through it unscathed. He had a bullet hole in his leg staining his trousers red with blood. "Ain't nobody left in town neither. Leastwise, not nobody we can count on. Sheriff Reese, he's been kilt."

"Do you think Jensen's comin' out here?" Potter asked, his voice reflecting his fear.

"Yes, sir, I'm sure he is."

"All right, Bozeman, you get down by the front gate. Hide somewhere, and when you see him comin', shoot him," Richards ordered.

Bozeman shook his head. "No, sir, I don't want nothin' more to do with it. Onliest reason I come back here to warn you was I was thinkin' maybe you might give me some money, enough to get out of here."

"You didn't do your job. Why should we give you anything?" Stratton asked.

"They was nineteen men got kilt for you three," Bozeman pointed out. "I got shot up for you. That makes twenty, and you can't even give me enough money to get out of here?"

"You did it for the reward money, only you didn't kill him. No, if you aren't going to help now, get out of here."

Bozeman pulled his pistol. "Give me some money," he demanded. "Or else I'll—"

Potter stepped up behind him and shot him in the back. Bozeman's eyes bulged out like they were about to pop from their sockets. The gun slipped from his fingers and thudded to the floor as he opened his mouth.

All that came out was a thread of blood before he collapsed on the floor.

"What do we do now?" Stratton asked.

"We've got to get out of here," Potter said.

"No," Richards replied, shaking his head. "I ain't runnin' no more. We've got too much at stake here to be run off like some rabid dog. Potter, you're wantin' to be governor. How's that goin' to happen if you're gone?"

"Yeah." Potter passed a shaky hand over his face. "Yeah, you're right."

"What's your plan?" Stratton asked.

"The first thing is, I'll meet him on the front porch, and I'll offer him ten thousand dollars to be on his way and leave us be."

"You know damn well he isn't going to take you up on that," Potter scorned.

"I know. That's why I said I'll meet him on the front porch," Richards said. "You two will be inside. Muley, you'll be just behind that window. Wiley, you'll be over there behind that window. As soon as you hear him turn down the offer, shoot. The moment he says no, both of you shoot at the same time."

At that moment the front door opened and, startled, all three turned to see Deputy Rogers.

"Rogers!" Richards said.

"I was listenin' to you out on the front porch. Bozeman is right. Reese and at least five more is dead in town. Ever'one else has left."

"Why didn't you leave?"

Rogers smiled. "I figure you'll pay me if I kill Jensen for you."

"All right, you get—"

"No," Rogers said, interrupting Richards. "I heard what you was sayin' to the others, and I plan on goin' out on the porch with you. I want you to know that I'm the one that kilt him. I been wantin' to kill Jensen ever since he come to town, even afore I knowed who he was."

"I don't know how smart a move that is," Richards said. "Jensen is very fast. I know because we've been trying to kill him for some time now."

Rogers disagreed. "No, you've been sendin' people to kill him. You don't have to send me. I'm already here."

"All right, Rogers. You're welcome company."

"Richards!" The call came from outside the house. "Richards, Potter, Stratton! Come on out!"

"That's him," Rogers said with an eager edge to his voice.

Richards nodded toward Stratton and Potter, and the two men got into position behind the windows. He looked toward Rogers, who loosened his gun in the holster, then nodded back.

The two men stepped out onto the front porch.

Smoke stood in front of the ranch house, easy and confident. "Where are the other two?"

"For the moment, you can deal with Deputy Rogers and me," Richards said. "Excuse me. Seeing as you killed Reese, that would be *Sheriff* Rogers, now."

"Where's Sally Reynolds?" Rogers asked.

"It doesn't make any difference to you where she is," Smoke said.

Rogers smiled. "Oh, yeah, it does. See, after this is all over, she's gonna be my woman."

Richards wasn't interested in that. "Jensen, suppose I give you ten thousand dollars? Would you ride away and never bother us again?"

A faint smile drew up the corners of Smoke's mouth, but his eyes glittered with hate and resolve. "I don't think so." He shook his head a little . . . and caught a fleeting glimpse of a gun appear in the window to his left. Drawing with lightning speed, he fired at that window, then swung his pistol to the right window and fired again. Potter tumbled out onto the porch from one of the windows, Stratton from the other.

When the shooting started, Rogers began his own draw, but he was too late. Smoke had already turned back to him and fired. One bullet into Rogers's forehead, and the deputy went down, dead before he hit the porch.

Richards managed to get his gun out and raised, but he wasn't able to pull the trigger before Smoke killed him with a single bullet.

Had anyone still been at the PSR Ranch, the four shots would have sounded like one sustained roar of gun thunder.

Except for Smoke Jensen, not one living person was anywhere on the ranch.

Bury

Leading two packhorses and with Sally riding astride beside him on a saddle horse he had bought for her, Smoke was ready to put Bury behind them forever. The two of them left the town, heading toward the High Lonesome.

Flora, Emma, and the other ladies of the Pink House stood on the front porch, waving good-bye. "Gee, I hate to see her go," Emma said. "She was such a good friend to all of us."

"Yes," Flora said, a little lump in her throat. "She was."

"It's too bad she was a schoolteacher. She's so pretty, she would have been really good at what we do here," Emma said.

Flora laughed out loud. "You know what? I think she would have agreed with you."

Summit County

"Do you like dogs, Mrs. Jensen?" Smoke asked as they reined their mounts to a stop and sat atop a hill overlooking the vast sweep of mountains, streams, and richly grassed valleys.

"Yes, I do," Sally answered.

"Good. I do, too. We'll have a lot of them at Sugarloaf."

"Sugarloaf?"

Smoke smiled at her. "That's what we're going to call our ranch." He nodded toward the paradise in front of them. "It's waiting for us out there, along with the rest of our lives."

TURN THE PAGE FOR AN EXCITING PREVIEW!

USA Today and *New York Times* **Bestselling Authors**
WILLIAM W. JOHNSTONE
with J. A. Johnstone

**THE GREATEST WESTERN WRITERS
OF THE 21ST CENTURY**

*The Kerrigans risked everything to stake a claim under a big
Texas sky. Now one brave woman is fighting to keep that
home, against hard weather, harder luck, and the West's most
dangerous men.*

A RANCH DIVIDED . . .

After a long hard journey up the Chisholm Trail,
Kate Kerrigan is in Dodge City, facing a mystery of
murder. A cowboy she hired, a man with a notorious
past, has been accused of killing a prostitute and
sentenced to hang. Kate still trusts Hank Lowry.
And when a hired killer comes after her, she knows
she has struck a nerve. Someone has framed Hank
for murder—in order to cover up a more sinister
and deadly crime spawned in the musty backrooms
of the Kansas boomtown . . .

Back in West Texas, the Kerrigan ranch is under siege.
A wagon train full of gravely ill travelers has come onto
the parched Kerrigan range, being led by a man on a
secret mission. With Kate's son Quinn manning the
home front, one wrong step could be fatal when the
shooting suddenly starts . . .

The Kerrigans, A Texas Dynasty
JOURNEY INTO VIOLENCE

Available August 2016, wherever
Pinnacle Books are sold.

CHAPTER 1

"She ran me off her property, darned redheaded Irish witch." Ezra Raven stared hard at his *segundo*, a tall lean man with ice in his eyes named Poke Hylle. "I want that Kerrigan land, Poke. I want every last blade of grass. You understand?"

"I know what you want, boss," Hylle said. He studied the amber whiskey in his glass as though it had become the most interesting thing in the room. "But wantin' and gettin' are two different things."

"You scared of Frank Cobb, that hardcase *segundo* of hers? I've heard a lot of men are."

"Should I be scared of him?" Hylle asked.

"He's a gun from way back. Mighty sudden on the draw and shoot."

Hylle's grin was slow and easy, a man relaxed. "Yeah, he scares me. But that don't mean I'm afraid to brace him."

"You can shade him. You're good with a gun your own self, Poke, maybe the best I've ever known," Raven said. "Hell, you gunned Bingley Abbott that time. He was the Wichita draw fighter all the folks were talking about."

"Bing was fast, but he wasn't a patch on Frank Cobb," Hylle said. "Now that's a natural fact."

"All right, then, forget Cobb for now. There's got to be a better way than an all-out range war." Raven stepped to the ranch house window and stared out at the cloud of drifting dust where the hands were branding calves. "I offered Kate Kerrigan twice what her ranch is worth, but she turned me down flat. How do you deal with a woman like that?"

"Carefully." Hylle smiled. "I'm told she bites."

"Like a cougar. Shoved a scattergun into my face and told me to git. Me, Ezra Raven, who could buy and sell her and all she owns." The big man slammed a fist into his open palm. "Damn, I need that land. I want to be big, Poke, the biggest man around. That's just how I am, how I've always been, and I ain't about to change."

The door opened and a tall, slender Pima woman stepped noiselessly across the floor and placed a white pill and a glass of water on Raven's desk.

"Damn, is it that time again?"

"Take," the woman said. "It is time." She wore a plain, slim-fitting calico dress that revealed the swell of her breast and hips. A bright blue ribbon tied back her glossy black hair, and on her left wrist she wore a wide bracelet of hammered silver. She was thirty-five years old. Raven had rescued her from a brothel in Dallas, and he didn't know her Indian name, if she had one. He called her Dora only because it pleased him to do so.

Raven picked up the pill and glared at it. "The useless quack says this will help my heart. I think the damned thing is sugar rolled into a ball."

Hylle waved an idle hand. "Man's got to follow the doctor's orders, boss."

Raven shrugged, swallowed the medication with a gulp of water, and handed the glass back to the Pima woman. "Git, Dora. White men are talking here."

The woman bowed her head and left.

"Poke, like I said, I don't want to take on a range war. It's a messy business. Nine times out of ten the law gets involved and next thing you know, you're knee-deep in Texas Rangers."

Hylle nodded. "Here's a story you'll find interesting, boss. I recollect one time in Galveston I heard a mariner talk about how he was first mate on a freighter sailing between Shanghai and Singapore in the South China Sea. Well, sir, during a watch he saw two ironclads get into a shooting scrape. He said both ships were big as islands and they had massive cannons in dozens of gun turrets. Both ships pounded at each other for the best part of three hours. In the end neither ironclad got sunk, but both were torn apart by shells and finally they listed away from each other, each of them trailing smoke. Nobody won that fight, but both ships paid a steep price." He swallowed the last of his whiskey. "A range war is like that, boss. Ranchers trade gunfire, hired guns and punchers die, but in the end, nobody wins."

"And then the law comes in and cleans up what's left," Raven said.

"That's about the size of it," Hylle said.

"I don't want that kind of fight. Them ironclads could have avoided a battle and sailed away with their colors flying. Firing on each other was a grand-stand play and stupid."

Hylle rose from his chair, stepped to the decanters, and poured himself another drink. He took his seat again and said, "Boss, maybe there is another way."

"Let's hear it," Raven said. "But no more about heathen seas and ironclads. Damn it, man, you're making me seasick."

Hylle smiled. "From what I've seen of the Kerrigan place it's a hardscrabble outfit and Kate has to count every dime to keep it going. Am I right about that?"

"You're right. The KK Ranch is held together with baling wire and Irish pride. She's building a house that isn't much bigger than her cabin. She's using scrap lumber, and the first good wind that comes along will blow it all over creation." Raven lifted his chin and scratched his stubbly throat. "Yeah, I'd say Kate Kerrigan's broke or damned near it."

"So answer me this, boss. What happens if her herd doesn't go up the trail next month?"

A light glittered in Raven's black eyes. "She'd be ruined."

"And eager to sell for any price," Hylle said.

Raven thought that through for a few moments then said, "How do we play it, Poke? Remember them damned ironclads of yours that tore one another apart."

"No range war. Boss, we do it with masked men—night riders. We scatter the Kerrigan herd, gun a few waddies if we must, but leave no evidence that can be tied to you and the Rafter-R. Stop her roundup and the woman is out of business." Hylle smiled. "Pity though. She's real pretty."

"So are dollars and cents, Poke. The Kerrigan range represents money in my pocket." A big, rawboned man, Raven's rugged face bisected by a great cavalry mustache and chin beard. He lit a cigar and said behind a blue cloud of smoke, "We wait until the branding is done and then we strike at the Kerrigan herds, scatter them to hell and gone before Kate can start the gather. Can we depend on the punchers?"

Hylle nodded. "They ride for the brand, boss."

"Good. A two-hundred-dollar bonus to every man once the job is done and I own the Kerrigan range." Raven slapped his hands together. "Do you think it can work?"

"No question about that. No cattle drive to Dodge, no money for the KK."

"Hell, now I feel better about things, Poke. It's like you're a preacher and I just seen the light. How about another drink?"

Hylle grinned. "Don't mind if I do, boss. We'll drink to the ruin of the KK and the end of pretty Mrs. Kerrigan's stay in West Texas."

CHAPTER 2

Kate Kerrigan stood on her hearthstone and watched the rider. He was still a distance off and held his horse to a walk. The weight of the Remington .41 revolver in the pocket of her dress gave her a measure of reassurance. The little rimfire was a belly gun to be sure, but effective if she could get close enough.

That Kate could stand on her hearthstone and see the man at a distance was not surprising since her new home was still only a frame and a somewhat rickety one at that. She'd scolded the construction foreman, but Black Barrie Delaney, captain of the brig *Octopus*, had assured her that he had inspected the work and the basic structure was sound. As she often did, Kate recalled their last conversation with distaste.

"I did not bring, all the way from Connemara, mind you, a slab of green marble for your hearthstone, Kate, only to

have your new house fall about your ears." Delaney wore a blue coat with brass buttons. Thrust into the red sash around his waist were two revolvers of the largest kind and a murderous bowie knife.

"Barrie Delaney, I'll never know why I let a pirate rogue like you talk me into building my house," Kate said. "Why, 'tis well-known that you should have been hanged at Execution Dock in London town years ago."

"Ah, Her Majesty Queen Victoria's mercy knows no bounds and she saw fit to spare a poor Irish sailorman like me."

"More fool her," Kate said. "You've sent many a lively lad to Davy Jones's locker and a goodly woman or two if the truth be known. Well, here's a word to the wise, Barrie Delaney, fix this house to my liking or I'll hang you myself or my name is not Kate Kerrigan."

Delaney, a stocky man with a brown beard and quick black eyes full of deviltry that reflected the countless mortal sins he'd committed in his fifty-eight years of life, gave a little bow. "Kate, I swear on my sainted mother's grave that I will build you a fine house, a dwelling fit for an Irish princess."

"Fit for me and my family will be quite good enough," Kate said.

Kate shook her head at the memory. As she watched the rider draw closer, she pushed on the support stud next to her. It seemed that the whole structure swayed and she made a mental note to hang Black Barrie Delaney at the first convenient opportunity.

Kate's daughters Ivy and Shannon, growing like weeds, stepped out of the cabin, butterfly nets in hand, and she ordered them back inside.

Ivy, twelve years old and sassy, frowned. "Why?"

Her mother said, "Because I said so. Now, inside with you. There's a stranger coming."

"Ma, is it an Indian?" Shannon asked.

"No, probably just a passing rider, but I want to talk with him alone."

The girls reluctantly stepped back into the cabin and Kate once more directed her attention to the stranger. He was close enough that she saw he was dressed in the garb of a frontier gambler and he rode a big American stud, a tall sorrel that must have cost him a thousand dollars and probably more.

The rider drew rein ten yards from where Kate stood and she saw that his black frockcoat, once of the finest quality, was frayed and worn and a rent on the right sleeve above the elbow had been neatly sewn. His boots and saddle had been bought years before in a big city with fancy prices and the ivory-handled Colt and carved gun belt around his waist would cost the average cowpuncher a year's wages. He seemed like a man who'd known a life and times far removed from poverty-stricken West Texas. His practiced ease around women was evident in the way he swept off his hat and made a little bow from the saddle.

"Ma'am." The man said only that. His voice was a rich baritone voice and his smile revealed good teeth.

"My name is Kate Kerrigan. I own this land. What can I do for you?"

"Just passing through, ma'am." He'd opened his frilled white shirt at the neck and beads of sweat showed on his forehead. "I'd like to water my horse if I may. We've come a fair piece in recent days, he and I."

Kate saw no threat in the man's blue eyes, but there was much life and the living of it behind them. His experiences, whatever they were, had left shadows.

"Then you're both welcome to water," Kate said. "The well is over there in front of the cabin and there's a dipper."

The man touched his hat. "Obliged, ma'am." He kneed his horse forward. His roweled spurs were silver, filigreed with gold scrolls and arabesques.

Kate fancied they were such as knights in shining armor wore in the children's picture books.

The rider swung out of the saddle, loosened the girth, and filled a bucket for his horse. Only when the sorrel had drank its fill did he drink himself, his restless, searching eyes never still above the tin rim of the dipper. Finally he removed his coat, splashed water onto his face, and then ran a comb through his thick auburn hair. He donned his hat and coat again, tightened the saddle girth, and smiled at Kate. "Thank you kindly, ma'am. I'm much obliged."

To the Irish, hospitality comes as naturally as breathing, and Kate Kerrigan couldn't let the man go without making a small effort. "I have coffee in the pot if you'd like some."

To her surprise, the man didn't answer right away. Usually men jumped at the chance to drink coffee with her and she felt a little tweak of chagrin. The man was tall and wide-shouldered. As he studied his back trail, there was a tenseness about him, not fear but rather an air of careful calculation, like a man on the scout figuring his odds. Finally he appeared to relax. "Coffee sounds real good to me, ma'am."

"Would you like to come into the house?" Kate said. "Unlike this one, it has a roof and four walls."

The man shook his head. "No, ma'am. Seems like you've got a real nice sitting place under the oak tree. I'll take a chair and you can tell your girls they can come out now."

"You saw . . . I mean all that way?" Kate said.

"I'm a far-seeing man, ma'am. I don't miss much."

Kate smiled. "Yes. Something tells me you don't."

After studying the cabin, the smokehouse, the barn and other outbuildings, the man said, "I reckon your menfolk are out on the range, this time of year. Branding to be done and the like." He saw the question on Kate's face and waved a hand in the direction of the cabin. "The roof's been repaired and done well, all the buildings are built solid and maintained. That means strong men with calloused hands. Your ranch isn't a two by twice outfit, Mrs. Kerrigan. It's a place that's put down deep roots and speaks of men with sand who will stick."

"And a woman who will stick," Kate said.

"I have no doubt about that, ma'am. Your husband must be real proud of you."

"My husband is dead. He died in the war." Kate smiled. "Now let me get the coffee."

As Kate walked away the man said after her, "Name's Hank Lowery, ma'am. I think you should know that."

She turned. "Did you think your name would make me change my mind about the coffee?"

"Hank Lowery is a handle some people have a problem with, Mrs. Kerrigan. They rassle with it for a spell and either run me out of town or want to take my picture with the mayor. Either way, they fear me."

Kate said, "Now I remember. I once heard my *segundo* mention you to my sons. A lot of unarmed men were killed in some kind of fierce battle, wasn't it?"

"The newspapers called it the Longdale Massacre, but it was a gunfight, not a massacre. The men were armed."

"We will not talk of it," Kate said. "You will drink your coffee, Mr. Lowery, and we will not talk a word of it. Does that set well with you?"

Lowery nodded. "Just thought you should know, ma'am."

"Well, now you've told me. Do you take milk and sugar in your coffee? No matter, I'll bring them anyway."

"Is the sponge cake to your liking, Mr. Lowery?" Kate asked.

The man nudged a crumb into his mouth with a little finger. "It's very good. I've never had sponge cake before, and seldom any other kind of cake, come to that."

"I'm told that sponge cake is Queen Victoria's favorite, one with a cream and strawberry jam filling just like mine."

Lowery smiled. "You're a good cook, Mrs. Kerrigan."

"No I'm not. I'm a terrible cook. I can't even boil an egg. The only thing I can make without ruining it is sponge cake."

"Then I'm honored," Lowery said. "This cake is indeed your masterpiece."

"Thank you, Mr. Lowery. You are most gracious. Ah, here are the girls at last and Jazmin Salas is with them. She's the one who cooks for the Kerrigan ranch, and her husband Marco is my blacksmith."

Kate made the introductions.

Aware of her twelve-year-old blooming girlhood, Ivy played the sophisticated lady and shook Lowery's hand, but seven-year-old Shannon was predictably shy and buried her face in her mother's skirt.

"Beautiful children, Mrs. Kerrigan," Lowery said. "They do you proud."

Jazmin's gaze lingered on the man's holstered Colt, fine clothes, and the silver ring on the little finger of his left hand. She guessed that Mr. Lowery had never done a day's hard work in his life. Although she had heard of such men, they were as alien to her as the strange little Chinamen who toiled on the railroads.

"Is the gentleman staying for supper, Mrs. Kerrigan? If he is I'll set an extra place at table."

Kate hesitated.

Lowery read the signs. "There's no need. I should be riding on."

"Of course you'll stay for supper, Mr. Lowery," Kate said, recovering from her indecision. "I will not allow a man to leave my home hungry." To lift the mood, she added, "We're having chicken and dumplings. Is that to your taste?"

"If it's as good as the sponge cake, then it most certainly is."

"Better," Kate said. "Jazmin is a wonderful cook."

"Will we eat in the dining room . . . again?" Jazmin said.

"Of course. Where else would we eat?"

Jazmin's eyes lifted to the table and chairs set up within the wobbly frame of the new house. "Yes, ma'am. Let's hope the weather holds and there is no wind."

If Hank Lowery was amused, he had the good manners not to let it show.

Connect with Us

Visit us online at
KensingtonBooks.com
to read more from your favorite authors, see books
by series, view reading group guides, and more.

Join us on social media

for sneak peeks, chances to win books and prize packs,
and to share your thoughts with other readers.

facebook.com/kensingtonpublishing
twitter.com/kensingtonbooks

Tell us what you think!

To share your thoughts, submit a review,
or sign up for our eNewsletters, please visit:
KensingtonBooks.com/TellUs.